*Around the World*
*in 100 Days*

# ·GARY· BLACKWOOD

# AROUND THE WORLD IN 100 DAYS

*Dutton Children's Books*

AN IMPRINT OF PENGUIN GROUP (USA) INC.

DUTTON CHILDREN'S BOOKS
A division of Penguin Young Readers Group

PUBLISHED BY THE PENGUIN GROUP

Penguin Group (USA) Inc., 375 Hudson Street, New York, New York 10014, U.S.A. • Penguin Group (Canada), 90 Eglinton Avenue East, Suite 700, Toronto, Ontario M4P 2Y3, Canada (a division of Pearson Penguin Canada Inc.) • Penguin Books Ltd, 80 Strand, London WC2R 0RL, England • Penguin Ireland, 25 St Stephen's Green, Dublin 2, Ireland (a division of Penguin Books Ltd) • Penguin Group (Australia), 250 Camberwell Road, Camberwell, Victoria 3124, Australia (a division of Pearson Australia Group Pty Ltd) • Penguin Books India Pvt Ltd, 11 Community Centre, Panchsheel Park, New Delhi - 110 017, India • Penguin Group (NZ), 67 Apollo Drive, Rosedale, North Shore 0632, New Zealand (a division of Pearson New Zealand Ltd) • Penguin Books (South Africa) (Pty) Ltd, 24 Sturdee Avenue, Rosebank, Johannesburg 2196, South Africa • Penguin Books Ltd, Registered Offices: 80 Strand, London WC2R 0RL, England

This book is a work of fiction. Names, characters, places, and incidents are either the product of the author's imagination or are used fictitiously, and any resemblance to actual persons, living or dead, business establishments, events, or locales is entirely coincidental.

Text copyright © 2010 by Gary Blackwood

The publisher does not have any control over and does not assume any responsibility for author or third-party websites or their content.

CIP Data is available.

Published in the United States by Dutton Children's Books,
a division of Penguin Young Readers Group 345 Hudson Street,
New York, New York 10014
www.penguin.com/youngreaders

Designed by Jason Henry

Printed in USA • First Edition
ISBN: 978-0-525-42295-2
1 3 5 7 9 10 2 6 4 2

*For Dante*
*whose pen is as quick as his hockey stick*

*A*S MANY READERS will realize, this is a sort of sequel to Jules Verne's famous 1873 novel *Around the World in 80 Days*. Verne was inspired by a newspaper article claiming that because of recent improvements in transportation—the Transcontinental Railroad in America, the Suez Canal, the linking of the railways in India—a traveler could conceivably circle the globe in eighty days. Verne's tale first appeared in serial form, in the French newspaper *Le Temps*. It was so popular that the newspaper's circulation tripled; steamship lines offered Verne handsome sums to mention their company's name in the story. He declined. Readers placed bets on whether or not Phileas Fogg would succeed; some even believed that Fogg and his journey were real, not fictional.

And, in fact, the novel inspired a spate of real-life attempts to duplicate Fogg's feat. In 1889, Elizabeth Cochran (using the pen name Nellie Bly), a reporter for the *New York World*, managed it in just over seventy-two days. American businessman George Train set a new record of sixty-seven days in 1890, the year before our story takes place. So why, you may ask, does this journey take so much longer? Well, Nellie Bly and George Train and Phileas Fogg all traveled almost entirely by ship and by rail. Our hero, Harry, does it the hard way.

# Contents

# ONE

## *In which*

# HARRY FOGG BEHAVES RECKLESSLY AND PAYS THE PRICE

**E**ven on a bright Sunday morning, the holding cell at the Marylebone station house was not a pleasant place. Indeed, it was at its absolute worst on Sunday mornings, for it contained the dismal dregs of London society, scraped from the gutters and sidewalks the night before. Most were weak-willed workingmen who, after drawing their paltry pay on Saturday afternoon, proceeded to squander the greater part of it at the nearest pub. They paid the true price later on, when they woke to find themselves sprawled on the floor of a dank, dirty cell, with their pockets empty and their heads pounding.

Locked up alongside these relatively harmless sots were actual criminals of every stripe, from the bug-hunters who robbed drunks of what few coins they had left, to cracksmen (burglars) and shofulmen (counterfeiters), to murderers with black blood still visible in the lines of their palms.

Certainly Marylebone jail was not the sort of place you would expect to encounter a young man of Harry Fogg's caliber. His clothing, speech, and manners all marked him as well-bred and well-to-do. And in fact, if he had told the police who he was, they would surely have let him off with no more than a warning. His father's name was still something of a household word, even though it was nearly two decades since Phileas Fogg had made his celebrated journey around the globe.

But Harry, anxious that no word of his predicament should reach his father's ears, had given the arresting officer a false name: William G. Grace. Actually, the name was real enough, it's just that it belonged to someone else—a noted cricket player who was one of Harry's heroes. And so here he stood, in his stocking feet, on the grimy stone floor of the corridor, while the warder unlocked the barred door of the cell. Harry had been advised to leave all his valuables, including his hat, waistcoat, and shoes, at the desk; if he didn't, the clerk said, they'd only be stolen by the other prisoners. And judging from the predatory looks cast at him by the men inside the cell, Harry suspected it was good advice.

Though it was barely midmorning, the jail was already stifling, and the stench of vomit and seldom-washed bodies nearly gagged Harry. Under his breath he cursed the drayman who, by carelessly pulling out in front of him, had caused the accident that brought him here. To be fair, though, it wasn't the poor fellow's fault; chances were, neither he nor his horse had ever encountered a steam-driven car before, or any sort of vehicle that moved faster than ten miles an hour—except a train, of course, and trains could be trusted not to come roaring down High Street at you.

No, Harry had to admit it was his own recklessness that had, as it so often did, landed him in hot water—or rather in warm beer, for that was what had spewed from the kegs when his motorcar struck the drayman's wagon. Well, perhaps Johnny Shaugnessey was partly to blame, for not designing better brakes. Then again, Johnny *had* warned him that the car still needed work and Harry, impatient to try it out, had scoffed at him for being too cautious.

When the cell door clanged open, the hungover prisoners grimaced and groaned and clapped their hands to their heads. "Right, then!" shouted the warder, causing more grimaces and groans. "Them as was haled in for being drunk, if you've somebody to pay your fine, you're free to go. I expect I'll see most of you again next Saturday." Those who had forgiving wives filed out of the cell, along with some who had had the sense to conceal a few coins in some private part of their person. As a scrawny fellow with bad teeth tried to exit, the warder held out his truncheon to stop him. "Not you, Swingle."

"But I was drunk as a piper, Your Honor," the man protested.

"You was also carrying a pocketful of jewelry. Get back in there, now." The warder glanced at Harry and jerked his head toward the doorway. "You too."

Harry stepped inside and the door closed behind him with a sound like the crack of doom. He swallowed hard and looked around at the half-dozen criminals who remained. To a man they stared back at him. Some seemed mainly curious, some suspicious, others glared at him with outright hostility. One burly man's gaze was difficult to read, for he had but a single eye; the other had been gouged out, possibly as recently as the night before.

Harry scratched his head—could the vermin that infested these places have found him already?—and cleared his throat. "So," he said, "when do they serve breakfast around here?"

The city of London has a well-earned reputation for being foggy, chilly, and damp. But sometimes in late summer it displays a different temperament altogether. This was one of those times. Gusts of hot, dry air swept through the streets, creating miniature cyclones of dust and grit that stung the eyes. They made fools of fashionable folk, tumbling gentlemen's hats just out of their reach and turning ladies' elegant parasols inside out.

Aouda Fogg, on her way up Marylebone Lane, just managed to keep her ivory tea hat in place by clutching the brim with both gloved hands, but could do nothing to keep the veil from whipping at her face. As she stepped from the curb and into the street, she reached down with one hand to lift the hem of her skirt. The wind took advantage of this unguarded moment to lift the hat from her head and send it sailing.

"*Kosana!*" she exclaimed as she watched it dance insolently along the cobbles. Though Aouda had studied English as a schoolgirl in Bombay and could speak it flawlessly, there were times when nothing but her native language could properly express her feelings. There were no men in sight whom she might prevail upon to rescue the hat, and it certainly wouldn't do for her to go chasing after it herself. She could easily afford a replacement, of course, but it had been her favorite hat.

Feeling exposed without the veil to mask her face, she crossed to the station house. When she opened the door, the wind threatened to tear it from her hands but she wrestled it closed, in as ladylike a fashion as possible, then smoothed down her tousled dress and hair and approached the desk clerk. "Good afternoon, sir. I understand that my son is being detained here."

The clerk gave her an impatient glance, then a second, more searching one. He was, she knew, taking note of her skin and of her hair, both of which were of a darker shade than is usually seen on English women.

She longed for the lost hat and the veil. "We haven't arrested any Indian boys lately," said the clerk. "That's what you are, I take it? An East Indian?"

"I grew up in India, yes. Now I am English."

The clerk gave a slight, sarcastic grin. "If you say so." He turned back to his paperwork.

"Would you please check to see if my son's name is on your list of persons being detained here?"

"They're called prisoners."

"Then would you please check your list of *prisoners*?"

The man sighed. "All right, madam. What's his name?"

"Harry. Harry Fogg."

He raised a skeptical eyebrow. "That's no Indian name."

"Nevertheless."

The clerk quickly scanned his blotter and shook his head. "No, there's no such person here."

"He is seventeen years old, perhaps five feet ten inches in height, with curly black hair—"

"I've told you, there's no one by that name. It must have been some other station. Now if you'll excuse me."

Aouda sensed that, like most Englishmen, he disapproved of anyone from a different culture or country— even one as nearby as Ireland or Scotland. But she also guessed that, like most Victorian men, he had been taught to treat all women with respect, and she played to that part of his nature. "Please, sir. I am a mother, asking for your help. I have reason to believe that my son is being held here. If you would kindly allow me to view the prisoners, I could see for myself whether he is among them."

The clerk frowned at her for a long moment. "The jail is not a fit place for a woman."

"If that is so," replied Aouda, "then it is not a fit place for my son, either."

The clerk shook his head again, but he called the warder. "Mr. Thompson, will you show this person to the holding cell?"

As they walked along the corridor, Aouda braced herself, expecting to find a scene of degradation and squalor. But nothing could have prepared her for what she actually witnessed when she stood before the bars of the cell.

Most of the prisoners were ranged in a half circle at one end of the cell. At the other end stood a huge one-eyed man, gripping a flat piece of wood perhaps three feet long—a bed slat, it appeared—as though about to hit something with it. Directly behind him were three more bed slats set upright with a fourth laid atop them.

In the center of the cell stood a barefooted Harry, making a windup motion with his arm. "All right, now, here it comes!" he called. A moment later he launched some sort of ball at the man wielding the bed slat. The man swatted the ball, which shot across the cell, past the other prisoners, and caromed off the wall.

"A solid shot!" exclaimed Harry. "Now run! Run!"

The man, still holding the bed slat, took off for the far wall, whacked the wood against it, then scrambled back to his original spot while another man retrieved the ball and flung it at the upright slats, missing them by a few inches.

"Two runs!" shouted Harry. "Good for you!"

While the one-eyed man thrust his arms in the air and roared in triumph, the others let loose a volley of raucous jeers and boos. Grinning, Harry flapped his hands in an attempt to calm them. "Gentlemen, gentlemen!" he called. "You'll all get your chance!" Just then he caught sight of the two figures who stood outside the cell and his face sobered. "Mother," he said.

"What are you doing?" demanded Aouda.

"Teaching these men to play cricket," said Harry, as though it were the most natural thing in the world.

"I see. Well, they seem to be enjoying it. But it's time for you to go." She turned to the warder. "Will you please release my son? I will pay whatever fines are owed, and I will pay for any damages that—"

She was interrupted by a chorus of protest from the prisoners. "You can't leave!" bellowed the one-eyed man. "We was just getting started!"

Harry shrugged apologetically. "Sorry, fellows. Another time, perhaps."

"Not unless you get nicked again," said the thief named Swingle, who then added confidentially, "Insulting an officer of the law is always good for a nice short sentence." He handed Harry the cricket ball, which, it now became clear, was made of the boy's rolled-up stockings. "Don't forget these."

As Harry started to exit, another prisoner, a stocky, bald-headed man, put a massive hand on his shoulder. "Wait a bit. That there's your mum?"

"Yes, it is."

"She's from Inja, ain't she?"

"Originally, yes, but—"

"I thought so. I served in Inja, you know, and, same as your da, I had me a *bibi*. But I weren't so daft as to drag her back to England with me." He peered through the bars at Aouda. "Although if she'd looked as good as that one, I must say, I'd've been tempted—" The man broke off in midsentence as Harry's fist caught him in the jaw. He staggered backward a few steps, then gave a long sigh and sagged to the floor.

The other prisoners descended upon Harry, scowling and grumbling, but when he picked up the makeshift cricket bat and turned to face them, they hesitated. "He had it coming, gentlemen," said Harry. "If he had insulted your mother, which of you would not have done the same?" With that, he tossed the piece of wood aside and slipped out into the corridor.

## HARRY RELUCTANTLY
## FACES THE MUSIC

**H**arry was fined ten shillings for careless driving and instructed to pay two pounds to the drayman for the damage done to his cart. The clerk handed him a printed leaflet. "If you plan to go on piloting motorcars, I suggest you read that."

It contained a set of rules for self-propelled vehicles: They were to go no faster than two miles per hour; they must be preceded by a person on foot, twenty yards ahead; they must emit no smoke or steam; at the sight of a horse, they must stop altogether. Harry had thoroughly broken all four rules. "Thank you," he said, and tucked the paper into his waistcoat pocket. Outside the station house, the wind had died down a little. "Would you like to take a cab?"

"Please," said his mother. "But first, let us walk that

way for a little distance and see whether we can spy my hat."

Harry laughed. "The wind claimed it, eh?"

Aouda wrinkled her nose. "I wish you would not use that term."

"What term?"

"You know."

"Oh, you mean 'eh.' It's a very useful term, Mother. Like the French phrase '*n'est-ce pas?*'"

"French has a refined quality. The other makes you sound like a day laborer."

"Well, I shall do my best to avoid it, if it displeases you." He leaned down and gave her a swift kiss on the cheek.

"You are a good boy, Harry, if only you would try to be a bit more . . ."

"Stuffy?" said Harry. "Stiff-necked? Straitlaced?"

She couldn't help smiling. "I was about to say cautious."

"But I do try. Honestly I do. I just can't seem to get the hang of it. Oh!" He suddenly broke into a run, startling Aouda until she saw where he was headed—toward a white object that had caught on the base of a lamppost. He snatched it up and came trotting back, grinning triumphantly.

Aouda shook her head and sighed. Her son was young yet, she reminded herself. Surely in a year or two his high spirits would begin to ebb and he would learn to behave suitably. As if reading her thoughts, he gave a gentlemanly bow when he handed her the hat. The brim was smudged with dirt and the veil was partially torn off, but all in all it had survived the adventure remarkably well.

Harry hailed a hackney and helped his mother inside. "Number Seven, Savile Row, please," he told the driver. As they clattered along, he said, "How did you learn where I was?"

"Your friend Jonathan told me."

"Jona—? Oh, Johnny. Well, I wish he hadn't. Does Father know?"

"Not yet," she said. "You must tell him before someone else does. And you must apologize to him."

"Apologize? It wasn't his wagon I ran into. And it wasn't his motorcar I banged up."

"No, but it is his reputation that you have damaged by your reckless behavior. And I hardly need to remind you that this is not the first time."

Harry certainly did not need to be reminded of his past transgressions, which had increased in severity as he increased in age. At six he had taken apart his father's pocket watch to see what made it tick—or rather what had once made it tick. When he was eight, the family lost a perfectly capable housemaid after she discovered the carcass of a cat boiling on the back of the stove. To Harry's credit, the animal had been dead when he found it; he had planned to salvage the bones and assemble them like the skeletons at the Natural History Museum.

At thirteen, he came home bruised and bloodied

from playing football with the working-class boys; though a doctor was called in to set his broken nose, it did not heal quite straight, giving him a slightly raffish look. At sixteen, he disgraced himself by flunking out of Eton, having spent far too little of his time studying the classics and far too much playing cricket.

It wasn't that he disliked learning; he just didn't seem to have the patience it required. A scholar might pore over dry, dusty volumes written in dead languages for years and have precious little to show for all his effort, whereas on the cricket field or the rugby pitch, a single second of brilliant play could make a fellow the toast of the school.

In the year since he effectively ended his academic career, Harry had not done much of any consequence, either to shame his family or to make them proud. Most of his time was spent on what he called "tinkering," and what his father called "wasting time." Since an early age he had been fascinated by machinery, and especially by vehicles—everything from windup toy helicopters to bicycles to electric submersible boats. His parents had tried diligently to steer him into more gentlemanly pursuits such as riding and shooting, but Harry continued to prefer gadgets to guns and horseless carriages to horses.

The cab stopped before a narrow, two-story brick town house. As Harry helped his mother down, he called to the driver, "Would you mind a bit of advice?"

"I s'pose not," said the man, warily.

"Harry!" whispered his mother.

He ignored her. "If I were you," he told the man, "I'd get myself a steam carriage, and soon; mark my word, within a year or two horse-drawn vehicles are going to be obsolete."

The driver was clever enough not to scoff at a customer outright, but he couldn't help smiling at this absurd notion. "Are they, now? Vell, I'll give that some thought, sir." As Harry walked away, the driver said, "You're forgettin' one fing, sir."

"Oh? What's that?"

"You 'aven't paid the fare."

By the time Harry reached his room, Hudson, his father's valet, had a warm bath waiting for him and a fresh suit of clothing laid out on his bed. Though Hudson was undeniably efficient, Harry sorely missed the old valet, Passepartout. The good-natured Frenchman had taught his charge how to juggle, how to fold a piece of paper into the shape of a frog, how to make and fire a slingshot—and how to glue the vase back together so that no one would even notice.

But the things that Harry loved and admired most about Passepartout were the very things that led to his dismissal. As his parents explained it, they felt the valet was having a "disruptive influence" on Harry. Phileas Fogg had given Passepartout enough money to set up a small tobacco shop near St. James's Square. The little

Frenchman had found himself an equally good-natured wife and seemed quite content.

Harry passed close by the shop on his way to the Reform Club, where he would have to confront his father and make a full confession. He considered stopping in to talk with his old friend for a moment, just to boost his own morale, but concluded it was best to get this over with as quickly as possible.

He prayed that Andrew Stuart would not be occupying his customary spot outside the Club; Harry didn't need another embarrassing confrontation. But as he approached the imposing building, the shabby, stooped figure was waiting there, still hoping against hope that one of his old Club cronies might take pity on him and invite him in for a drink. They never did. Most turned their heads away and pretended not to recognize him; a very few stopped to ask how he was—knowing well enough that he was miserable and destitute—and, under the guise of shaking his hand, passed him a shilling or two.

Harry suspected that if he tried to give Stuart money, the man would refuse it—most likely spit on it, in fact. So he only nodded and said, "Good afternoon, Mr. Stuart."

"For you, maybe," snarled the man. Harry hurried on, but Stuart's rasping voice followed him. "You're ashamed to face me, aren't you? And well you should be, after—" His tirade was cut short by a fit of coughing.

Harry rolled his eyes at the doorman, who shrugged sympathetically and held the door for him.

It wasn't necessary to ask where he might find his father. Phileas Fogg lived his life according to a precise schedule that seldom varied—with the notable exception of his round-the-world voyage. According to friends, Mr. Fogg had once spent most of his waking time at the Club and taken all his meals there, but since his marriage almost twenty years earlier, his habits had changed somewhat. Now he had only luncheon there, after which he retired to the library to read the day's papers until the stroke of three. He then proceeded to the card room for a few rounds of whist with friends; at precisely five-forty, he rose—often in the middle of a game—and went home for supper.

Since the clock in the entry hall read a quarter to three, Harry went up the main staircase to the library, a favorite gathering spot for the more literary-minded members, including the amiable Arthur Conan Doyle. Though medicine was his real profession, Dr. Doyle had penned some historical novels—Harry had not read them—and two detective stories that Harry had rather enjoyed. At the moment, Dr. Doyle appeared to be napping. Phileas Fogg was in his habitual spot, in an armchair by the window that overlooked the courtyard.

Harry took a deep breath and started across the room. As he passed Dr. Doyle, the man glanced up at him. "Ah, Harry, you rascal. What's this I hear about a motorcar mishap?"

## OUR IMPULSIVE HERO MAKES A WAGER HE IS UNLIKELY TO WIN

**H**arry groaned inwardly. He might have known the news would make the rounds quickly. When it came to spreading gossip, society matrons were poor amateurs compared with the men of the Reform Club. He was tempted to lay all the blame on the careless drayman, but his sense of fair play wouldn't let him. "Yes, a wagon pulled out from an alley right in front of me and I couldn't stop in time. It was my fault, I suppose, for driving so fast. But you know, you can't rein in a motorcar the way you do a horse; they'll run away with you if you're not careful."

Dr. Doyle laughed. "No, I'm afraid I *don't* know. I've never ridden in one. I must say, I wouldn't mind it, though. It sounds like great fun."

"Oh, it's splendid! I'll tell you what, Doctor; the

next time I take her for a spin, you may come along."

"The next time?" said a dry voice. "It seems to me you've done quite enough damage." Phileas Fogg's words betrayed no particular feeling, not even disapproval. His voice was even and matter-of-fact, as always. And as always, it totally unnerved Harry. He would have much preferred to have his father storm and shout, for when a storm blows over the air is clear again. This was like the eerie calm before a storm that never came.

"I know," said Harry. "And I'm sorry, sir. But it won't happen again. Next time we'll tow her somewhere where there's plenty of open space and—"

The small, florid-faced man who sat on the sofa lowered his copy of the *Times*. "You'd better tow it to Bodmin Moor, then. The city is no place for these devil-wagons and their infernal noise."

"On the contrary, sir," Harry replied, a bit too sharply, "ours makes very little noise. She is not one those flimsy contraptions that resemble an overgrown baby perambulator with a clattering gasoline engine. Ours is substantially built and driven by steam—a sort of smaller version of the steam coaches that were popular fifty or sixty years ago."

The man gave a dismissive laugh. "I would hardly say steam coaches were *popular*. In point of fact, they were a dismal failure."

"Of course they were," said Harry. "But only because the railroad interests saw them as a threat and did everything in their power to destroy them."

The man's face turned even redder and he flung aside his paper. "See here, young man—"

"I'll handle this, Julius," put in Phileas Fogg. He turned to Harry. "You owe this gentleman an apology."

"I only spoke the truth," Harry protested.

"I believe Mr. Hardiman is in a better position to know about such things than you are. He is, after all, president of the Great Southern Railway."

"Oh." Harry gave an embarrassed grin. Though he was quick to fly off the handle, he was also quick to make amends. "I do apologize then, sir. I didn't mean to be discourteous. It's just that . . . Well, it gets my back up when people speak of motorcars as if they're merely a nuisance, some sort of frivolous toy."

"Aren't they?"

"No, sir. I believe they are the most practical form of transportation ever invented, and within a very few years, half the population of London will own one."

Hardiman gave an incredulous snort. "Really? So you think they will replace the locomotive, do you?"

"I don't know. But they will surely replace the horse."

The railroad man laughed again, and most of the others joined in—with the exception of Phileas Fogg.

"Not the motorcars I've seen, I'm afraid," said Dr. Doyle. "The few that actually work travel no faster than a man can walk, and they get bogged down in a large mud puddle."

"You're quite right," said Harry.

"Ah, he agrees!" crowed Hardiman.

"But," Harry went on, "as I said, the *Flash* is a different sort of motorcar altogether."

"The *Flash*?" echoed Hardiman with a chuckle.

"Yes. We haven't given her a proper road test yet, but she has plenty of power and not much weight. We fully expect her to do thirty miles per hour or more and ford a stream or climb a hill better than a team of Clydesdales."

"I think perhaps you exaggerate," said Phileas Fogg.

"You haven't seen her in action, Father!" Harry exclaimed. Then, knowing how Phileas Fogg disliked displays of emotion, he added more calmly, "I really don't feel I'm exaggerating in the least, Father."

Fogg regarded his son evenly for a moment. Just as he seemed about to respond, the clock struck three. He rose automatically from his chair, as though he himself were run by clockwork. "Pardon me, gentlemen. I have an appointment in the card room."

Harry wondered what his father had been about to say. Was he curious at all about what Harry's motorcar could do? Or did he feel, too, that the machines were useless? Was he truly ashamed of his son's unconventional behavior and attitude? Or did some part of him secretly admire Harry's spirit? Guessing what lay beneath that calm, composed exterior was like trying to fathom what the Buddha was thinking, or the Mona Lisa. No wonder the man was such a formidable card-player; his opponents could have no inkling of what sort of hand he held. Unfortunately, neither could his partner.

The other club members, seeing the opportunity for a rousing discussion, had pulled their chairs closer. "So," said Mr. Sullivan, the banker, "this *Flash* of yours. Is she built any better than these—what did you call them? Overgrown perambulators?"

"Oh, far better. Johnny's given her a frame of ash, like the best carriages, and made the body from light-weight sheets of aluminum."

"Johnny?" said Dr. Doyle. "You don't mean Johnny Shaugnessey?"

Harry nodded enthusiastically. "My friend is a genius at this sort of thing."

"The boy who was kicked in the head by a horse?" said Mr. Flanagan, the brewer. "I'd hardly call him a *genius*."

"I know, I know," said Harry. "When he's dealing with people he's slow and awkward. But when it comes to machines he has a . . . a sort of *instinct*."

Flanagan laughed. "Instinct? I thought that was the province of animals."

"Whatever you call it," said Harry impatiently, "he knows how to build things. When we've got the kinks worked out, this motorcar will be able to go anywhere. Why, if I wanted to, I daresay I could drive her around the world."

For a moment there was dead silence in the room. "Well, now," said Hardiman, the railroad man. "That's a wildly extravagant statement. You wouldn't care to retract that, would you?"

Harry hesitated. Perhaps it had been a grandiose claim. But he didn't like the condescending tone of these men, the way they made fun of Johnny and of the machine to which the two of them had devoted hundreds of hours of greasy, backbreaking, knuckle-skinning work.

He looked Hardiman in the eye. "No, sir," he said. "I am confident that she would be up to the task."

"Really?" said the railroad man. "Just how confident are you?"

"What do you mean, sir?"

"I mean, would you be willing to bet money on it?"

"Certainly."

"How much?"

"Whatever sum you propose."

"How does two thousand pounds strike you?"

The truth was, it struck him almost dumb; though it might seem a reasonable wager to the president of a railroad, for him it was a huge one—roughly ten times the amount he had spent building the *Flash*. But his pride wouldn't let him back down. He bowed slightly. "Two thousand it is."

With a self-satisfied smirk, Hardiman turned to the other members. "Perhaps some of you gentlemen would like to propose wagers of your own?"

"Not I," said Dr. Doyle. "A poor physician and struggling author can't afford such immoderate gestures. And frankly, Harry, I'm not sure that you should be—"

"Count me in," interrupted Flanagan, eagerly. "I have another two thousand that says you'll never make it."

"If the boy is willing," said Sullivan, "I'm in for an equal amount."

"The more you gentlemen wager, the more I stand to win," said Harry staunchly. Though six thousand pounds was a staggering sum, his confidence in the car and in himself remained firm.

"Excellent!" Hardiman rubbed his hands together. "Shall we shake on it, then?"

"One moment," said Sullivan. "Perhaps we should set some sort of parameters, here. After all, if we give him an unlimited amount of time, of course he can do it. He could rebuild the car as many times as necessary. That wouldn't prove anything."

Harry did a quick series of calculations in his head. He knew from repeatedly tracing the route of his father's famous journey that the distance around the world was roughly 25,000 miles. He could count on the *Flash* to average at least 25 miles per hour. If he drove ten hours each day, that was 250 miles per day.

Two hundred and fifty divided into 25,000 was: "One hundred days," he said.

"I beg your pardon?" said Sullivan.

"Does one hundred days sound like a fair allowance of time?"

The men glanced at one another. "You really think that's enough?" said Flanagan.

"Don't argue with the lad," said Hardiman. "If he says he can do it that quickly, let him prove it. When will you start?"

"Within the week."

"Excellent!" Hardiman repeated, gleefully. "Dr. Doyle, would you please make a note of all of this, for the record? Six thousand pounds. One hundred days."

"One more thing," said Sullivan. "We should clearly stipulate that the vehicle must go the entire distance under its own power—that is, not aboard a flatcar or a ship, or towed by horses."

"You can hardly expect me to drive across the ocean," said Harry. "Or across rivers."

"Of course not," said Hardiman. "Let the record state, then, that you may ship the motorcar across any and all bodies of water, but otherwise the motorcar must travel under its own power. Agreed?"

"Agreed." Harry shook the hands of the three men in turn. "And now, if you will excuse me, I have quite a number of preparations to make."

As he left the library, he heard Hardiman say snidely

to the others, "He needs to prepare himself all right—to lose this wager!"

Harry's heart was racing and he felt flushed and vibrant, the way he did after bowling a strenuous inning of cricket. "Go ahead and laugh, gentlemen," he muttered under his breath. "The last laugh will be mine."

He was halfway down the stairs before a thought occurred to him that dampened his buoyant mood. If he was going to travel all the way around the world, he would need a certain amount of money for expenses— just how much money, he wasn't sure. According to Harry's mother, her husband had spent something on the order of ten thousand pounds in making his epic journey, but that was an extreme case. After all, in addition to paying for his passage and Passepartout's, Fogg had purchased a whole ship, not to mention an entire elephant.

Harry's expenses would be far more modest. Fuel was no problem; the *Flash* would burn nearly anything, from kerosene to wood chips. Nor was lodging; he could sleep in the car. But he would need food and steamship tickets and that sort of thing.

Every cent of his own income had gone into building the *Flash*, and, though his mother had ample money for personal and household expenses, she had nothing put by.

There was no option but to approach his father.

# FOUR

*Showing that*

## ALTHOUGH PHILEAS FOGG DOES NOT DRIVE A MOTORCAR, HE DOES DRIVE A HARD BARGAIN

Of the twenty thousand pounds he had won as a result of his famous wager, Phileas Fogg had put five thousand into a trust fund for his son, where it had sat for nearly two decades, collecting three percent interest per annum. Harry himself couldn't draw upon the fund until the age of twenty-one. But perhaps he could persuade his father to advance him a small portion of it.

Harry would have been wise to wait until five-forty, when Phileas Fogg's customary whist-playing time was over. But Harry was not known for his wisdom; he headed at once for the card room.

His father was seated at a table with three other men, all of whom glanced up and greeted Harry. Phileas Fogg seemed oblivious of his presence. The man's attention was entirely on the game. "Sir?" said Harry softly. There was no response. "Father? I need to talk to you."

"I'm listening," said his father, without looking up from his cards. "Six diamonds."

"It's . . . it's a private matter."

"Is it urgent?"

"Yes, sir." Well, that was true, in a sense. After all, he had only a week in which to do everything.

"Will you excuse me, gentlemen?" Fogg led his son to the private drawing room that adjoined the card room. "Is something wrong?"

"Not exactly. You see . . ." Whenever Harry was in a tight spot, he took the same approach he did in cricket: No use shilly-shallying, just deliver the ball and take what comes. "Well, sir, after you left, I bet Hardiman and his friends that I could drive the *Flash* around the world."

"The motorcar?"

"Yes, sir."

Phileas Fogg showed no surprise or alarm, in fact no emotion in particular. "I see. Is there money involved?"

"Yes, sir. Six thousand pounds."

"That's a considerable sum."

"You once wagered far more than that," Harry reminded him, "and from what I've heard, you didn't blink an eye."

"That's true. But there was a major difference between my situation and yours. Had I lost—and, you will recall, I came very near to it—I had the funds to make good on my wager."

"It would have left you practically penniless."

"Nonetheless, I could have done it. If *you* lose, you can't possibly pay, which means I shall be responsible for your debt."

Harry winced slightly; he hadn't thought of that. "The money from my trust fund would cover it, would it not?"

For the first time, a touch of irritation found its way into Phileas Fogg's voice. "That money was put aside to help you set yourself up in life, not to pay off an ill-considered bet."

"I know that," said Harry, rather meekly. Then he took a deep breath and soldiered on. "In any case, I have no intention of losing. The *Flash* is fast and she's reliable. My main concern is how to finance the trip."

"You receive a rather generous allowance—two pounds a week, if I am not mistaken. I would have thought you could manage to save some of it."

"No, sir. I've put it into building the *Flash*. I was hoping you might see your way clear to advance me a few hundred pounds."

"From the trust fund."

"Yes, sir."

"The same trust fund with which I am expected to pay your debt."

"Only if I lose."

Hands clasped behind his back, Phileas Fogg gazed

down at the horse-drawn traffic on Pall Mall. At last he said, "Have you thought at all about your future?"

Harry was thrown off balance by this sudden change of topic. "My—my future, sir?"

"What you'll make of yourself. Even if you don't lose it on this wager of yours, five thousand pounds won't last forever. You'll need to settle on a profession of some sort."

"Profession?" said Harry. "To be honest, I hadn't thought about it." He had grown up with the vague notion that being a gentleman was a profession in itself—one that, admittedly, he was not very good at. "You have no profession, sir," Harry pointed out, "or none that I'm aware of."

"Not presently, no. But when I was a young man, I did actually work for a living."

"You did?"

Phileas Fogg turned to him with a thin, almost imperceptible smile. "How did you imagine I amassed my wealth, such as it is?"

"I—I was not sure. I assumed that you inherited it, I suppose. What sort of work were you engaged in, then?"

"That is not the issue here. The question was, what do *you* intend to make of yourself? You might, of course, do as so many other well-born young men have done, and go on living off the family fortune for as long as it lasts. But I expect—or at least I hope—that your sense of pride would not let you be content with that."

"No," said Harry. "Of course not."

"I had thought at one point that you might go into law, or perhaps medicine," said Phileas Fogg. He might have added, *That was before you flunked out of Eton*, but he did not. "I don't suppose that is likely to happen."

"No, sir. Offhand, I can think of no profession that truly appeals to me."

Phileas Fogg stared out the window again. After a time, he said, "With whom did you make this wager of yours?"

"With Mr. Hardiman, Mr. Sullivan, and Mr. Flanagan. Each of them wagered two thousand pounds."

"You are aware, I suppose, that the latter two were among the very men who bet that I could not circle the world in eighty days."

"No! I thought your wager was with Andrew Stuart!"

"He was the one to start it rolling, but four others climbed aboard, including Sullivan and Flanagan. Their fortunes were large enough to recover from the loss; Stuart's was not. Stuart has never forgiven me, as you know."

Harry nodded. "He harangued me yet again, outside the Club."

"Yes, well, I believe the others still nurse a grudge as well. I suspect that they seized upon this as an opportunity to take their revenge."

"Then they'll be extremely disappointed, for I intend to win."

"You seem very certain."

"As certain as you were when you made your wager."

Phileas Fogg fixed that unnerving, inscrutable gaze upon Harry. "Very well," he said, finally. "Here is what I propose. I shall advance you the money you require for the trip, and, should you lose, I shall pay your debt." Harry's face broke into a relieved grin, which faded only a little when his father added, "On one condition. You must agree that, if you *do* lose, you will abandon all this *tinkering* and this squandering of money, and take up some profession appropriate for a gentleman— not grudgingly, not halfheartedly, but cheerfully and diligently."

Harry had the unfortunate habit of hearing only what he cared to hear and disregarding the rest. His father had said that he would finance the trip; that was the important part. Anything else could be dealt with later. "You have my word, Father." They sealed the bargain, as gentlemen do, with a firm handshake. "I'd better go and break the news to Johnny."

"You'll want to hire an experienced driver, of course. Perhaps I can help locate one."

"No, no," said Harry hastily. "That's all taken care of." The experienced driver he had in mind was himself, but his father probably did not need to know that.

# FIVE

*In which*

## HARRY'S PLANS ARE SERIOUSLY ALTERED, IF NOT RUINED ALTOGETHER

**H**arry's parents had dismissed a valet because they considered him a bad influence on their son; unfortunately, they could do nothing about Harry's choice of friends.

Gentlemen were expected to associate with others of their class. Johnny Shaugnessey was not even close. His mother was a naive farmgirl who came to London to better her lot. She married Michael Shaugnessey, an honest blacksmith who, for all his hard work, could barely keep them fed and clothed. Within a year, she died giving birth to his son. When Johnny was twelve, an Irish mob began demanding protection money from the artisans and merchants of York Court, most of whom were also Irish. Michael Shaugnessey refused to pay them, so they beat him brutally with his own hammer; he died a week later.

Even at that age, Johnny was as large and strong as most men. He found work with a friend of his father's, a carriage maker, and was beginning to show some real promise as both a craftsman and a designer when an accident ended his career. One day a young gentleman arrived to pick up a fast phaeton that the firm had built to order for him. Johnny harnessed the customer's high-strung bay mare to the carriage, then crouched down to check the whiffletree, which wasn't moving as freely as it should. The horse lashed out with a rear hoof, catching Johnny on the top of the head, caving in his skull.

A surgeon at London Hospital Medical College managed to save the boy's life by cutting away the broken bone and covering the resulting hole with a thin metal plate. But he could do nothing to repair the damage done to the brain. Though Johnny recovered most of his faculties to some degree, he never quite returned to normal.

At the same time, the accident left him with one ability he had not possessed before: He developed an uncanny rapport with all things mechanical, from clocks to steam engines. He seemed to understand instinctively not only how they worked but how they could be made to work better. It was as though, by virtue of the metal plate screwed into his skull, he had become part machine himself and spoke the language, as it were.

Johnny led a Spartan existence, sleeping in one corner of his father's old shop, cooking his scanty meals on the forge. Despite his slow, sometimes sullen manner, his skill as a mechanic and blacksmith earned him a fair amount of business—more than he would have liked, actually. He did not deal well with people; he much preferred to spend his time in the rickety shed at the rear of the smithy, tinkering with machines. For the past year, most of his efforts had, like Harry's, been focused on a single project, his most ambitious to date—a steam-driven motorcar.

When Harry arrived, direct from making his devil's bargain with Phileas Fogg, he found Johnny sitting on the dirt floor of the shed, soldering copper pipe with an acetylene torch. Harry examined the right front fender of the *Flash*, the one he had caved in when he struck the beer wagon. Johnny had pounded it out so skillfully that the damage was barely visible. "Splendid work, my lad," said Harry. Though Johnny was probably at least twenty, Harry always thought of him as being younger, and often spoke to him in an almost parental fashion. "What's that you're making?"

"Condenser," mumbled Johnny.

"A condenser? Oh, I see. For the steam. We're going to catch it, cool it, and recirculate it, back into the water tank." Heedless of the dirt, Harry sat on a packing crate. "Here, let me help." He held one length of pipe while Johnny soldered another to it.

"With this, I figure . . ." Johnny paused, as if he needed to work out the words in his head before he spoke them. "I figure she'll go two hundred miles. Maybe more."

"On one tank of water?" Harry whistled. "That's impressive. I was just wondering what I'd do if I had to drive through a long stretch of country with no water. I was afraid I might have to relieve myself in the tank."

Johnny gave him a crooked grin and shook his head. Then a suspicious look came over his slightly lopsided face. "Why would you?"

"Why would I what?" said Harry innocently.

"Go someplace with no water."

"Oh, that. No reason. I was just wondering. It's what you call a hypothetical situation."

Johnny got to his feet, dusting the dirt from his trousers. "Liar."

Harry eyed the burning torch. "Would you please shut that thing off?"

"I may have to use it," said Johnny. "If you don't tell me."

Harry laughed. "All right, all right. But you might want to sit down again."

"Why?"

"Because what I have to say is staggering in its import." He paused for dramatic effect. "I've entered the *Flash* in a race."

"A race? With who?"

"Not against other motorcars. Against a time limit."

"How long?"

"One hundred days."

Johnny stared at him blankly. "The distance, I mean."

"Oh, that. A mere twenty-five thousand miles. More or less." Harry made a circular motion with his hand. "Around the world, actually."

Johnny was in fact feeling a sudden need to sit down; he perched on the bumper of the *Flash*. "You're joking again."

"It's true, I swear it."

Johnny was silent a moment, then said softly, "You never asked me."

"What do you mean? Oh, I see. You mean that I didn't consult you before making the wager. Well, I suppose I felt it was my decision to make, since it's my money we've been using to build the *Flash*." The reproachful look on Johnny's face made Harry a bit ashamed. "I'm sorry, that was unfair; you've done the lion's share of the work. She's your motorcar as much as mine." He shrugged. "Perhaps I should have asked you first. But I just assumed you'd *want* to race her. After all, think of what it will mean if we win, lad. It'll prove to everyone once and for all what the motorcar is capable of!"

"We don't know."

"Don't know what? Oh, what she's capable of." Harry gave the fender of the *Flash* a confident pat. "Well, then, it looks as if we'll find out, eh?"

◆　◆　◆

Though Harry was known to exaggerate, when he had bragged that the *Flash* was a different sort of motorcar altogether, he was not overstating the case. Over the previous half-century, inventors had come up with a wide variety of self-propelled vehicles. But the steam-driven ones, with their huge boilers and heavy cast-iron engines, were too slow and ungainly to be practical. The newly developed internal combustion engine was far lighter, but also far less powerful, so "petro cars" tended to be small and rather flimsy, totally unsuited to high speeds or long distances.

To propel the *Flash*, Johnny had built a boiler of thin-gauge steel wrapped with piano wire for strength; at ninety pounds, it weighed half as much as the standard boiler, yet could handle three times as much steam pressure. With the help of a machinist, he had designed and created an engine that weighed a mere fifty pounds but was more efficient than engines four times its size.

Since most of the mechanical parts were concealed beneath the seats or the floorboards, the *Flash* looked much like any other large carriage. The difference lay in how it performed. The ash-wood frame was strong and flexible yet lighter than steel, and the body was made of aluminum, so the motorcar weighed no more than a typical four-horse coach. But its steam engine had the power of twenty or thirty horses—theoretically, at least. How reliably it could deliver that power had yet to be seen.

There was no time to road test the car and make

improvements or adjustments. Harry had promised to be ready in a week—just enough time to complete the tasks they already knew were necessary: hooking up the condenser, putting better lining on the brake shoes, replacing a faulty steam valve, getting the water gauge to work, adding a cyclometer to measure the miles, fashioning an extra set of wheels, and, of course, purchasing all the equipment and supplies Harry would need.

"Bully beef!" Johnny called from beneath the motorcar, where he was installing a new oil line.

"Is that a new form of cursing?" said Harry. "Or did you want me to buy some?"

"Buy some."

"You mean the sort in tins?" Harry grimaced. "I don't like it."

"I do."

"Well, that's fine. But I'm getting food for the trip, and you're not coming."

"Yes, I am."

Harry knelt and peered under the car. "I'm the one who tells the jokes around here."

"'Tis no joke."

"Johnny, it was I who made the bet. You're not obliged to help me. This trip won't be any picnic, you know. There's not much in the way of roads, and precious few hotels or pubs. I'll be driving ten to fifteen hours a day and sleeping in the car, or in a tent, in all sorts of weather. It'll be dirty and miserable and exhausting."

Johnny turned his head to look at Harry. "So," he said, "why should you have all the fun?"

Harry sat back on his heels and scratched his head. "You know, now that I think about it, it might not be a bad idea. She's a fine car, but she's bound to have problems sooner or later, and I may not always be able to fix them. The only thing is . . . I mean, do you think . . . that is, are you certain you're up to it?"

"I'm certain."

"It's just that sometimes you have those . . . spells."

"I'm certain!" shouted Johnny, so vehemently that Harry flinched. After a minute or two, he heard his friend murmur, "I'm sorry. You said she's my motorcar, too. I should get to go."

"No need to apologize. You're quite right. You should get to go, and go you shall." Harry got to his feet. "How much bully beef do you want?"

Before Johnny could reply, there was a knock at the door of the shed. "Who could that be?" Harry lifted the latch and swung the door open to find three gentlemen in morning coats and bowler hats, looking wholly out of place in these rather shabby surroundings. One was a stranger to Harry, a blond youth of about his size and age. The others were all too familiar. "Mr. Sullivan. Mr. Hardiman. What brings you to York Court?"

Sullivan the banker took a long Havana cigar from between his teeth and blew a ring of smoke. "We thought we'd have a look at this motorcar of yours."

"I see. You're wondering whether there's any chance I might actually win, is that it?"

"Not at all," said Hardiman irritably. "We merely wanted to make certain you'd be ready within the week, as agreed."

"Oh, we'll be ready. As for whether or not you may look her over, I'll have to ask Mr. Shaugnessey." He called to Johnny, "The men who made the wager are here. Is it all right if they examine the *Flash*?"

"I guess," grumbled Johnny. "Don't let them touch nothing."

"You may look but not touch," Harry told the visitors. The three slowly circled the vehicle, doing their best not to brush against the assorted parts that leaned against the walls or step on the tools and piles of oily rags that littered the floor.

"I must say," the railroad man grudgingly admitted, "she's built far better than I expected."

"Thank you, sir."

"Mind you, I still don't believe she'll make it around the world. If you're lucky, you might get across the United States. But you'd better take along a lot of spare parts."

"I'll keep that in mind."

Hardiman shoved aside a pile of filthy rags with the polished tip of one shoe and approached Harry. "Good.

I know machines, and I know what I'm talking about. Here's another piece of advice. If you should by some miracle manage to reach Asia, take the shortest possible land route from there. If I were you, I'd catch a steamer to Hong Kong and go across southern China and northern India. That should cut nearly a thousand miles off your journey."

"I see. But why are you telling me this, sir? I should think it would be in your best interest for us to take as *long* a route as possible."

"Because," put in Sullivan, "we want you to have every chance to succeed, so that when you lose, there will be no excuses, no crying foul."

"There will not be, I assure you. Now, if you will excuse me, gentlemen, I am on my way to purchase equipment and supplies for the trip."

"Before you go," said the railroad man, "let me introduce my son, Charles Hardiman."

Harry shook the blond youth's hand cordially. "Pleased to make your acquaintance." The boy's handshake was limp and his palm felt cold against Harry's.

"Likewise," said Charles with a slight lisp, but without the least hint of pleasure. He withdrew his hand, glanced at it, then rubbed at his palm with a handkerchief.

"I've talked it over with your father," said Julius Hardiman, "and we feel it would be best if you took along an impartial observer."

Harry stared at him. "What do you mean?"

"I mean that Charles will be going with you, to make certain there are no . . . infractions, shall we say? No bending of the rules?"

"I agreed to the terms," Harry said, heatedly. "I gave you my word!"

"When your father made his famous wager, he also agreed to the terms. But apparently there was some question as to whether or not he lived up to them."

"He showed up at the Reform Club on the specified date!"

"That's true," said Sullivan. "He did circle the globe in eighty *calendar* days. But only because he crossed the international date line and thus gained a day. The fact remains, the actual elapsed time was eighty-*one* days."

Harry felt his fists clenching, and he thrust them in his pockets. "Well, you needn't worry, sir, because I'll be traveling west, so I'll actually be *losing* a day."

"That's not such an important issue, here, since you have more time," said Hardiman. "Our main concern is that the motorcar go the entire distance under its own power. To make certain of that, we need to have an observer aboard."

"An *impartial* observer, you said. What reason do I have to believe that your son would be impartial?"

"You have my word on it," said Charles coolly.

"Oh, so *my* word isn't good enough, but *yours* is?"

"Your father has already agreed to this," said Hardiman, "so I'm afraid it's all settled."

"He had no right to speak for me! This is my wager!"

"Ah, but you had no money to back it up."

Though Harry was seething, he managed to say, in a fairly civil tone, "Perhaps you should leave, now. We have a good deal of work to do, and you might get your fine clothing dirty."

As Harry strode up the street toward Fortnum & Mason's department store, he caught sight of another figure he thought he recognized. When he stopped and turned to make certain, the man disappeared down a side street. Harry went on, reciting under his breath a litany of ungentlemanly things he should have said to that lobster-faced midget, Hardiman, and his foppish son, and to that smirking money-grubber, Sullivan.

An hour later he returned, this time riding in a hackney and surrounded by crates and packages—a veritable cornucopia of tinned meats, soups, and milk, plus a variety of desiccated fruits and vegetables. Selecting these supplies would have taken most people an entire day; Harry had simply snatched up a bit of this and a bit of that. He had also bought a splendid sports knife that could be transformed into a variety of useful tools, including a screwdriver, a saw, scissors, an awl, a file, a corkscrew, and a drill.

As they drew near the blacksmith shop, the driver shouted, "Cor! There's summat afire up ahead!"

Harry thrust his head out the cab window. Roiling clouds of black smoke were rising from the vicinity of the shop. "Drive on!" he ordered. "Quickly!" He had the door open and was leaping from the cab before it rolled to a stop. He dashed around to the rear of the shop to see one corner of the shed engulfed in flames. "Find a fire station or an alarm box!" he called to the cabdriver.

"What'll I do wiv your purchases, then?"

"Never mind that! Just go!"

The door of the shed flew open and Johnny stumbled out, coughing. "The *Flash!* We got to save her!"

"Come on, then!" Harry yanked a handkerchief from his vest pocket. Covering his nose and mouth, he plunged into the smoky interior. Luckily, all the car's wheels were currently attached. Harry began pushing the vehicle, only to jerk his hands away as the hot metal seared his skin. He put one shoulder against the car and heaved. For all their efforts to make the *Flash* as light as possible, it was no featherweight. Harry couldn't budge it.

He glanced furtively at half a dozen metal cans filled with kerosene, which they'd been using for fuel. If the flames reached those, the shed and everything in it would be incinerated instantly. He seized one of the cans and flung it through the nearest window.

Johnny appeared beside him, a filthy rag pressed to his face. Together they tossed out the rest of the kerosene cans, then turned to the car. Just above their heads, the roof rafters were ablaze. "On three!" called Harry. "One! Two! Three!"

The *Flash* rocked forward slightly, then settled back. "Again! One! Two! Three!" It still refused to move.

"The gear stick!" said Johnny.

Harry groaned. He hadn't checked to see whether the driving gear was engaged. He flung himself over the top of the passenger door and whacked the gear stick painfully with one hand until it disengaged. At once, the *Flash* began to roll.

Just as they got it through the doorway, part of the shed roof collapsed, so close behind them that sparks stung the back of Harry's neck. "Keep going!" he cried. "Get her as far away as possible!" Ahead was a board fence that marked the edge of the adjoining property. They mowed it down and kept pushing until the front bumper rammed up against the neighbor's privy.

The friends sank to the ground, drawing ragged breaths punctuated by racking coughs. Through his own wheezing, Harry heard the sound of a clanging bell. "The fire brigade," he gasped.

"Too late." Johnny nodded toward the shed. The remainder of the roof caved in, sending up an enormous billow of greasy smoke. The horse-drawn fire wagon drew up before the blacksmith shop; firemen scrambled to hook up the hand-operated pump and direct a jet of water onto the flames.

"Did we lose anything crucial?" asked Harry.

Johnny stopped sucking on his burned fingers long enough to reply, "My tools."

"Those can be replaced. We saved the *Flash*; that's the important thing. And you, of course. Do you have any idea how it started?"

Johnny shrugged. "Oily rags?"

"Something had to set them off. You weren't using the acetylene torch?"

"No."

"And you weren't smoking your pipe?"

"No."

Harry stared at the smoldering ruin. "Wait a moment. I know who *was* smoking—Sullivan. When he arrived, he had a cigar. I don't recall seeing it when he left."

"You think he did it a-purpose?"

"There's no way of knowing. He and Hardiman seemed surprised that the *Flash* was so well built; perhaps they realized we might actually win, and decided to destroy our chances by destroying the car. However . . ." Harry paused to think. "It is possible that the culprit may have been someone else altogether. Did you see anyone skulking around after I left?"

Johnny shook his head.

"Did you leave the shed at all?"

"I went to the privy."

"That might have given him enough time."

"Who?"

"As I was heading up Baker Street earlier, I thought I caught a glimpse of someone I know. Or, more accurately, someone my father knows. Someone who hates my father—and by extension, our whole family—so much that I suspect he'd jump at any chance to strike back at us."

"Who?" repeated Johnny.

"His name is Andrew Stuart."

# SIX

## AOUDA FOGG REVEALS AN UNPLEASANT SECRET FROM HER PAST

**T**he cabman returned with Harry's supplies and drove him home. Harry had meant to have it out with his father over this "impartial observer" business. But, though the boy's temper could flare up quickly, it died down almost as quickly. There was really no point in arguing the matter, anyway. Once Phileas Fogg made up his mind about something, he was like the *Flash* with its gears engaged—immovable.

His mother tended to his burned hands, smearing them carefully with salve and binding them with gauze. "Now perhaps you will call off this trip of yours," she said.

"Of course not. Why would I?"

"Because it is dangerous!" she said, so sharply that Harry blinked in surprise. "You might have been killed!"

"The fire was an accident, Mother." Well, it *could* have been an accident. There was no proof that it had been set deliberately. "It had nothing to do with the trip."

"Well, in any case, how will you drive a motorcar with your hands like this?"

Harry shrugged. "I'll manage. I'll wear heavy gloves. Besides, Johnny can do some of the driving."

"Why do you not hire a driver, as your father suggested—someone more experienced?"

"Motorcars are such a new invention, I'm afraid no one has much experience driving them. Besides, with Johnny and Charles Hardiman aboard, we'd scarcely have room for another person."

"You do not mind taking the Hardiman boy?"

"I'm not thrilled by the prospect. He's rather a cold fish."

"I hope you two will get along. He was here with his father. He seems a pleasant enough boy, and very well mannered. Perhaps it will do you good to spend some time with him."

"Maybe some of his fine manners will rub off on me, you mean?"

Aouda gave a wry smile. "I would not mind if they did. Nor, I suspect, would your father. However, the real reason he agreed to let Charles Hardiman go along was to avoid any misunderstanding as to whether or not the rules were followed."

Harry threw up his hands, then winced at the pain it

caused. "So Father thinks I'm going to cheat as well?"

"Of course not. He only wants to be certain that you will not be accused of it."

"Why don't those men trust me? I agreed to their rules. We shook hands on it. Father always says that an English gentleman's word is his bond, but it doesn't seem to be good enough for them."

"I think that perhaps . . . perhaps they do not quite consider you an English gentleman."

Harry laughed. "Why? Because I couldn't make the grade at Eton? Because I have dirt under my finger-nails? Because I'm not a Little Lord Fauntleroy, like Charles Hardiman?"

"Those things may be a part of it. But I believe that the main reason is your heritage."

"You mean . . . because I'm half Indian?"

She nodded.

The notion took Harry by surprise. Not that he was any stranger to prejudice. In his younger years, he had thrashed at least half a dozen boys for calling him or his mother a "wog." That was one reason he took to playing with the working-class lads. They didn't know much about his background, and didn't particularly care, as long as he could kick a football. At Eton, he had not bothered to mention that his mother came from India, and his skin was light enough that no one was likely to guess.

After years of fitting in, of feeling no different from any other well-bred English lad, it was something of a shock to find that, in the eyes of the people he considered his peers, he was still somehow inferior, and not to be trusted.

It suddenly occurred to him that his mother must face that same attitude each time she left her house, and had no doubt done so ever since her arrival in England twenty years before. He had always wondered why she went out so little, why she had so few friends—only a half-dozen artists and musicians who were considered too Bohemian for polite society.

Aside from Mr. Gandhi, a law student who was a distant relation and who sometimes took dinner with them, she made little effort to associate with London's sizable Indian population. In fact, she seemed at times to be deliberately avoiding her countrymen. Harry supposed that this was her way of trying to protect him; she was fiercely determined that he should be as English as possible.

"You know," said Aouda, "that I am unhappy about your making this trip."

"Yes, but—"

She held up a hand to silence him. "However, I have not told you the true reason." And she did not tell him now. After a pause, she said, "Have you decided what route you will take?"

"We'll land in New York, drive the most direct route to San Francisco, then take a steamer to Asia."

"And then?"

"Well, Mr. Hardiman said we would cut a thousand

miles off the journey if we drove across southern China and northern India."

Aouda nodded solemnly. "That is what I feared."

"Feared? What is there to fear about it?"

"Your father told me that, when he was traveling around the world, the newspapers all printed reports of his progress. Will the same happen with your trip?"

"I suppose so. It's the first time anyone's tried to take a motorcar around the world, after all."

"Then people in India will read about it, in the English papers."

"So?"

She sighed heavily. "I have never spoken of this to anyone but your father. Now I suppose I must. You know that I grew up in Bombay."

"Yes."

"When I was little older than you, my parents died and my cousin arranged a marriage for me, to a wealthy prince from the province of Bundelkund. This may not sound like such an awful fate, but the man was three times my age. He died within a year and, to make certain I would inherit none of his fortune, his family conspired to be rid of me.

"Traditionally, when a Hindu man died and was cremated, his widow was burned alongside him, a practice called *sati*. My husband's family attempted to revive the practice; they drugged me with opium and I would have perished on the funeral pyre had your father and Passepartout not rescued me.

"According to my cousin, who now lives in Europe, the prince's relatives have never forgiven me for escaping their clutches." She smiled wanly. "Apparently they fear, even now, that I might return to claim my inheritance and wreak vengeance upon them. My cousin has never gone back to India; because we are related, the prince's family might try to harm him, or perhaps kidnap him in order to have some hold over me. They are a fanatical lot, and I would put nothing past them." She laid her hand gently on Harry's bandaged ones. "You see now why I do not wish you to go. If they were to learn that my son is passing through India . . ."

Harry patted her hand reassuringly. "You needn't worry, Mother. If they did try to abduct me, they'd have a deuce of a time doing it. The *Flash* can outrun the fastest horse. And even if they were to catch me, I can handle myself. Besides, I'll have Johnny along for reinforcement, and you know how strong he is. It's possible that the Hardiman brat may even be of some use; we're taking firearms with us, and I assume he knows how to shoot."

Aouda was silent for a moment, gazing so intently at him that he felt uncomfortable. Finally she said, "I can see that you are determined to go, and that nothing I say will deter you."

"I'm afraid not."

To Harry's surprise, her mouth formed a slight, wry smile. "I wish you truly *were* afraid. I know that I am." She gave a sigh of resignation. "But I also fear what will happen if you remain here, drifting aimlessly along as you have been. If this will give you some sense of direction, perhaps it is for the best."

Harry laughed. "I hope I have *some* sense of direction, Mother, or I may not make it as far as Liverpool."

After dinner, Harry excused himself, saying, "There are still a number of items I need to purchase for the trip." That was true. His actual destination, however, was not Fortnum & Mason's but the blacksmith shop. Armed with an old carbine that had belonged to Johnny's father, he kept watch over the motorcar for several hours while Johnny caught some sleep. At eleven, Harry went home, leaving his friend to stand guard through the night.

They repeated this ritual the following night, and the night after. Every hour of daylight was spent getting the *Flash* in shape for the long, grueling journey—well, in truth, not *every* hour, for the press had now gotten wind of the wager, and reporters from the *Times*, the *Standard*, the *Morning Post*, the *Daily News*, the *Daily Telegraph*, and the *Illustrated London News* descended upon them, demanding details about the motorcar and its drivers.

Johnny sullenly ignored the newspaper men and women. It was up to Harry to satisfy them and their readers—not that he really minded. He had always relished being the center of attention, perhaps because he received so little from his father. Despite his dismal academic record, he had been something of a celebrity at Eton. He was driven to excel at everything—as long as it did not involve studying or memorizing—and had often been carried off the cricket field or rugby pitch on the shoulders of his teammates for bowling the final out or kicking the winning drop goal. For the past year he had been out of the limelight altogether; it was good to be back.

His enthusiasm quickly faded when he realized that the reporters were less interested in him and his motorcar than in comparing his journey to the one made by Phileas Fogg. He was asked the same few questions over and over: "Will you try to beat your father's record?" "Do you think you'll be attacked by wild Indians, as your father was?" "How does your father feel about motorcars?" Harry was tempted to reply, "Why don't you ask *him*?" But of course his father would never consent to be interviewed by a newspaper.

Only the reporter from the *Standard*, a brash fellow too young to remember Phileas Fogg's famous feat, had a fresh question: "Have the New Luddites come by to harass you yet?"

"Luddites? Are they still around?" Though Harry's knowledge of history was no better than his command of math, he had heard of the Luddites, a group of fanatics bent on destroying all sorts of machinery because, they said, it put people out of work. The movement had died out around 1815, after a dozen of its members were hanged.

"Well, it's a different set of them, of course. Only now they're not interested in breaking up knitting machines; they're after bigger game: locomotives and printing presses and electric lighting—and, of course, motorcars."

"Why? None of those is a threat to people's livelihood."

"Ah, but they're destroying the world, or so say the New Luddites. Locomotives and motorcars foul the air and jangle the nerves; electric lights blot out the stars; newspapers devour the trees and litter the streets."

"The same could be said of books and of gaslights—and when it comes to fouling the air and littering the streets, horses are the worst offenders."

"Well, this lot apparently have no objection to horse droppings; that's part of nature, you see. So I gather they haven't bothered you yet?"

"The horse droppings?" said Harry.

The reporter laughed. "I meant the Luddites."

"No."

"Well, keep an eye out for them. They can be nasty. They broke into the press room at the *Standard* last week—knocked one of our men unconscious and flung hot lead from the linotype machine all over. You're sure it wasn't them who burned down your shed?"

"I don't think so."

"Any damage to the car?"

"No. She's in splendid shape."

The reporter nodded at Harry's bandaged hands. "I suppose you'll wait for those to heal before you set off?"

Harry grinned. "This is nothing. I once bowled two innings of cricket with a broken index finger. We leave tomorrow morning."

# SEVEN

## In which

# A BORING SPEECH IS AVOIDED BUT MORE SERIOUS TROUBLE IS NOT

**W**hen news about the motorcar and its builders appeared on the front pages of the papers, Hardiman and his cronies were disturbed. The stories portrayed Harry and Johnny not as impetuous upstarts who had bitten off more than they could chew, but as underdogs: clever, spunky lads bravely taking on a seemingly impossible challenge—just the sort of thing Victorian readers relished. No one had even bothered to interview the three stodgy men who represented the wealthy elite.

Hardiman promptly announced that the car would officially begin its journey in front of the Reform Club at 10:00 A.M. sharp on Thursday, and that he personally would make a speech, generously wishing the young travelers well—and, of course, slipping in a few references to his railway, Sullivan's bank, and Flanagan's brewery.

Hardiman didn't bother to consult Harry and Johnny before making the announcement. It would serve the man right, Harry thought, if they left directly from the blacksmith shop before the sun was up. Of course, that would mean leaving without Charles Hardiman—not a bad idea, really, but Harry didn't care to defy his father's wishes.

On Wednesday evening they loaded the food, tools, and other supplies in the storage space behind the rear seat and once again took turns standing guard. At dawn, they began making their final preparations. Depending on the fuel they used, it took only twenty or thirty minutes to get up a full head of steam; they spent the rest of the time making sure everything was in working order.

Ordinarily Harry would have done his share of the work, but his burned hands made him clumsy and tentative. By the time they adjusted the burner for the umpteenth time, resoldered a leaking condenser line, and greased the balky steering linkage, it was nearly ten o'clock. "If there's anything else," said Harry, "we'll fix it later. Let's go!"

Johnny yanked his workman's cap down until it touched his ears to make sure the jagged scars on his scalp were hidden from sight; then he climbed into the passenger seat. Harry pulled on a clean pair of gloves to protect his hands, engaged the gears, and slowly pulled out the throttle. Smoothly, almost silently, the *Flash* rolled into the street; the crunch of the rubber-rimmed wheels on the stones made more noise than the soft chugging of the engine.

When they reached Pall Mall, Harry said incredulously, "Great heavens, Johnny! Will you look at that?" The pavement before the Reform Club was packed so tightly with people that there was no room for the car to pass. When the *Flash* approached, a cheer went up; slowly the wall of bodies began to separate into two masses and Harry carefully guided the car between them.

They were surrounded by smiling faces; eager hands reached out to pat the *Flash*'s fenders or shake the boys' hands. Someone knocked Johnny's cap askew and he frantically yanked it back in place. A pretty girl bent over and gave Harry a swift kiss on the cheek. Another flung a bouquet of flowers that landed in Johnny's lap.

Though all this adulation was like ambrosia to Harry, he knew how excruciating it must be for his reclusive friend. "Stiff upper lip, lad," he said. "I'll get us out of here as quick as ever I can."

On the steps of the Reform Club stood Julius Hardiman and his son, along with Sullivan and Flanagan and half a dozen dignitaries Harry didn't recognize. There was no sign of his father, but Harry spotted Aouda Fogg on the fringes of the crowd and waved to her. She raised one hand tentatively, as though not quite certain it was her son driving the car.

Charles Hardiman, lugging an enormous leather portmanteau, wormed his way through the throng. With great effort he flung his bag into the car, then stood there looking baffled. Since the rear seat had been added as an afterthought to accommodate their unwanted passenger, no door led to it. "How do I get in?" asked Charles.

"However you like," replied Harry. He watched with amusement as the boy placed one foot on the running board, swung the other awkwardly over the side of the car, and toppled unceremoniously into the seat. His bowler hat went flying. The crowd laughed and applauded.

"Better put some stirrups on her!" called one man.

On the steps of the Reform Club, Julius Hardiman was waving his hands and shouting over the din, "Ladies and gentlemen! May I have your attention, please! I would like to say a few words on this momentous occasion!"

Harry groaned. "Time to go," he murmured to Johnny and pulled out the throttle. The car leaped forward, a bit more eagerly than he had expected, sending spectators scattering. "Sorry!" he called. "She has a mind of her own!"

Charles, who had been thrown back in his seat and lost his hat again, said heatedly, "That was rude of you, Fogg! My father was about to make a speech!"

"Oh, was he?" said Harry innocently. "My apologies. These motorcars; they're so unpredictable, you know." Just when it seemed that they had left the crowd behind, Harry saw another group of a dozen or so blocking the street ahead of them. They seemed to have something more in mind than just gawking at the celebrated motorcar. Some of them brandished sticks; others clutched paving stones in their hands. Several carried wooden signs with crudely painted messages. "What the deuce—?" said Harry.

"They look as though they mean to attack someone," said Charles.

"They do," said Harry. "Us." As the mob drew nearer, he could hear them chanting "Down with the devil-wagons!" and he could make out the messages on the signs: STEAM IS DEDLY; MACHINES ARE THE WORK OF MADMEN; THE SMOKE OF THERE TORMENT ASENDETH UP FOR EVER & EVER & THEY HAVE NO REST.

A stone sailed through the air and bounced off the fender of the *Flash*. "Do something!" cried Charles.

"Turn!" shouted Johnny. But they were in the middle of a block; the only side streets were narrow alleys. If they got stuck in one of those, they would be at the mob's mercy.

Harry glanced around. Just ahead of them, a horse-drawn delivery van was pulled up to the curb. "I've a better idea." He reached for a small handle that protruded from the dashboard, next to the throttle.

"I'm getting out!" said Charles.

"Don't move!" Harry yanked on the handle. An ear-assaulting shriek rent the air. The horse harnessed to the delivery van reared up, let out a whinny nearly as piercing as the steam whistle, and bolted. The New Luddites scrambled for the sidewalks, clearing a path for the terrified animal and the careening wagon—and the motorcar that roared along right behind them. "Heads down!" Harry warned his passengers. A stone struck the glass windscreen, cracking it; another caromed off the leather hood that was folded, accordion-like, behind the rear seat.

A moment later they were out of range of the Luddites' missiles. "It's a lucky thing they hate machines so much!" Harry gloated. "If they'd brought a catapult, we'd be in trouble!"

"We'd be in a good deal more trouble if they had guns," said Charles sourly.

"Oh, I'm sure they meant us no personal harm; they just wanted to bang the car up a bit."

"I daresay they'd have banged us up a bit as well. We should have abandoned it. I'm not a coward, you know. I just can't see risking my own skin for the sake of a machine."

Harry gave him a stern glance. "See here, Hardiman. Let's get one thing straight right from the beginning. The *Flash* is more than just a machine. Johnny and I have put a devil of a lot of sweat and blood into building her, and we'll do whatever it takes to protect her, even if it means risking our own skins. If you're not willing to do the same, you may as well get out now."

Charles took a moment to adjust his hat and his tie before answering. "I'm willing," he said, coolly. "Up to a point." He opened his portmanteau and drew out a leather-bound diary and a fountain pen. Checking his pocket watch, he made a note of the time, then consulted a small 1891 calendar printed in the front of the diary. "We left the Reform Club—rudely—at ten-fifteen A.M. on Thursday, the sixth of August." He counted ahead one hundred days. "So. In order to win this bet of yours, you and of course your machine—sorry, your *more*-than-a-machine—must appear at the foot of the Club steps no later than ten-fifteen A.M. on the fourteenth of November. Correct?"

"Is that calendar days or elapsed days? We'll lose a day when we cross the Pacific Ocean, you know."

"If we get that far."

"Oh, we'll get that far, I promise you."

"According to my father, you are to have one hundred calendar days."

Harry nodded. "All right. Just so I know where we stand. I hope I can trust you to keep an accurate count of the days."

"Of course."

Though Harry had his doubts, he kept them to himself. As irksome as young Hardiman was, there was no point in antagonizing the boy. Like it or not, they were stuck with him for the next one hundred days. Well, actually, only ninety-nine. But Harry feared that they would be very long ones.

## THE STEAM CAR MAKES
## A GOOD SHOWING AND HARRY
## MAKES A FRIEND

**H**arry knew a good deal about steamships, but it was mainly their size and weight and speed and construction that interested him. He knew nothing at all about traveling on one; he had let his father make those arrangements. Phileas Fogg had booked passage for him and his companions on the steamship *Aurania*, which departed from the port of Liverpool at noon on the eighth of August.

The distance from London to Liverpool was no more than two hundred miles and they had two full days before the ship sailed; barring a major breakdown, they were sure to make it. With that in mind, Harry drove slowly and carefully—for perhaps half an hour. Once they were out of the city, with the open road ahead of them, he felt an irresistible urge to see what the *Flash* could do and he pulled out the throttle—not all the way; though he might be impetuous, he was not a complete fool.

The car leaped forward like a horse who feels the sting of the driver's whip. Harry laughed gleefully. "She's got muscle, Johnny, and plenty of it!"

Johnny could be nearly as inscrutable as Phileas Fogg, but Harry thought he detected a smile on his friend's lopsided face. "Just don't strain her muscles."

Harry consulted the cyclometer on the dashboard. "Ten miles down! Only twenty-four thousand nine hundred ninety to go!" Happy to be really rolling at last, he burst into a chorus of "Chucka-roo-choo-choo," a rollicking music-hall song.

Charles Hardiman, holding his hat tightly on his head, peered over the seat back. "How fast are we going?" he asked, sounding a little anxious.

Harry shrugged. "There's no way of telling, unless we time her. Does your watch have a second hand?"

"Yes."

"Start timing when I say 'go'." When the last digit on the cyclometer hit zero, he called, "Go!" When it rolled around to zero again, he said, "Stop!"

"One minute, fifty seconds."

"Harry," said Johnny.

Harry ignored him. "So that's . . ." He couldn't quite manage the math in his head.

"Just over thirty miles per hour," said Charles rather smugly.

"Harry," said Johnny.

Harry paid no attention. "That's as fast as most locomotives! And she's nowhere near full steam!"

"Harry!" said Johnny.

"Yes, Johnny, what is it?"

"You missed the turn for Liverpool."

Harry had assumed they would leave their celebrity status behind as soon as they left London. But in each town they passed through, dozens of people, sometimes hundreds, were lined up along the highway, waving and cheering.

Even in Liverpool, a city that saw strange and exotic travelers come and go every day, the "intrepid young motorists" (as the papers were fond of calling them) caused a considerable stir. On Saturday morning, a large crowd gathered to watch the "marvelous machine" (as the papers were fond of calling it) being lowered into the hold of the SS *Aurania*. Though Johnny would much rather have kept out of sight, he stoically stayed by the *Flash*'s side, making certain she was properly cared for.

By the time the *Aurania* pulled away from the pier, there was such a press of people that two poor chaps were accidentally pushed into the water and had to be fished out by longshoremen. Cries of "Bon voyage!"

and "Good luck!" filled the air. Harry stood at the rail on the second-class deck, grinning and waving as though he were Henry Irving or some other celebrated stage actor.

A soft, melodious voice next to him said, "My goodness, what a turnout. There must be someone famous aboard." Harry gave a brief sideways glance, followed by a second, much longer look. The speaker was a young woman of perhaps twenty, wearing a long linen duster and a rather masculine-looking wide-brimmed felt hat—not the most fashionable attire, but on her tall, slender frame it was quite attractive. She craned her long, graceful neck this way and that, searching for the cause of all the commotion.

Though he had an appetite for attention and acclaim, Harry was neither boastful nor conceited. He did not acknowledge that he himself was the cause. "Perhaps it's royalty," he suggested. "I saw someone earlier who was a dead ringer for the Prince of Wales."

The young woman laughed gaily, almost musically. "I don't expect it was, though. I believe he has a ship of his very own." She was interrupted by a blast from the ship's steam whistle, which had a far deeper, mellower tone than the *Flash*'s. She grimaced and held her ears. "That always frightens me a little. I'm afraid it's the boiler, or whatever it is, blowing up."

"Oh, you needn't worry," said Harry. "Steam engines are actually quite safe."

"Really? I seem to recall an American steamboat blowing up and killing something like two thousand passengers."

Harry nodded. "Such accidents are nearly always due either to human error or to poor design. A properly built boiler has a pressure relief valve, plus a fusible plug that melts if the steam overheats."

"You seem to know a good deal about steam engines."

"Not compared to my friend Johnny; he knows them inside and out, backward and forward. He's built a steam-driven motorcar that's going to revolutionize the field of transportation."

"A motorcar?" Most young women, when he mentioned machines, smiled politely and quickly changed the subject. This one seemed genuinely interested. "Does it actually run?"

"Yes, of course. We drove it here from London."

"Really? Were you taking part in a road race?"

"In a way, yes. We mean to drive her around the world, you see."

"Around the world? Is that even possible?"

"All I know is, we're going to give it a devil of a try. Pardon my language, Miss—"

The young woman held out her hand, which was unfashionably bare. "Elizabeth."

Harry was surprised at the firmness of her handshake. "Harry Fogg. I'm pleased to meet you. But I don't feel I know you well enough to call you by your first name."

"If you don't mind, I'd prefer not to reveal my family name." Elizabeth leaned into him and said confidentially, "It's one you'd readily recognize, you see, and I'm traveling incognito."

"I don't mind. But if you have a chaperone, she may object to my being so familiar."

"I'm traveling alone, actually."

"Is that safe?"

"I can take care of myself," the young woman said, rather haughtily.

"Yes, I daresay you can." Harry leaned against the rail and gazed at the distant docks. The crowd had drifted away. He wondered whether their interest in him would fade, too, now that he was out of their sight. He rather hoped the public and the papers would forget about the journey, or at least stop comparing it with Phileas Fogg's. The point was not to duplicate or surpass what his father had done, but to prove the worth of the *Flash* and of motorcars in general. "I can understand your not wanting to give your family's name. There are times when I'd just as soon people didn't know who my father is, or what he's done."

"Oh?" said Elizabeth, her eyes wide. "What *has* he done?"

"You don't know?"

"I'm afraid not. Is it something dreadful? Never mind, you needn't tell me. We'll *both* be incognito."

"Good. Just call me Harry, then." He laughed. "Of course, there's really no way I can prevent you knowing about my father; all you have to do is pick up a London paper."

"I don't read newspapers. I prefer a good book." As if she'd seen enough of England for a while, she turned her back to the railing. "I'd like to know more about this motorcar of yours, Harry. Is it on the ship?"

"She's in the hold. Would you like to see her?"

"Very much. One thing, though."

"What's that?"

"Would you mind not referring to it as 'she'? I find it insulting to be placed in the same category as a machine."

"Oh. Sorry. It's just that I think of h—of *it* as something more than a machine—a living thing, almost."

"Really. Well, feel free to call it 'he' if you like. I don't object to that."

# JOHNNY IS UNUSUALLY FRIENDLY AND HARRY IS UNUSUALLY FLUSTERED

**O**ne of the crew escorted them to the hold, but stayed at a discreet distance. Harry suspected that he mistook them for sweethearts; they looked near enough in age. He didn't disillusion the man; he rather liked being seen as the beau of such an attractive, self-assured young woman.

Elizabeth kept a tight grip on Harry's arm as they made their way between the piles of packing crates. Though there were several electric lamps overhead, they cast more shadows than light. "I should warn you," Harry said. "We may come upon Johnny Shaugnessey. If we do, he's likely to behave a bit . . . well, oddly. He doesn't like people very much, particularly strangers."

"Oh, he'll like me," said Elizabeth. "Everyone does."

The *Flash* sat between two stacks of wooden barrels,

its wheels secured to the floor by chains. There was no sign of Johnny; Harry assumed he had retreated to their cabin.

Elizabeth seemed eager to learn all about the steam car, and Harry was happy to oblige. He opened a metal door on the side to show her the boiler. "You see, it has both a kerosene burner and a firebox, which can be fueled with almost anything, from coal to corncobs."

"What a good idea. You're not likely to ever run out of fuel, then. Where is the engine?"

"Under here." Harry leaned over to lift the rear seat, only to discover a body curled up there, half hidden in the shadows. "Johnny?" he whispered.

Johnny shook his head urgently, as if to say *Just pretend I'm not here.* But it was too late. Elizabeth had climbed up on the running board and was gazing down at him.

"Hello. You must be Johnny." She held out her hand. "I'm Elizabeth."

Johnny ignored her and gave Harry a pleading look.

"I expect he's been having a nap," said Harry, "and is still a bit groggy. Perhaps we should let him be."

"Of course. It's just that . . . Well, I was hoping you might be willing to answer a few small questions I have about your motorcar, Mr. Shaugnessey."

Harry hid a smile. The young woman was smart. She didn't address Johnny the way most people did— as though he were feebleminded, or a child. And she guessed rightly that the surest way to bring the lad out of his shell was to display an interest in the *Flash*.

Johnny sat up hesitantly, pulling his cap down so that it hid not only his scar but the tops of his ears. "What?" he murmured warily.

"For one thing, I was wondering how many pounds per square inch of steam she can handle."

"We've had her up to four hundred," said Johnny.

"You've fitted her with a pressure gauge?"

Johnny nodded and pointed out the gauge. "Water-level indicator, too."

"Very clever," said Elizabeth. "How much water does she use?"

"Twenty-five gallons, London to Liverpool."

"That little? How did you— Oh, I see. You've equipped her with a condenser."

Johnny and Harry traded glances that said, *This young lady knows a thing or two.*

Elizabeth rapped the fender with her knuckles. "That's not steel. Aluminum, I'm guessing?"

Assuming that Johnny was about talked out, Harry answered. "That's right."

"She must be very lightweight."

"Three thousand pounds," said Johnny.

"Really? And how many horsepower?" asked Elizabeth.

"Not sure. Thirty, maybe."

"How do you manage that, with such a small engine?"

This was beyond Johnny's capacity. He glanced at Harry.

"Well," said Harry, "in addition to the two high-pressure cylinders, there's an extra set of low-pressure cylinders; they make use of the power that would be wasted otherwise, you see." Fearing this might be over her head, he added, "Does that make sense to you?"

"Just because I'm woman," she said, "it doesn't necessarily follow that I'm stupid."

Harry felt uncharacteristically flustered and awkward. "I—I wasn't suggesting you were. I was only—"

She smiled sweetly and put a hand on his arm. "I know. I forgive you." She turned to Johnny. "One more question, if you don't mind." Johnny shrugged. Elizabeth moved so close to him that he drew back a little; in a low voice, as though inquiring about some secret matter, she said, "How fast will she go?"

Now she had Johnny flustered—not a difficult thing to do. "I—I—"

"We had her up to thirty miles per hour on the open road," said Harry.

Her eyes widened and, even in the dim light, Harry could see that they were a deep blue, like the gemstone called lapis lazuli, which was the centerpiece of his mother's favorite necklace.

"Thirty miles per hour? It sounds exhilarating."

"Oh, yes, it's splendid fun. I wish you could take a ride in her. Him. It."

"Well, who knows? Perhaps I shall, when we reach New York. I wouldn't want to delay you, of course. You have such a terribly long trip ahead of you; I'm sure you'll want to set out at once."

"We could always deliver you to your destination, if it's on our way."

"Thank you for the offer," she said. "I'll consider it."

"There's lots of room," put in Johnny.

"Yes," said Harry. "There are only three of us, so there's an empty seat."

"Three of you?"

"Charles Hardiman is the third. I don't know what's become of him."

"Hardiman? The son of the railroad magnate?"

"You know him?"

"I know *of* him. I find it hard to imagine that he would enjoy traveling around the world in a motorcar."

"Yes, well, so do I. I'll be surprised if he lasts much beyond Philadelphia."

Elizabeth laughed. "I believe *I'd* enjoy it. Perhaps I should go along in his place."

Harry realized that she was only joking, and he joined in the laughter. At the same time, he rather wished it were possible. "It won't be any cakewalk," he said. "In any case, I'm sure you have far better things to do." But if she did, she declined to reveal them.

"Thank you, gentlemen, for showing me your motorcar. And now, if you will excuse me, I should find my cabin and freshen up."

"I'll accompany you," Harry said.

"No," she replied brusquely, then added, more civilly, "Thank you. I'm quite capable of finding my way." As she walked away, Harry saw the crewman speak briefly to her—probably offering to escort her as well, for she shook her head emphatically and proceeded up the stairs to the upper decks.

"Well," said Harry. "What an extraordinary girl."

"She's beautiful," said Johnny.

"Do you think so? Her nose is a bit small and turned up for my taste, and her lips rather too thin. Interesting, though, definitely interesting."

"Will we see her again?"

"No doubt. Second class is not exactly a vast realm, and we'll be sharing it for six or seven days. We're sure to run into her—in the dining room, if nowhere else."

"Oh," said Johnny, glumly.

Harry glanced at him in surprise. "I thought you liked her."

"I did."

"Then what's the—? Oh. I see. It's the prospect of eating in a dining room that has you worried, eh? Too many people, I expect."

Johnny nodded.

"Well, you can have your meals in the cabin if you like." He nudged his friend playfully. "Unfortunately, Miss Elizabeth won't be there."

To Harry's surprise, Charles Hardiman was not in the cabin, nor was his huge portmanteau. There was, in fact, no sign that he had ever been there. When four o'clock came, Harry headed for the dining room, certain that a young gentleman as conventional as Charles would never miss afternoon tea.

He was wrong. Just when Harry began to fear—or, more accurately, to hope—that something had happened to his companion, a steward handed him a message that read, in precise, careful script: *Fogg: The cabin was too cramped and dreary to be borne. Have taken a berth in first class. H.*

Well, at least they would be spared Hardiman's company for a few more days. It would have been better had he abandoned them altogether, but Harry was thankful for small favors. As he piled his plate with tiny cucumber sandwiches and smoked salmon, he glanced at the passengers grouped around the linen-covered dining tables. Though there were several attractive young women, Elizabeth was not among them. Harry felt an unfamiliar pang of disappointment.

He lingered awhile longer, on the off chance that Elizabeth might turn up. At last he shrugged and headed back to the cabin, balancing Johnny's plate of food, whistling a lively chorus of "There's a Good Time Coming" to show that he was his usual carefree self.

# TEN

## *In which*

# HARRY REVEALS HIS TRUE NAME AND ELIZABETH HER TRUE COLORS

O ne of the items Harry had purchased back in London was a brown tweed suit for Johnny; knowing his friend would never visit a tailor, Harry had bought a reach-me-down, or ready-made suit, and guessed at the proper measurements.

He coaxed Johnny into donning the jacket and trousers and joining the other second-class passengers for dinner, assuring him that Elizabeth would be there. She was not. Johnny, his cap jammed on his head, wordlessly wolfed down a plateful of roast mutton and potatoes, then retreated to the cabin.

The blowsy, overdressed woman opposite Harry said indignantly, "Such coarse behavior! His sort belong in steerage, not second class! I believe I shall speak to the captain."

"I wouldn't do that if I were you, madam," said Harry.

"And why not?"

"Hasn't anyone told you?" Harry glanced around furtively, then said, in a near-whisper, "You've heard of Thomas Edison?"

"The American inventor? Of course."

"Well, that was his son, Thomas Junior."

"Oh, my. Really?"

Harry nodded earnestly. "He's an eccentric genius. Do you know, he recently invented an electrical device that stimulates certain areas of the brain, dramatically increasing a person's intelligence."

"Really?" said the woman again.

"Yes. I highly recommend that you purchase one."

Later that evening, in need of fresh air—the cabin was filled with smoke from Johnny's foul-smelling meer-schaum pipe—Harry took a stroll on the deck. As he stood at the rail, staring at the dark water, a soft voice said, "Hello, Harry."

He jerked around in surprise. "Elizabeth!" He took a moment to collect himself before he went on. "I didn't see you at tea or at dinner. I was wondering what had become of you."

"I've just been in my cabin, reading."

"Books are all well and good, but you can't eat them."

She laughed. "The steward brought a meal to my cabin."

"I didn't know they did that, in second class."

"They do if you pay them enough." She leaned on the rail next to him. "What deep thoughts were you thinking, before I interrupted them?"

"Nothing very profound. Only wishing the ship would go faster."

"Oh? Why are you in such a hurry?" She gave him a sly glance. "Perhaps you don't enjoy the company of the other passengers."

"No, no, it's not that at all. It's just . . . Well, we have to complete our trip by a certain date, and each day at sea is one day less of driving time."

"What happens if you don't finish by that date?"

"I lose six thousand pounds. And I don't have it to lose."

"Your family would be responsible for your debt, then?"

He nodded. "I have every intention of winning. But you see why I'm so eager for the ship to make good time."

"Yes. Yes, I do see." She gazed intently out over the water, as if searching for land. "It's a worrisome thing, having your whole future ride on the outcome of a wager."

Harry had not said that his whole future was at stake, but in a way it was true. Until that moment, he had conveniently forgotten his promise to his father: If he lost, he would quit tinkering and take up some gentlemanly profession. It had been a stupid promise, rather like agreeing to spend his life in jail for a crime he had not committed. Harry pushed the thought out of his head. No point in fretting over what might happen if he lost; he was not going to lose.

"Harry," said Elizabeth.

"Yes?"

"Is that short for Harold or for Edward?"

"Neither. It's just Harry." He paused, not certain he wanted to reveal his actual name. It would mean also revealing his origins. But for some reason, he wanted Elizabeth to know. Perhaps it was a sort of test, to see how she would react, whether it would matter to her. Or perhaps it was due to the sense of intimacy that occurs between shipboard acquaintances who know that, once the ship docks, they will never see each other again. "In actual fact," he said, "it's Hari, with an *i*. It's an Indian name. According to my mother, it means 'the sun.' S-*u*-n, not s-o-n. But apparently it can also mean 'the monkey.'"

Elizabeth snickered. "You're making that up."

"No, honestly. When I started school, my mother insisted that I spell and pronounce it the English way. She wanted me to appear as British as possible. Didn't want me to go through what she went through, I suppose."

"I'm sure it was difficult for her, trying to fit into a world so different from the one she was used to."

Harry glanced at her, curiously. "You sound as if you know her."

"No, of course not. I was just assuming she grew up in India." Elizabeth shivered. "It's turned a bit chilly. I think I'll go back to my cabin and my book."

"I'll walk with you, then."

"Please don't bother."

"It's no bother, really—" Harry started to say, but she was already walking away, calling over her shoulder, "Good night, Monkey."

The next day, Harry had a leisurely breakfast in the dining room, as well as a long luncheon, afternoon tea, and dinner, certain that Elizabeth would turn up for at least one meal. She did not. Harry could only assume that the book she was reading was awfully compelling— or that she was deliberately avoiding him.

But that evening, as he wandered about the deck, trying to walk off his growing impatience, she approached again, with a smile that implied she was genuinely glad to see him. For nearly an hour they talked companionably, mostly about books and motorcars. Then she returned to her cabin, again refusing to let him escort her.

They played out a similar scene the next night, and the next. Though she revealed nothing about her background or her reason for traveling to America, he did at least learn the title of the book she found so fascinating—*Adam Bede*, written by George Eliot, who was apparently a woman. Elizabeth promised to pass it on to him when she was done. But the truth was, Harry felt no need for a book; mulling over the mystery of this young woman was more than enough to occupy his mind.

Harry had tried hard to respect Elizabeth's wishes and let her remain anonymous. But on the fourth day out of Liverpool, his curiosity overrode his conscience; he talked the head steward into showing him the list of all the passengers in second class. Three Elizabeths appeared on the roll; two were accompanied by their husbands, and one was a child.

Unless his Elizabeth was married or lying outrageously about her age, Harry could think of only one satisfactory explanation: She was, in fact, traveling first class and—unlike Charles Hardiman—chose to fraternize with the less exalted passengers for a brief while each day.

That evening, when they met in their usual spot at the rail, Harry lost patience with her attempts to keep the conversation in safe, neutral territory and blurted out, "Why are you pretending to be a second-class passenger?"

She blinked her blue eyes at him. "Whatever makes you think that?"

"I looked at the passenger list."

"Oh."

"Why didn't you tell me?"

"Why does it matter?" she countered. "To you, of all people?"

"What does that mean?"

"You know what it's like to be looked down upon. I wouldn't have expected you to be guilty of it yourself."

"I'm not looking down upon anyone."

"Yes, you are. Because I'm in steerage, you act as though—"

"Steerage? I thought you were in first class!"

Elizabeth laughed. "And how did you imagine I'd afford *that*?"

"When you said your family name was a familiar one, I naturally assumed—"

"You assumed they were rich and influential."

"Yes."

"Well, they're not, I assure you." There was a bitter edge to her words, as though she sorely resented the fact. For a minute or so she stood drumming her fingers thoughtfully on the wooden rail. When she spoke again, it was in that soft, melodious voice Harry had come to enjoy. "You like me, don't you?"

For once, Harry was cautious; he wasn't ready to admit just how much he liked her. "You said yourself, everyone likes you. Even Johnny."

Elizabeth gave a gratified smile. "Does he?"

"I actually managed to lure him to the dining room with the promise that you'd be there."

"I'm sorry. They don't allow steerage passengers to dine in second class."

"I'm surprised they let you on this deck at all. They're not supposed to, are they?"

"No. But I'm something of a special case."

"In what way?"

She hesitated so long that Harry wasn't sure she would answer at all. Finally she reached into her reticule, drew out a business card, and handed it to him. Harry moved close to one of the deck lights to read it:

---

### ∗ PRESS PASS ∗
LONDON *Daily Graphic*
**Annie Laurie**
CORRESPONDENT

---

"This is . . . this is you?"

"It's not my real name, of course. It's a nom de plume, like Nellie Bly or Bessie Bramble. Perhaps you've seen my newspaper stories."

"I don't read the *Daily Graphic*."

"Well, it's rather a new rag. We're working hard to increase our circulation."

Harry nodded grimly; at last he understood what her game was. "And you thought that a personal interview with the intrepid young motorists would be just the thing."

"Yes."

"Or, even better, a personal conversation with the son of the famous Phileas Fogg. I expect you knew all along who my father was."

"Yes."

"Then why not just *ask* me for an interview? Why go

to all the bother of pretending that we were friends?"

Elizabeth showed no sign of shame. She unflinch-ingly returned his gaze. "Because. I wanted more than just a single news story. I want to chronicle your entire journey." She reached out and placed a hand on his. "I want to come with you," she said.

# HARRY LOSES AN ARGUMENT AND THE *FLASH* GAINS A PASSENGER

**H**arry thrust the press pass into her hand. "I'm afraid not. I don't like it when people lie to me. It makes me distrust them."

"I don't make a regular habit of lying, you know."

"Only when it suits your purpose."

"Oh, and you never say anything that isn't perfectly true, I suppose?"

"I try to avoid it."

"You didn't, for example, tell anyone that Johnny was Thomas Edison, Junior?"

Harry shifted uncomfortably and scratched his head. "How did you hear about that?"

"It's all over the ship," she said. "You should have told someone who was more discreet."

"It was meant as a joke. I wasn't deliberately trying to deceive anyone, the way you have been."

"Tell me this, then: If I had asked you, on the first day we met, whether I could accompany you and your friends around the world, what would you have said?"

"I'd have said no, of course."

"There you are."

"Yes, well, I'm saying it now, in any case. So all your deception, all your—your fake friendship didn't accomplish a thing, did it?"

"Oh, yes, it did," said Elizabeth acidly. "It made me realize what a prude and a hypocrite you are, and how intolerable it would be to spend even a few days in your company, let alone several months!" She turned on her heel and strode off across the deck. For once, Harry did not offer to escort her to her cabin.

Over the course of the next two days, Harry wished a hundred times that he had had the foresight to bring along an interesting book. It might have distracted him, kept him from replaying over and over every conversation he'd had with Elizabeth—if that was, in fact, her name—and wondering how he could have been so naïve. He should have realized all along that, if she was so fascinated by him and by the *Flash*, there must be some good reason.

This was hardly the first time he had been betrayed or disappointed. No one makes it through childhood and school without the pain of having a playmate or a classmate suddenly turn against him. Harry had had more than his share of such experiences. Sometimes a friendship soured because he had carelessly revealed his Indian heritage; other times friends grew resentful when Harry outshone them at sports. In spite of it all, he had gone on trusting people too much, believing the best of them. Well, if he expected to make it around the world without losing his money or his motorcar, or worse, that would have to change. Somehow he would have to learn to be more cautious, less trusting.

The *Aurania* was scheduled to reach New York on the fifteenth of August. On that morning, as Harry was having breakfast, Charles Hardiman unexpectedly appeared at his table. "May I?" said Charles, gesturing at a chair.

Harry grinned wryly. "If you're sure you can bear such a cramped and dreary dining room."

Charles brushed something from the seat of the chair and lowered himself onto it carefully. "I need to talk to you," he said solemnly.

"Having second thoughts about the trip?"

"No, not at all. It's about Annie Laurie, actually."

"Aha. So, she's risen all the way up to first class, eh?"

"Yes. I first made her acquaintance two days ago, and we've spoken at length several times since then."

"I see. And what sort of lies has she been telling you?"

Charles scowled. "See here, Fogg, it's not good form to insult a lady."

"She's not a lady. She's a reporter."

"I know that."

"Oh? What else did she tell you?"

"That she asked to accompany us on the trip, and that you refused her."

"I did." Harry set his scone aside; the marmalade on it suddenly tasted bitter to him.

"Did she tell you why she was so anxious to come with us?"

"Not in so many words. But isn't it obvious? If she did a series of exclusive reports on our heroic efforts, it would increase her paper's circulation—and, of course, make her reputation in the bargain."

Charles waved his words aside. "No, no, you don't understand. There's more at stake than that. The *Daily Graphic* didn't give her this assignment, you know. In fact, the editor didn't believe she could handle it. She had to practically beg him to give her a chance. And she's had to pay her own way. She gets no salary at all from the paper until she begins sending in stories. If we don't even let her aboard the *Flash*, she's going to look a fool; it'll badly damage her career, if not ruin it altogether. You should have seen her, Fogg, when she was telling me all this. She was practically in tears."

Harry wanted to scoff, to say that it was undoubtedly all a show, designed to win Charles over. But he couldn't bring himself to believe that Elizabeth was really that cold and conniving. Neither could he bring himself to forgive her entirely. "I'm sorry. It's just not possible."

"Why not?"

"Do you still imagine this is going to be some sort of pleasure jaunt, Hardiman? It's going to be dirty and miserable and exhausting, and the last thing we need is a woman along. I mean, think about it. Where would she sleep? What would she eat? I bought supplies with two people in mind, not four. Where would she . . . you know? There won't be any facilities."

"We can work all that out."

"When? We arrive in New York today; we'll be on the road first thing tomorrow morning." Harry shook his head vehemently. "No. No. It's just not possible."

"Have you considered the fact," said Charles, "that it's not your decision to make? The three of us are in this together. I move that we take a vote."

"Why should you have any say at all? This was never your idea; you came only because your father told you to."

"Well, what about Shaugnessey, then? Have you asked him?"

Harry sighed. He hadn't bothered to mention the matter to Johnny. Though his friend was a genius where machinery was concerned, he didn't know the first thing about people, particularly women. He was obviously smitten with Elizabeth and would welcome her company without considering the problems involved.

Clearly, Elizabeth was a clever and capable woman. But this trip would demand more than cleverness. It would require unflagging determination and fortitude, and there was no way of knowing whether she had those qualities.

Of course, when it came to toughness and tenacity, she probably had the edge on Charles Hardiman. And, now that Harry thought about it, a reporter for a major London newspaper might prove to be a real advantage. As Elizabeth had demonstrated, a press pass sometimes opened doors that were firmly closed to ordinary people.

"If she did come," said Harry, "—and I'm not saying she *will* come, but supposing she did—she would have to provide her own food and pay for her own lodging . . . if there is any."

"She fully expects that. And should she run short of funds, I can easily afford to lend her some."

"No doubt. Unless, of course, we're attacked by Chinese bandits who beat us senseless and take all our money."

Charles looked startled. "Do you think that's likely?"

Harry sighed again. "This is not the Cotswolds we'll be traveling through, Hardiman, or the Lake Country. Anything is likely. Anything at all."

If Harry had been truly adamant—had he, for example, refused to drive the car if Elizabeth was in it—he might have had his way. But, though he did not approve of her impulsive and foolhardy plan, he could not bring himself to spoil it, now that he knew how much it meant to her. Besides, he was hardly in a position to condemn anyone for being impulsive or foolhardy.

And so it was agreed that Elizabeth would join them on a sort of trial basis. If she proved too much of a liability, Harry reserved the right to drop her off at the nearest train station; from there she could make her own way home.

Thanks to the transatlantic telegraph cable, news now crossed across the ocean far faster than any ship. For a week, New Yorkers had been reading about the *Flash*'s imminent arrival, and hundreds had gathered to welcome the car and its crew; a squad of policemen had been brought in to keep them from mobbing the intrepid young motorists.

While Harry and Johnny oversaw the unloading of the motorcar, Charles accompanied Elizabeth to the nearest Western Union office, where she sent a triumphant telegram to the *Daily Graphic*, informing the paper that she had won—or, more accurately, finagled—a seat in the car; the editor promptly cabled her ten pounds for expenses.

She at once began composing her first dispatch:

**New York, New York, August 15** ─────────
The daring young motorists who are to attempting to circumnavigate the globe have generously agreed to let a representative of the *Daily Graphic* ride with them. In the weeks to come, this fortunate reporter will be providing the

*Graphic*'s readers with a series of regular and exclusive eyewitness reports on the adventures of the *Flash* and its crew.

It promises to be a grueling journey, even for us passengers. As we are expected to provide our own food and shelter, your humble correspondent purchased a canvas tent and several cases of tinned food, only to discover that there was no room for them in the vehicle. Thankfully, Mr. Shaugnessey, the ever-obliging mechanic, offered to attach a wooden crate to the rear of the "car," for the purpose of carrying such supplies.

Since it was by this time late in the day, Mr. Hardiman gallantly suggested that some among us might prefer to spend the night in a hotel, as it might be the last opportunity to do so for some time. He referred, of course, to the female contingent, who made it clear that she expected no special treatment, and that she would be perfectly content to set out without delay. And so we did. It must be admitted that your correspondent had an ulterior motive; if we leave at once, we will avoid the unwelcome attentions of rival newspaper reporters.

Though our readers will undoubtedly be curious to know what route we will follow across America, the young pilot of the *Flash*, Mr. Fogg, has asked that the *Graphic* not reveal this information. He fears that, if we are beseiged by well-meaning well-wishers in every town along the way, it will slow his progress, and that is something he can ill afford. As of this date, Mr. Fogg has a mere ninety days remaining in which to cross all of North America, Asia, and Europe, or lose his extravagant wager.

# TWELVE

## *In which*

# THE MOTORISTS BEGIN THEIR JOURNEY IN EARNEST, OR AT LEAST IN AMERICA

Fom talking to the longshoremen, Harry learned that, instead of driving through Manhattan—and through the daunting mass of well-wishers—he could put the motorcar on a ferry, cross the Hudson River to New Jersey, and head west from there. It would mean missing the chance to see one of the world's great cities, unfortunately. But this was not a sightseeing tour; it was a race against time.

They filled the *Flash*'s ten-gallon fuel tank with the last of the kerosene and lit the burner; in fifteen minutes, they had enough steam to drive the car aboard the ferry. A chorus of disappointed cries arose from the vast welcoming committee, who wanted a closer look at the car and its crew.

Since everyone had assumed the travelers would be going by way of Manhattan, there was no fanfare when they disembarked in Hoboken, and no crowd of admirers to slow them down. They took a second ferry to Newark and by five o'clock were in the open countryside, cruising along an old toll road at a gratifying speed.

A regular network of these former turnpikes was strung out across New Jersey and Pennsylvania. They had once been the main arteries between cities, but the coming of the railroad had changed all that. The turnpikes were still used by farm wagons and by cyclists, though, so most were in reasonably good repair, and many were marked on maps.

Harry didn't have much use for maps. He had been blessed with a good sense of direction, so he preferred to trust it and, if he got in trouble, ask for directions from the locals—who, it stood to reason, should know the neighborhood better than some printer in a city hundreds of miles away.

Charles, on the other hand, hated leaving anything to chance. He had purchased a map of the area and spent much of his time either peering nearsightedly at it—he had eyeglasses but was too vain to wear them, particularly in front of Elizabeth—or attempting to keep it from blowing out of the car.

Harry would not have minded so much, had Charles not insisted on calling out at regular intervals something on the order of "Now, when we reach New Brunswick, you'll want to take the road to the right; otherwise we'll end up in Atlantic City." When he sensed one of these comments coming, Harry tried to find a bump or a pothole that would rattle the boy's teeth.

Elizabeth was not fazed by this in the least. She merely hung on to her hat and cried "Whoo!" as though she were on a roller coaster. Aside from these deliberate jolts, the ride was so smooth that she asked, "What sort of suspension did you put on her, Mr. Shaugnessey?"

Johnny had pulled a kerchief over his head and was tying it under his chin to keep his cap in place. "Coil springs, ma'am," he mumbled. "One on each wheel."

"Coil springs? Is that your own invention?"

"You might say he reinvented them," Harry put in. "Coil springs have a tendency to break; these are made of a special alloy."

"Well, they work superbly," said Elizabeth.

Charles raised his eyes from the map. "According to this—" he started to say, but the breath went out of him as the car lurched over a half-buried rock.

Harry was not much on planning, either. He hadn't thought to inquire whether Americans might have some laws about motorcars. But he had learned his lesson back in Marylebone about sharing the road. When he overtook a bicycle or a hay wagon, he slowed down and made a wide detour, calling out, "Motorcar coming! Motorcar coming!"

Despite his precautions, horses sometimes panicked at the sight of a large, self-propelled vehicle belching smoke. And more than one cyclist, either startled or fascinated by the *Flash*, went careening into a ditch.

Gradually the traffic thinned out, until at last the turnpike stretched ahead of them, unoccupied and unobstructed, all the way to the horizon. Harry, who was admittedly not burdened by cares even at the worst of times, felt such a fierce sense of freedom that he let out a whoop of delight.

"What the deuce is wrong with you?" demanded Charles.

"Wrong? *Nothing* is wrong. That's the point! For the next one hundred days, we'll have no responsibilities, no rules, no demands, no parental disapproval, only the open road before us. Isn't it splendid?"

"*Ninety* days," Charles reminded him. He glanced up at the darkening sky. "And it won't be so splendid when those clouds decide to let loose."

To Harry's disgust, Charles's gloomy outlook proved accurate. All afternoon, the sky grew more and more threatening; as they crossed the bridge over the Delaware River, they were caught in a drenching downpour. Harry halted and helped Johnny put up the rain hood, which had lain folded up accordion-style behind the rear seat. The leather cover was attached to a framework of steel rods; when the hood was raised, the rods locked into place to support it. As the wind picked up and began blowing rain into the cab, they pulled down the leather side curtains, which had small windows made of isinglass—thin sheets of mica.

When they reached Philadelphia, Charles took a hotel room, but Elizabeth remained with the others. "I don't want any special treatment," she insisted. "Besides, I can't afford a hotel."

When they tried to rent space in a livery stable, the owner regarded both the motorcar and Harry's English banknotes with disdain. "I don't take no foreign money. And even if I did, I wouldn't share my roof with the very thing that's going to put me out of business one day, would I?"

Elizabeth lifted the side curtain and showed the man her press pass. "You will be out of business far sooner," she said sweetly, "if I tell my readers how you refused shelter to the son of the famous Phileas Fogg."

When they were seated on bales of straw, drinking coffee and eating ham sandwiches provided by the stableman's wife, Harry said, "That was quick thinking. Thank you."

"You're welcome."

"You gave yourself away, however."

"In what way?"

"When we met, you told me that you knew nothing about my father."

Elizabeth shrugged. "I didn't want you thinking I

was interested in you only because you were Phileas Fogg's son."

"Yes, well, in future could you please leave my father's name out of it? I don't like always feeling that I'm riding on his coattails."

"All right," said Elizabeth. "Next time I'll tell them you're the son of the famous Thomas Edison."

Harry couldn't help laughing. "We've got one of those already." He nodded at Johnny, who had taken up his oilcan and was lubricating everything on the car that could be lubricated.

"True. But he's Mr. Edison's *older* son, Thomas Junior. You can be the younger and less mechanically gifted son . . . Monkey Edison."

Among Harry's enviable qualities was the ability to fall asleep anywhere. He gathered straw into a soft though prickly mattress, spread a blanket over it, and was out like one of Mr. Edison's electric lights. Ordinarily he would have slept soundly until morning, but halfway through the night he woke with the distinct sense that something was wrong.

He lay listening to the muted sounds around him—the horses sighing, the raindrops skipping along the roof, Johnny snoring—until he heard one that seemed out of place. It sounded like metal scraping metal and it seemed to come from the far end of the stable, where the *Flash* sat alongside half a dozen ordinary carriages.

Harry crept down the aisle toward the car. As he passed the adjacent horse stall, its occupant gave an uneasy snort. Harry froze in place, but it did no good. The skittish animal snorted again and danced nervously about, bumping the sides of the stall.

The scraping sound stopped. A moment later, a dark form slid from beneath the motorcar. Harry nearly called out, "Johnny?" But though Johnny had been known to work on the car at odd hours, he wouldn't do so without an acetylene lamp. Besides, Harry could hear his friend's familiar guttural snore issuing from the next stall.

But who else would be fiddling with the *Flash*, and why?

# THIRTEEN

## *In which*

# EVIDENCE IS FOUND
# AND ACCUSATIONS MADE

**H**arry would have been wise to sneak up and catch the intruder unaware, but it was not in his nature to be sneaky. He stood and called out, "You there! What are you doing?"

The shadowy form sprang to its feet and ducked behind one of the horse-drawn carriages. By the time Harry reached the spot, the figure had vanished; the only clue to where it had gone was the open door of the stable, flapping in the wind.

The disturbance had upset the horses, and their anxious whinnies roused the stableman; he appeared in the doorway with a kerosene lantern in hand, water streaming from his slicker and rain hat. "What's going on?" he demanded.

"I caught someone messing about with our motorcar," said Harry. "Did you see anyone leave the stable just now?"

"Not a soul," said the stableman. "You sure you weren't just having a bad dream?"

"Perfectly sure. Here, let me borrow that." He took the lantern and, kneeling next to the car, examined the ground. Scuff marks in the dirt showed that someone had been scrambling about in the spot. He shone the light beneath the *Flash* but could see nothing out of place.

The stableman snatched the lantern and went to check on his horses. When Harry returned to the stall that served as their bedroom, Johnny was still sound asleep. "Is something wrong?" said a soft voice. "I thought I heard shouting."

"We had a visitor."

"A visitor? Who?"

"I wish I knew. I suspect someone was trying to sabotage the *Flash*."

"Oh, dear," said Elizabeth. "I hope he didn't succeed."

"Not as far as I can tell. We'll examine her more closely in the morning."

"You didn't get a look at the culprit, then?"

Harry shook his head. "Too dark. You may as well go back to bed. All the excitement's over—I hope."

She put a hand on his arm. "You get some rest, too, Harry. We don't want you falling asleep at the wheel."

"Yes, all right." But instead of stretching out on his straw bed, Harry curled up in the rear seat of the *Flash*, where he dozed fitfully until dawn.

When it was fully light, they pushed the car into the stable yard and Johnny crawled under to make certain nothing had been damaged. When he emerged, Harry said, "Did you find anything?"

"No. But I have a feeling."

"A feeling?"

"Something's wrong."

"With the car, you mean? What sort of something?"

Johnny scowled. "I don't know."

"Well, we may as well fire her up. If there is anything amiss, we'll know soon enough."

While the *Flash* built up steam, Harry searched the bay where the car had sat. He found, crammed beneath one of the carriages, a ragged old peacoat. The back was covered with dirt. Clearly, it had been worn by the unidentified intruder.

The obvious suspect was the stableman. When Harry confronted him, the man admitted the coat was his. "I keep it hung on a nail by the door; I use it whenever there's dirty work to be done. Mind you, it wasn't me who messed with your motorcar. I was in the house, sound asleep, until I heard all the ruckus."

Harry was inclined to believe the man. After all, why would he would run away, only to grab up a lantern and rain gear and come right back to the scene of the crime? But who else had a reason to want the car disabled?

The answer was so obvious that Harry mentally kicked himself for not having seen it before. He was so deucedly naive, it had never occurred to him that Julius Hardiman might have sent his son along not to keep Harry honest but to make certain that he lost.

Harry stuffed the peacoat under one arm and strode across the alley. Just as he reached the back door of the hotel, Charles appeared, glancing up at the sky. "Thank heavens that beastly rain has let up."

Harry thrust the dirty coat under his delicate nose. "I'm onto you, Hardiman!"

Distastefully, Charles pushed the coat away. "Well, I'll thank you to get *off* me. What is that smelly object?"

"The coat you wore last night!"

"Are you out of your mind, Fogg? You couldn't force me at gunpoint to wear such a repulsive garment."

"Don't try to deny it! You used it to keep your fancy clothing clean while you crawled under the car!"

Charles appeared genuinely puzzled. "Why on earth would I do that?"

Harry flung down the coat. "I may be gullible, Hardiman, but I'm not a complete fool! Now I see why your father wanted you aboard the *Flash*! So you could sabotage her!" He raised a fist, tempted to knock the disdainful look off Hardiman's face.

Charles flinched, but stood his ground. "My father is

a gentleman, sir. He would never resort to such tactics. Even if he did, I would not carry them out." Charles straightened the lapels of his well-tailored tweed jacket. "I believe you owe me an apology."

Harry's fit of righteous anger quickly lost steam. "And I will gladly tender one . . . if you can prove that you were not in the stable last night."

"I can't *prove* it. But I give you my word, I did not try to sabotage your machine."

Harry took a deep breath and blew it out again. "All right. I'll accept that. For now." He scooped up the coat. "Mind you, I'll be keeping a close eye on you, all the same." He started for the stable.

"Just a moment," said Charles. "You never properly apologized, you know."

"Yes, all right, if it will make you feel better, I apologize."

"Thank you. Oh, by the by, I've changed some money into American dollars. Perhaps you'd like a bit."

"You're giving it away?" Harry said. "How kind of you."

"I expect English currency in return."

With two of the bills, Harry purchased twenty gallons of kerosene from a drugstore. Another two went to the stableman, and a half-dollar to his wife for some ham sandwiches and fruit. Harry and Johnny wasted no time on eating; too many hours of daylight had escaped them already. They topped up the fuel and water tanks and set off.

Once they left the paved streets of Philadelphia, they found that the heavy rains had turned the dirt roads to something resembling glue. Harry tried in vain to muscle the motorcar through the mud. "I suppose we'll have to put on the other set of wheels," he said.

While he and Johnny labored at this task, Charles sat in the *Flash*, jotting in his journal.

### Sunday, August 16

*Though our mechanic, whom I have mentally nick-named Quasimodo, does not appear overly bright, he has proven more practical-minded than his friend Fogg. He had the foresight to construct a pair of steel wheels, designed for use where extra traction is needed. Rather than the usual hard rubber tyres, they are equipped with metal cleats, like those one sometimes sees on steam tractors. Fogg asked for my help in installing them; I reminded him that I am neither a motorist nor a mechanic, merely an observer.*

*Elizabeth has taken advantage of the halt to get a bit of exercise. When she climbed from the car, I offered to assist her, but she declined. As she stepped down, she hiked the hem of her skirt nearly to her waist. I averted my gaze, but need not have, for beneath the dress she wears a pair of baggy trousers gathered just below the knee— bloomers, I believe they are called.*

*The cleated wheels are installed. I'm glad I sat*

*this one out; Fogg and Quasimodo resemble golems, so caked with mud are they. They have turned up the burner, and we will be on our way soon. Or perhaps not. Fogg is indicating that something is amiss, signaling us all to be silent. Ah, yes; I hear it now—a distinct hissing noise coming from beneath the motorcar. It sounds very much like escaping steam.*

# FOURTEEN

*In which*

## THE *FLASH* CHALLENGES
## A LOCOMOTIVE

**H**arry had plenty of time for a ham sandwich after all—any number of them, in fact. He sat helpless for an interminable two hours while Johnny repaired the line that fed steam to the engine. The pipe had not actually been cut, only filed down so that it would burst under pressure.

Through the smudges of dirt, Harry could see that his friend's face had an unhealthy pallor. "Your head's hurting, isn't it?" he said.

Johnny nodded slightly, then grimaced with pain. He had put so much of himself into the *Flash* that, when anything went wrong with the car, something went wrong in Johnny's head. Ever since the accident with the horse, he had been subject to blackouts and violent headaches. They were unpredictable, but seemed to occur most often when he was under stress.

"I'll put your tools away," Harry said. "You stretch out on the grass and relax for a while."

"We need to go," Johnny protested weakly.

"I was thinking of stopping for a few hours anyway, until the roads dry out."

"Liar."

"Well, in any case, it wouldn't hurt. Go lie down, now. Or have a sandwich; that might help."

"Nothing helps." Nevertheless, Johnny lay down in the shade and draped an arm over his eyes to block the light.

"Is he ill?" Elizabeth asked quietly.

Harry nodded. "He gets these pains in his head. He says it's like having his head squeezed in a vise and pounded with a chisel."

Elizabeth clucked her tongue sympathetically. "I have something that may help." She retrieved her carpetbag from the box on the back of the car and took out a bottle labeled DR. PEMBERTON'S SYRUP. "Give him two capfuls of this," she said. "I mean the bottle cap, of course, not the cap on his head."

"Thank you for clearing that up," said Harry.

Whether it was due to the medicine itself or simply to the power of suggestion, within half an hour Johnny was feeling well enough to take his seat in the motorcar. Harry relit the burner, and they set off again.

Beyond Lancaster, the roads began to improve. Though he hated stopping, Harry knew they would make better time with the rubber-tired wheels, so he pulled over and got out the jack.

When Charles made no move to help, Elizabeth gave him a reproachful glance, then said to Harry, "I'll assist you, if you like."

"No, no," Charles said hastily. "I'll do it. It's no job for a lady." As he climbed awkwardly from the car, Harry and Elizabeth exchanged a small conspiratorial smile.

To Charles's dismay, they didn't stop in Harrisburg to clean up and change clothing. Harry insisted on driving well after dark; the acetylene lamps on the fenders cast a dim light for ten or fifteen yards.

Until now, the land had been relatively level, but once they crossed the Susquehanna River they began to climb into the mountains—the Appalachians, according to Charles's map. The most practical route through the mountains was the one chosen by the engineers who built the railroad line from Harrisburg to Pittsburgh. When the wagon road they were following crossed the railway, Harry impulsively turned onto the tracks.

Knowing they would be driving over rough terrain, Johnny had equipped the motorcar with forty-inch wheels. Smaller tires would have dropped into the gaps between the wooden sleepers, but these rolled over the ties with a rhythmic, almost soothing thumping sound.

Charles took advantage of the relatively stable ride to jot another entry in his journal:

**Sunday, August 16**

*We have resorted to driving on the tracks of the Vanderbilt Railroad. I am not at all certain that this is a good idea. I inquire what we will do if we happen meet a train. Fogg blithely replies that either it will have to get off the tracks or we will. I ask how we will accomplish that. He replies that we will simply pick up the motorcar and move it. I cannot make out whether he is being frivolous or serious.*

*It certainly does not seem a very practical plan to me. I helped replace a wheel earlier in the day, and it alone must have weighed a hundred pounds. I did not bother to argue, however, not wishing to give ~~Elizabeth~~ the others the impression that I am fainthearted. Besides, what are the chances of encountering a locomotive out here in the wilderness? It would surprise me if as many as two or three trains pass over this godforsaken stretch in the course of a week. I will try to put the matter out of my mind.*

For a time, it seemed that they would have the track all to themselves. They thumped along without incident for hours on end. Harry nearly dozed off more than once, but then the wheel would drop off the end of the sleepers and jar him awake.

Around ten o'clock or so—it was too dark for Charles to read his watch—they crossed a trestle over a deep river gorge. On the other side lay a steep mountain, impossible to cross had the railroad not cut a tunnel through it. Harry silently thanked the Vanderbilt Line's engineers for making his journey so much shorter and easier.

His good mood abruptly vanished. As he entered the tunnel, he heard the chilling shriek of a steam whistle, then saw a bright light coming toward him. "Hang me!" he breathed. "Where did *that* come from?"

He tromped on the pedal that shifted the valves and made the engine run in reverse. The *Flash* was quick to respond, but not quick enough to suit Harry. "Come on, girl!" he urged. "Faster! Faster!" He twisted his head around, trying desperately to keep the car on track as it barreled backward across the trestle. There was no roadbed here; if the wheels slipped off the ties, there would be nothing for them to land on except the bottom of the gorge.

Harry heard the locomotive's wheels grating against the rails as the engineer applied the brakes, but he knew the train could never stop in time. Unless he got out of the way, it would run them down. Unfortunately, there was nowhere for him to go.

In the light from the train's headlamp, he saw the terrified look on Charles's face. Elizabeth's eyes were wide, but she seemed less frightened than exhilarated, as if she knew the danger they were in, but trusted him to get them out of it. Harry hoped her trust was not misplaced.

At the end of the trestle, there was solid ground on each side, but Harry couldn't simply drive the car off the tracks; though the *Flash*'s wheels were large, they wouldn't roll over a rail six inches high. He yanked on the hand brake and they skidded to a halt. "What are you doing?" cried Charles. "You can't stop! The train's still coming!"

"Get out!" ordered Harry.

Charles didn't have to be told twice, nor did Elizabeth. They scrambled from the car and up over the ridge of earth next to the tracks. When Elizabeth saw that Harry and Johnny were still with the car, she started back. "Are you insane? Come on!"

Harry waved her away. "It's all right!" He bent down, grabbed hold of the car's wooden running board, and yanked it upward. Johnny did the same on the passenger's side, and they laid the boards alongside one of the rails to form a sort of ramp. Harry leaped into the car and ran the *Flash*'s wheels up over the ramp and off the tracks—none too soon. A moment later the locomotive thundered by with the engineer still sounding the whistle, scolding them for their recklessness.

Elizabeth hurried to Johnny, whose hands were clamped over his ears to shut out the noise. "Are you all right?" Johnny nodded bashfully, flattered by her concern. She hiked up her skirt, strode over to the car, and punched Harry in the arm, hard.

"Ouch," said Harry. "What's that for?"

"For not telling me what you were doing. I thought the car was going to be demolished, and you two along with it."

"Well, we didn't know whether or not the ramp would work. We never had a chance to try it out."

"And what if it *hadn't* worked?"

"But it did."

"But what if it *hadn't*?"

"What if the train had come along ten minutes later?" countered Harry. "Or ten minutes earlier? Things happen the way they happen. What's the point in wondering how they *might* have happened?"

Elizabeth stared at him, clearly at a loss for words. "Well," she said, at last, "it will make a good story, at any rate."

Though Charles practically pleaded with Harry not to take them across the trestle again, there really was no alternative. Charles insisted on walking ahead, to make certain there were no approaching trains.

"What do you suppose he'll do if a train does come?" said Elizabeth. "Dive into the river?"

They made it through the tunnel with no trouble. Harry drove another few miles and then, bone weary, pulled the car off the tracks. "Surely we're not stopping *here*," said Charles. "It's only fifty miles to the next town."

Harry yawned. "You may go on if you like. We'll pick you up in the morning." It was too late to bother setting up the tents. They used the woods as a privy and slept sitting up in the car. At first light, Harry filled the water tank from a stream and drove on.

In Pittsburgh, Harry allowed the crew two hours to wash up and have a decent meal—and, in Elizabeth's case, to send a dispatch to the *Daily Graphic*—then they set out again. Though the roads had dried considerably, they were still badly rutted, and Harry's arms ached from wrestling with the steering wheel. Luckily, his hands were nearly healed.

Charles had purchased yet another map and insisted on giving directions periodically. Though Harry didn't like to admit it, their nattering navigator did keep him from making a wrong turn more than once. When they crossed the Ohio River, the land leveled out into vast stretches of farmland with few houses and even fewer towns.

Just before dark, they spied a steam-powered combine mowing down a field of wheat. "Hold your ears," Harry warned, and pulled the handle that operated the steam whistle. An answering blast came from the man on the combine. They were, thought Harry, like two members of some exclusive society, exchanging a secret countersign.

Harry was growing too weary to control the car. He would have turned it over to his friend, but Johnny had said at the outset that he didn't trust himself to pilot the *Flash*; if he suffered one of his spells, he might lose control.

Harry was not about to let Elizabeth or Charles take the wheel. He parked in a meadow, and they set up the tents. Elizabeth slept in one and, though he was distinctly unhappy about the arrangement, Charles shared the other with Johnny. Harry stretched out on the rear seat of the *Flash*.

# FIFTEEN

*In which*

## THE *FLASH* CHALLENGES ANOTHER MOTORCAR

**T**he days that followed were blessedly uneventful. Lacking anything of real interest to spice up her newspaper story, Elizabeth spent several paragraphs complaining, in a genteel way:

**Des Moines, Iowa, August 21** ————————
The heroic round-the-world racers have spent the past three days struggling along six hundred miles of so-called highway that has ranged from the almost tolerable to the atrocious. Perhaps there is little need for decent thoroughfares, as they do not serve to connect anything much. At the risk of offending the good people of the American Midwest, it must be said that we have

passed through not a single town truly worthy of the name.

Not that it matters; with a full fortnight gone from his allotted span of one hundred days, Mr. Fogg is reluctant to stop at all, and on those rare occasions when he does, it is long enough only for a hurried meal and an even more hurried washup. Even where there are comfortable lodgings to be had, we seldom avail ourselves of them; we get our sleep in small doses, mostly in the seat of the motorcar.

We have discovered that, outside of the major cities, the supply of kerosene is extremely limited and proportionately expensive. Druggists and hardware merchants carry only enough for their customers' oil lanterns; they are not accustomed to sell twenty or thirty gallons at a time.

According to Mr. Fogg, the *Flash* will burn nearly anything "from coal to corncobs," but since kerosene is the most efficient and least bothersome fuel, he is willing to pay the exorbitant price of thirty cents per gallon. One wonders whether he has stopped to consider the wisdom of this. It has been subtly suggested several times that Mr. Fogg take stock of his finances and prepare some sort of rudimentary budget so he will not find himself wholly without funds somewhere in the middle of Persia or Romania, but he remains unconcerned.

•  •  •

Des Moines was the first really civilized place they had encountered since leaving Cleveland. They had been driving all day through what Harry referred to as a typhoon, a relentless downpour like the ones his mother recalled from her childhood in India. The leather hood couldn't keep out all that water, and the four motorists were damp and chilled. What's more, the roads, not much account to begin with, had turned to quagmires.

"I suppose we'd better stay the night," said Harry, grudgingly.

"Thank God," said Charles. "Surely, even in America, a town this size must have a decent hotel."

The Hotel Victoria seemed up to his standards. Unable to face another night in a livery stable, Elizabeth could not resist taking a room as well. While Johnny braved the rain to find somewhere to store the car, Harry escorted Elizabeth upstairs. "Surely," she said, "you and Johnny could afford to stay in a hotel just this once."

"I suppose so," said Harry. "But we can't leave the *Flash* unguarded."

"I hardly think the car is in any danger. No one will even know where we are until my story appears, and by then we'll be long gone."

"I prefer not to take any chances."

Elizabeth gazed at him a moment, then said softly, "You still think Charles is trying to sabotage it, don't you?"

"I think it's possible. Don't you?"

"I don't know. I do know that Julius Hardiman has a reputation for being ruthless in his business dealings. I think he'd stoop to nearly anything to make certain you don't win."

"So would Mr. Sullivan, I suspect. Or Mr. Flanagan. Or Mr. Stuart. They were all parties to my father's famous wager."

"So I've heard," said Elizabeth. "It seems a lot of people would like to see you fail."

Harry laughed. "More than you know. There are also my mother's relatives in India; she thinks they're bent on kidnapping me, or worse."

"Why would they want to do that?"

"Well, it's rather a long story, but I'll try to make it brief. You see, my mother was once married to an Indian prince."

"Really? Was he was named Monkey, as well?"

"I seriously doubt it. All I know is that he was the Rajah of Bundelkund."

"A rajah? So your mother could have been living in a palace, but she chose to run off with your father, instead?"

"You make it sound like some sort of illicit affair. My father saved her life. The rajah had died, and his relatives wanted Mother to do likewise so she couldn't inherit his fortune."

"I didn't know that. I'm sorry."

"Apology accepted. My mother believes that her old

in-laws are still nursing a grudge, and that they'll be lying in wait for me."

"Only if you go by way of India."

"It's the shortest route. Don't worry, I'm sure the rajah's relatives have all died off by now, or forgotten the whole matter."

"I'm not worried," said Elizabeth. "In fact, I think it's quite exciting. I'll have to tell my readers all about it."

Harry winced. "Actually, I'd rather you didn't. My mother was reluctant even to tell me her story; she certainly won't want the whole world to hear it."

"I won't write about it if you don't want me to. There'll be plenty of other exciting bits." She was silent a moment. "You know, it surprised me, what you said about your father saving your mother's life. I've always considered him something of a scoundrel, spiriting a woman away from her husband and winning a wager by dubious means. You make him sound almost . . . heroic."

"Perhaps he was, in a way—at least for a time." They halted before one of the doors that lined the third-floor hallway. "You seem to know a good deal about me and my family," said Harry.

"Any reporter worth her salt researches her subject thoroughly in advance."

"That's not fair."

"Why not?"

"Well, you've revealed nothing at all about yourself—

not even your last name. It's not actually Laurie, I presume."

"No." She toyed thoughtfully with her room key. "Perhaps I shall tell you more about myself . . . eventually. For now, I prefer not to. I've agreed to let your mother's past remain a secret; you must allow me the same courtesy." She unlocked the door and stepped inside. "Good night, Prince Hari. I'll see you in the morning."

Harry grinned as he headed back down the stairs. Prince Hari. He liked the sound of that.

A carriage maker had given them permission to use his barn. Harry and Johnny bedded down in the vehicle and, in the morning, gave the *Flash* a good going-over. They had covered over 1,200 miles in just seven days, and the grueling pace had taken its toll. As Johnny went through his routine of lubricating everything in sight, he discovered a leak in the differential—the set of gears that transmitted power to the wheels. Not only had the leather gasket developed a crack, the grease in the gearbox had deteriorated badly and needed to be replaced.

While Johnny was off buying more grease, Elizabeth appeared carrying a bag of muffins and a container of tea. "Since you didn't come to breakfast," she said, "I decided to bring it to you."

"Smashing!" said Harry, surprised at her thoughtfulness. As he reached for a muffin, he noticed his grimy hands. "We've been working on the *Flash*." He rubbed at the grease and dirt with a rag that was only marginally cleaner than his hands.

"Nothing major, I hope?"

"A cracked gasket on the differential."

"May I look?"

Harry shrugged. "There's not much to look at; just some gears."

"I like seeing how things work." She spread a horse blanket on the ground and crept beneath the jacked-up car. Through the floorboards, Harry heard her say, "The gears don't appear to be damaged. Shouldn't the differential be full of grease, though?"

"Johnny's gone to get some." When she didn't reappear, Harry said, "What on earth are you doing under there?"

Elizabeth emerged, dusting her hands. "Looking at the frame and the coil springs." She patted the fender of the *Flash*. "It's an impressive piece of work. I'm beginning to think it could actually make it round the world."

"Meaning that, up until now, you *didn't* think so."

"No," she admitted. "Not really."

"Then why were you so determined to come along? Why write about an enterprise that's sure to fail?"

"My readers don't want to hear about things that are certain to succeed. They want stories about people struggling courageously against impossible odds."

"I hope you're making us sound sufficiently coura-geous."

"Oh, yes. I'm sure my readers are hanging on every word."

Johnny hurried in, carrying a tin of grease. "Harry! Come look!"

"What is it, lad?"

"You'll see."

The intrepid travelers had not encountered another horseless carriage since leaving London. But when they emerged from the barn they were nearly run down by one. The machine was so quiet, they had not heard it coming.

The driver, a portly man with more hair on his face than on his head, yanked on his hand brake, sprang from the car, and doffed his broad-brimmed hat. "My apologies to you, gentlemen, and to you, miss. I didna see you till I was almost upon you."

"There is no harm done, sir," said Elizabeth.

"I got word that there was another motorcar in town, and I was anxious to see it before it left."

"That would be ours," said Harry.

"You dinna say so! You built her yourselves? Do you mind if I have a wee look at her?"

"Not at all. And I hope we may examine your ve-hicle?"

"By all means. My name is Morrison, by the by. If you hadna guessed, I'm a transplanted Scotsman. And I'm guessing you're Londoners."

"An excellent guess," said Harry.

Morrison's machine was much better built than the other motorcars Harry had come across, and certainly far quieter. "She can't possibly have a gasoline engine," said Harry. "But I see no smokestack, either."

Morrison beamed at them. "Nay, nay, she runs on electricity, my friends." He lifted the seat to reveal an electric motor powered by twenty-four dry storage batteries. "She has but five moving parts."

Johnny surveyed the bulky battery bank. "'Tis a lot of weight," he murmured.

"Yes," said Harry. "I don't suppose she goes very far or very fast."

"She doesna need to go far," said Morrison. "I just drive her around the streets of Des Moines, and, as you may have noticed, it's not exactly London, or even Edinburgh. As for her speed . . ." He eyed the *Flash*, which looked far heavier than it actually was. "I'll wager that, over a short distance, she can outrun your machine."

Harry laughed. "I wouldn't wager very much, if I were you."

His remark clearly irritated Morrison. "How does a thousand dollars sound?" said the man sharply.

Harry stared at him. "Are you serious?"

"Perfectly."

"I'm afraid I don't have nearly that much in American dollars."

"I'll accept British notes."

Harry did a quick mental calculation. A thousand dollars was roughly the equivalent of two hundred pounds—about one third of what remained in his money belt. Remembering how he had neglected to consult Johnny when he made his original bet, Harry turned to his friend. "What do you think?"

Before Johnny could reply, Elizabeth said softly, "I wouldn't, if I were you. The *Flash* is powerful, but I'm not sure she's fast enough."

Johnny gave her a hurt look. "She's plenty fast."

"He's right," said Harry. "We can beat that battery-powered perambulator without even trying." Johnny nodded in agreement.

Elizabeth raised one delicate eyebrow dubiously. "I'll believe it when I see it."

"Then watch closely." Harry turned back to Morrison. "All right," he said. "Let's have a race."

# SIXTEEN

*In which*

## THE ADAGE "THE RACE IS NOT TO THE SWIFT" IS PROVEN TRUE

**W**hile Morrison went off to his bank to withdraw money for the wager, Johnny took Harry aside. "We will win, won't we?"

Harry patted his shoulder reassuringly. "We can't possibly lose, lad."

They packed the differential with fresh grease and installed a new leather gasket. As they were cleaning up, Charles finally appeared on the scene. "Everything shipshape and Bristol fashion?"

"Yes," said Harry, "but we won't be leaving for a while yet. We're going to race the *Flash* against an electric car. You're just in time to place your bet."

"I am not in the habit of throwing away money on bets."

"Why am I not surprised?" said Harry. "You might want to reconsider. This is a sure thing."

"There are no sure things. I suppose you've made a wager of some sort."

Harry nodded. "A thousand dollars."

"Why am I not surprised?" said Charles. "See here, Fogg, do you really think you can afford to waste time racing other motorcars? You have a more important contest to worry about."

"I'm not worried. We've plenty of time. Besides, I undertook this whole trip in order to show what the *Flash* can do. This is just another way of demonstrating that."

Morrison led them to a level, well-maintained stretch of road bordered by hay fields, just west of town. "Would you consider a mile a fair distance?" he asked Harry.

"One mile or a hundred, it makes no difference."

"You see the barn with the silo? Let's call the silo our finish line, shall we?"

"I suppose we three should get out," said Elizabeth. "You'll want the car as light as possible."

"There's no need," said Harry. "She can easily carry twice your weight."

Charles started to climb out of the car. "I agree with Elizabeth. The lighter the better."

"I'm staying," said Johnny.

Elizabeth, her eyes sparkling with anticipation, tied the string of her hat tightly under her chin. "So am I."

"Oh. Well, in that case." Charles took his seat again.

"Can you handle a pistol?" Harry asked.

"Of course. Why?"

"There's one under the seat. You may be the starter. All right with you, Mr. Morrison?"

"Aye."

When the road was clear of wagons and carriages, the motorcars lined up side by side. Harry engaged the gears and released the hand brake. "Ready . . ." said Charles. "Steady . . ." The instant the pistol went off, Harry yanked out the throttle. The *Flash* leaped forward like a greyhound in pursuit of a rabbit.

"Where's Morrison?" he demanded, not wanting to take his eyes off the road.

"Almost even with us!" called Elizabeth. "And he's gaining!"

"I'll be bound! I never dreamed he'd be that fast!" Harry pulled the throttle out almost to its limit and the *Flash* surged ahead. "Where is he now?"

"He can't keep up!" said Elizabeth gleefully, holding on to her hat. "He's dropping back!"

Harry gave a triumphant laugh. He couldn't resist glancing over his shoulder at his opponent. Just as he did, Elizabeth gasped and put a hand to her mouth. "Oh!" she cried. "Look out!"

Harry jerked his head around to see two large dogs, one chasing the other, come loping out of the hay field and directly into his path. "Hang it!" He wrenched the wheel to the left. The car bounded into the ditch and out again, nearly flinging its passengers from their seats; it mowed down a sizable swath of hay before Harry managed to stop.

Morrison was so far behind that the dogs presented no danger to him; totally oblivious of the trouble they had caused, they disappeared into the field across the road. As he sped past the sidelined *Flash*, the Scotsman laid on his electric horn; it gave an irritating, insulting bleat.

"Well," said Charles. "So much for your sure thing."

Elizabeth swatted him with her hat. "Oh, do stop gloating. I think it was admirable of you, Harry, to care more about the dogs' lives than about winning the race."

"Yes, well, they're quite valuable dogs," said Harry.

"Really?" said Charles. "They looked rather like mangy mongrels to me."

"Perhaps. But each of those mangy mongrels is now worth five hundred dollars."

When Harry had paid up, his money belt felt alarmingly thin. As they headed west again, he said to Elizabeth, "I suppose you'll recount all this in your next dispatch."

"Of course. Why? Are you afraid of looking foolish?"

"Not at all. I just want your readers to know that the Flash *would* have won, except for the dogs."

"Apparently the papers here aren't following our

progress," said Charles. "No one I spoke to had heard anything about us."

"It's just as well," Harry said. "America may have its equivalent of the Luddites. I wouldn't want to run into them again."

"Luddites?" said Elizabeth.

Charles nodded grimly. "Didn't you hear about our narrow escape back in London?" He pointed at the cracked windscreen. "That's a souvenir of it."

"I should fix that," muttered Johnny.

"So," said Harry. "What did you think of Morrison's electric vehicle?"

"It's very clever, I suppose," put in Elizabeth. "But I don't think it would make it round the world."

"It might," said Johnny, almost to himself. "With some way of charging the batteries."

Harry laughed. "We'll work on that when we get home."

"*If* you get home," said Charles. "I'll be interested to see how you manage to cross the Pacific Ocean, Asia, and Europe with what meager money you have left. I trust you don't expect any help from me. I'm only an observer, remember."

"I wouldn't dream of it," Harry said calmly. Somehow he could not bring himself to worry about such mundane matters. For now, the car was running well and the path before them was straight and smooth. What more could a person ask?

The road was, in fact, so decent that Charles managed to make a fairly legible entry in his journal.

### Saturday, August 22

*I wonder if Fogg has any notion how much he sounds like Dickens's hapless Mr. Micawber: "Something will turn up." Though I suppose it is in my best interests—or at least my father's best interests—to see this venture fail, I have no desire to be stranded somewhere in the American wilderness.*

*We paused in Omaha, the eastern terminus of the Union & Central Pacific Railroad, barely long enough to eat, buy fuel, and take on water from a horse trough. I did manage to secure both a detailed map of the railroad's route and a train timetable. In the rear of the timetable I discovered an even more useful sort of schedule—one that lists the departure times and destinations for all the major steamship lines that dock in San Francisco.*

*Fogg has apparently made no arrangements for getting us across the Pacific. He does at least have a destination in mind—Hong Kong—but only because my father suggested it. Consulting the steamship schedule, I see that the next steamer for Hong Kong sails on September 5th at 2 p.m.—a mere fourteen days from now. Thirteen days and twenty hours, to be precise. And San Francisco is still some 2,000 miles away, which means that we must cover roughly 143 miles each day.*

*Fogg considers that, in his words, "a walk in the park." Both Shaugnessey and Elizabeth seem to share his unconcern. Why am I the only one aboard with any sense?*

*We are scarcely an hour out of Omaha, but already there are no houses in sight, nor any trees, only empty prairie. The only sign that anyone has ever passed this way before is the braidlike pattern of interlaced ruts that has been accumulating for half a century, since the first covered wagons crossed the plains to California and Oregon.*

The giddy sense of freedom that had come over Harry on their first day in America returned like a gust of wind; the dull ache that had settled in his arms and back from the long hours of driving seemed to melt away. Back in London, he had seen this country in the same way he saw the Atlantic Ocean—as something to be crossed as quickly as possible. Now he found himself almost wishing that he had no deadline hanging over him, that he could simply go on driving across this uncluttered landscape with no concern at all for actually getting anywhere.

It was a feeling that he had experienced before, on the cricket field and rugby pitch. As much as he loved the taste of victory, acheiving it meant an end to the game. There were times when he would have liked to go on playing endlessly, for the sheer enjoyment of it.

By the same token, winning this wager would mean

that the journey would end, that he would return to his life in London. It was not a bad life, by any means. But even he, with his talent for living in the moment, knew that the aimless, irresponsible existence he was accustomed to could not go on indefinitely, any more than the seemingly boundless prairie could.

Harry felt his sense of elation fade and the ache in his arms return. He shook the sober thoughts from his head and struck up a determinedly cheery chorus of "There's a Good Time Coming."

Near dusk they spied a windmill in the distance, spinning furiously in the rising wind, pumping water for some remote ranch. "There's what Morrison needs!" said Harry. "He could erect one on the back of his car and run a dynamo with it."

"He'd generate plenty of power today." Elizabeth clutched at her hat, which threatened to take flight. "It's a pity you didn't equip the *Flash* with a sail." She leaned forward so the breeze wouldn't whip her words away. "Didn't your father travel in a wind-driven vehicle at some point? Sorry, I forgot. You don't like talking about his exploits."

Harry sighed. "It seems there's no escaping it. As he described the thing, it was a sort of sledge with sails." He surveyed the boundless expanse of grass, undulating like waves in the wind. "As a matter of fact, it would have been on this very stretch of the prairie." Harry was silent for a time. Though he seldom gave a thought to the future, he couldn't help wondering whether his own children—assuming he had any—would be asked continually about the epic journey of the *Flash*, and whether they would resent it.

"I'm afraid a sail wouldn't do us much good, in any case," he said. "The wind's blowing in the wrong direction."

## SEVENTEEN

*In which*

# DISASTER LOOMS
# ON THE HORIZON

**T**wo days out of Omaha, there was still no end to the prairie in sight. Harry's wish to go on driving across it forever had given way to a festering impatience. He felt as though they were stuck in a stage play, with the same bit of scenery being cranked past in the background, over and over. He found himself almost wishing for some sort of trouble, just to break the monotony.

Ever since Des Moines, Johnny had had the vague feeling that something was not right with the *Flash*. But the engine kept chuffing along tirelessly and the big wheels rolled without hindrance over the sandy soil and across the few shallow streams they encountered.

At Lexington, a hardware dealer sold them ten gallons of expensive kerosene from a rusty-looking drum. Later that day there was a flurry of excitement when they overtook a prairie schooner; though caravans of these wagons had once stretched from horizon to horizon, now it seemed like a quaint relic of an earlier age. On the flapping canvas cover was painted the motto THE PAXTONS, ILLINOIS TO OREGON. The driver stared at them in awe, like someone who has caught a glimpse of the future.

"Well, finally," said Elizabeth, "something mildly interesting for my next dispatch. If this keeps up, my editor may decide my stories are too tedious to print."

"Why don't you invent something?" suggested Harry. "You could have us meet up with Buffalo Bill, or perhaps the Dalton Gang."

"I am a reporter, not a novelist. It's rather a shame, really, that the Indians have all packed it in. An Indian attack would be just the thing to capture my readers."

"Provided *you* weren't captured first," said Charles. He laughed, then—an event so rare that Harry turned to see whether something was wrong. "I was just thinking about a story I read when I was perhaps nine or ten," said Charles. "I can't recall the title, but I remember it was absolutely rife with Indian attacks. Curiously enough, it also featured a steam-driven vehicle. What was it called? Something about a hunter . . ."

"*The Huge Hunter; or, the Steam Man of the Prairies*," said Harry.

"That's it! You've read it, then?"

Harry grinned. "Only about fifty times. I wouldn't have thought it was your sort of book."

"Oh, it was ripping!" Charles turned to Elizabeth. "The hero is a fifteen-year-old dwarf who also happens to be a genius. He invents a huge mechanical man powered by steam and capable of pulling a wagon and he drives the contraption all over the West, fighting off Indians at every turn."

"It sounds fascinating," said Elizabeth.

Harry and Charles failed to notice the sarcasm in her voice. They proceeded to recall all their favorite scenes from *The Huge Hunter*. Even Johnny put in a few words; though he had never learned his letters, Harry had told him about the boy genius—also named Johnny—and his Steam Man so often that it seemed he had read the book himself.

Elizabeth let them go on for half an hour before her patience ran out. "Oh, for heaven's sake! If you're going to discuss books, at least talk about something with a shred of literary value!"

Harry gave her a wounded look. "It may not be great literature, but that book made a profound impression on me."

Elizabeth's disapproval had put a damper on Charles's enthusiasm. "No, she's right, Fogg. We were mere boys when we read that. Now that we've studied the classics, I daresay it would seem like pretty poor stuff."

"I wouldn't know," said Harry. "I didn't manage to make it through many of the classics."

Charles laughed rather disdainfully. "Of course not. You were too busy playing rugby and cricket."

"How do you—?" Harry turned to glance at him. "Oh. You were at Eton, were you?"

"I didn't suppose you would remember me. I was a year ahead of you, and we didn't move in the same circles. Besides, as I recall, you weren't there for long."

Their feeling of camaraderie had faded. They fell silent. Elizabeth seemed unaware of the tension and of her role in creating it. She seemed, in fact, quite cheerful, pointing out the few sights that appeared on the mostly featureless plain—a patch of wildflowers, a prairie dog village, a herd of pronghorn antelope, the gloomy clouds gathering on the horizon.

"It looks as though we may be in for another typhoon," she said.

Charles unfolded his latest map purchase. "Perhaps we can make it to North Platte before it hits."

"How far is it?" asked Elizabeth.

"Twenty or thirty miles."

"Oh, dear. I'm afraid I can't wait that long."

"What do you mean?"

She gave him an uncomfortable look. "*You* know."

"Oh!" Charles blushed deeply. "Oh, I see." He tapped Harry on the shoulder. "Fogg, I must ask you to stop."

Though Harry had overheard their exchange, he saw no harm in making Charles squirm. "Stop? Whatever for?"

"For . . . for personal reasons."

"Don't tell me; you've lost your map."

Elizabeth spoiled the fun by saying brusquely, "If you must know, I require a bit of privacy. I won't be long, I assure you."

They stopped next to a small rise—what passed for a hill in these parts—and Elizabeth disappeared over it. "We're running low on fuel, anyway," said Harry. "We may as well fill up the tank."

"Maybe we should strain it," suggested Johnny.

"I don't see the point. Every other batch we bought has been clean enough. You worry too much, lad."

Though Johnny had lit up his pipe, he wasn't smoking it; he sat rubbing his forehead with one large hand. "Are you all right?" asked Harry. "Do you want another dose of Dr. Pemberton's Syrup?"

Johnny shook his head. "I still feel something wrong."

"We checked everything on the car that can be checked. Maybe it's the weather that's bothering you."

Elizabeth scrambled over the rise, holding her long skirt aloft to clear the tall prairie grass. "Look over there!" She pointed to the southwest. Beneath the dark gray storm clouds was a lighter band the color of smoke. "I think the grass is burning!"

Harry gave a low whistle. "Hang me! Into the car, everyone! Now!" He upended the kerosene can, then tossed it into the back of the car and sprang into the driver's seat. "The fire is still a good way off," he said, as they gained speed. "I'm sure we can outrun it."

"If nothing goes wrong with the car," Elizabeth added.

"Nothing will. She's running fine."

"I hope you're right."

Harry glanced over his shoulder. She gave him a quick smile that seemed cheerful and confident, but it was undermined by the look of anxiety—alarm, almost— in her blue eyes. It was not like her, Harry thought, to be daunted by danger. "Don't worry," he said. "We'll make it."

"I'm not worried," she replied, so carelessly that he almost believed her.

At first they seemed to be heading out of harm's way. But the wind picked up, urging the flames into a faster pace. And then, so gradually that Harry scarcely realized it, the *Flash* began to lose power. Harry pulled out the throttle as far as it would go, but the car didn't respond.

"The pressure's dropping," said Johnny, consulting the gauge. "'Tis down to two hundred."

Elizabeth gripped Harry's shoulder with surprising strength. "What is it? What's the matter?"

"Deuced if I know. It's not the water; we're showing over half a tank."

"You were having problems with the differential. Could that be it?"

"I shouldn't think so. We'd better stop and have a look, eh, Johnny?"

"*Stop?*" cried Charles. "You can't *stop*! The prairie's on fire!"

"You can keep going if you want," said Harry. "I only hope you're a fast runner."

It took Johnny no more than a minute to locate the problem. "Burner's clogged. Dirt in the fuel, is my guess."

Harry groaned. "You were right, lad. I should have strained it."

"Can you clean it?" asked Charles.

Johnny ignored him and fetched his toolbox.

"We could," said Harry. "If we had a couple of hours to spare."

"A couple of hours? We're lucky if we have ten minutes!"

Harry glanced at the line of flames, which was so near now that they could hear the crackling of the parched grass as it caught fire. Rabbits and mice and prairie dogs scurried all around them, heedless of humans when a greater danger threatened. "Perhaps less than that," said Harry. He snatched a large knife from the toolbox and thrust it it into Charles's hand. "Here."

"What am I supposed to do with this?"

"Start cutting grass."

## THE CREW OF THE *FLASH* FIGHTS FIRE WITH FIRE

**W**hat good will that do?" demanded Charles. "We can't possibly cut enough for a decent firebreak!"

Harry unfolded the serrated blade of his sports knife. "It's not for a firebreak. It's for fuel." He grabbed a bunch of the tough prairie grass and sawed off the stems. "Twist it together in a tight bundle, like this, then double it over and tie it with one of the stems."

"I'll help." Elizabeth fished a wicked-looking stiletto from her carpetbag and began hacking off grass and twisting it deftly into miniature sheaves.

Charles fumbled awkwardly with his bundle. "You really think this is going to work?"

"I'd prefer to use wood, but I don't see any trees, do you?"

"What about buffalo chips?" said Charles.

"Buffalo chips?" Elizabeth echoed.

"Dried manure," explained Charles. "That's what the wagon trains used."

"I don't see any buffalo, either," said Harry.

"Got it!" Johnny called, triumphantly holding up the disconnected burner.

"Excellent work, lad!" Harry tossed his grass bundles into the firebox.

Johnny struck one of the lucifer matches he used to light his pipe; the wind promptly blew it out. A second was snuffed out just as fast. "The devil take it!" he muttered.

"Here, I'll shelter you!" Elizabeth raised the hem of her long skirt high in the air, creating a barrier that blocked the wind. The third match did the trick. The bundles burst into flames, which licked at the bottom of the boiler.

The prairie fire was now no more than a hundred yards away. The smoke from it set them coughing and rubbing at their eyes. Elizabeth transformed her skirt from a windscreen into a basket, scooping into it the rest of the grass sheaves.

"We'll need to feed them in a few at a time," said Harry.

"You drive. I'll feed." She climbed onto the running board.

"It's too dangerous!" protested Charles. "You'd better let me—"

"Get in!" she ordered, in a tone that forbade further discussion.

There was enough steam pressure to get them rolling, but just barely. "We would have been better off running!" said Charles.

"Give her a minute or two," Harry replied calmly. "Johnny designed her to heat up quickly."

"If we don't get moving, we're all going to heat up *very* quickly!"

"Let's have some more fuel," Harry called. Elizabeth clung to the car with one hand and, with the other, stuffed a bundle into the firebox, singeing her fingers.

Though he couldn't see much through the pall of smoke, Harry knew the flames were almost upon them. If they stayed on the trail, which ran perpendicular to the path of the fire, they were surely lost. He yanked the steering wheel to the right and set off across the open prairie, bounding over abandoned prairie dog mounds. The *Flash* struck a foot-high anthill, leaped into the air, and came down with a thud that would have broken an ordinary set of springs. "We've lost Elizabeth!" cried Charles. "Go back!"

Harry glanced over his shoulder. Elizabeth was on her feet and scrambling after them, still clutching the grass bundles in her skirt. "She'll catch up," said Harry.

"She's injured herself! Look, she's limping! You've got to go back, Fogg!"

Harry pushed in the throttle a bit, and the *Flash* slowed enough so Elizabeth could overtake them. The moment she was back on the running board, he gave the engine full steam. "More fuel, please."

Red-faced and panting, Elizabeth crammed another sheaf onto the fire. "There are only a few left!" she gasped.

"That's all we'll need." Harry pointed ahead, where the ground dropped down into a shallow ravine with a line of trees. He barreled down the slope, slackening his speed only a little when they reached the shallow brook at the bottom. The *Flash* plunged into the water, sending up sheets of spray that drenched them all, then bounded up the far bank.

They stopped at the top of the hill and surveyed the scene behind them. The line of flames swept down the slope as swiftly as the car had. But though the creek was neither wide nor deep, it halted the progress of the blaze. Frustrated, the fire clawed at the trees, scorching bark and low-hanging leaves; when it had consumed all the most flammable fuel, it was reduced to a smoldering mass of blackened grass.

"Well," said Elizabeth, still breathing heavily. "I certainly have plenty to write about, now."

"Sorry you were thrown off," said Harry. "The grass was so high, I couldn't see the bad spots."

"I told him to go back for you," put in Charles. "He refused."

"No, no, you were right not to stop, Harry. I promised I wouldn't be a hindrance to you."

"Not only were you no hindrance," said Harry, "you were a considerable help." Taking her wrist, he examined her burned hand. "That must hurt."

"It does. I was too busy to notice."

He retrieved a jar of Holloway's Ointment from their medical bag and gently applied some to her red, blistering fingers. She gave a sharp intake of breath. "Sorry," said Harry.

"It's all right. I'm surprised you thought to bring along something so practical as a medical kit."

"Well, to be perfectly truthful, it would never have occurred to me. My mother insisted upon it." He wrapped her fingers carefully with gauze and snipped the fabric off with the scissors on his sports knife. "That was quick thinking, holding up your skirt as a windscreen that way."

"Well, women's clothing is mainly a nuisance; it's nice that, for once, it actually proved useful."

"If you two are quite finished," said Charles irritably, "may I remind you that it's going to pour rain any moment now? I think we should be going."

"My, my," whispered Elizabeth. "I believe someone is just the slightest bit jealous."

"I'm afraid he's not the only one," Harry replied softly.

Elizabeth glanced at Johnny, who was staring sullenly in their direction. "Oh, the poor boy."

"Don't pity him," said Harry. "He hates that."

"I won't." As they resumed their seats in the *Flash*, Elizabeth said, "How on earth did you remove the burner so quickly, Johnny?"

"'Tis made that way," Johnny muttered. "You just loosen a couple of fittings."

"Well, it was very clever of you. So was designing a boiler that will burn anything. Without it, we'd have been in serious trouble."

Johnny blushed deeply. Harry glanced back at Charles. He was gazing at Elizabeth as though waiting for her to praise him, too. When she did not, Harry said, "Good work back there, Hardiman. You pitched in and did your part."

"Oh," said Charles uncertainly. "Well. Thank you." Apparently he was unaccustomed to praise. Harry doubted that Julius Hardiman was the sort to offer much approval or encouragement. Well, that made three things the two boys had in common: Eton, *The Huge Hunter*, and a disapproving father.

"As I recall," said Charles, "Johnny Brainerd had some close calls, too, when he ran out of steam."

Harry laughed. "He did at that. It nearly got him scalped, in fact."

"Who on earth is Johnny Brainerd?" asked Elizabeth.

"The fifteen-year-old dwarf, remember?"

"Oh, bless me," groaned Elizabeth. "Not him again."

# NINETEEN

## Showing that

# HARRY, UNLIKE THE STEAM
# MAN, IS ONLY HUMAN

**E**lizabeth's account of their adventure was quite dramatic, and only slightly exaggerated.

**North Platte, Nebraska, August 24**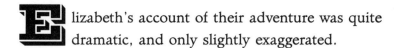

. . . and so it was we narrowly escaped being roasted like so many suckling pigs. Though this reporter's clothing was considerably charred and her skin badly blistered, she feels fortunate to be alive.

For all its flash and bluster, the storm did not amount to much. By late afternoon we drove out of it, and onto a highway that, for a change, was paved with something more than just potholes. Signs began to sprout up alongside the road, most promoting some business or other. The largest and least crude read WELCOME TO NORTH PLATTE, HOME OF BUFFALO BILL CODY.

Your correspondent had hopes of providing the *Daily Graphic*'s readers with a personal profile of the famed frontiersman, but alas, it was not to be. It appears that Mr. Cody is not in Nebraska but in England, touring with his celebrated Wild West Show.

An exhausted Harry let himself be talked into spending the night in North Platte. As usual, Charles and Elizabeth took hotel rooms while the more intrepid young motorists made do with the livery stable. After a frugal supper of bread and tinned meat, Harry set about cleaning the kerosene burner.

Though the *Flash* was back to its speedy self the next day, they barely got into Wyoming before night fell. They set up the tents by the light of the car's acetylene headlamps. "I've seen lamps like those before," said Elizabeth, "but I've never understood how they work."

Harry grinned and shook his head.

"What?" she said.

"Nothing. It's just that most women wouldn't have the slightest interest in how an acetylene lamp works."

"I'm not most women. Haven't you figured that out yet?"

"Oh, yes. Long ago." He cleared his throat. "Well, it's not much different from a gaslight, really. There's a tablet of calcium carbide inside, and a small reservoir of water. When the water drips onto the carbide, it gives off acetylene gas, which you burn to make the flame."

"Thank you, Professor Monkey. May I use one of them to read by?"

"Actually, I'd rather you didn't. The carbide disappears rather quickly, and there's no telling when we'll find more. Sorry."

"No matter. I've brought candles."

This caught the attention of Charles, who was picking listlessly at some tinned beef. "Do you have an extra?"

"Of course." She took a white taper from her carpetbag. "Would you like a book, as well? I've some Brontë, some George Eliot, even some Ouida."

"*Ouida?*" said Harry. "She writes sentimental romances and dog stories. I thought you read only great literature."

Elizabeth was not shamed in the least. "I make a point of reading only women writers; sadly, there are not many to choose from."

"I'm not in a reading mood," said Charles. "I wouldn't mind a game of cards, however. Do you play bezique, Fogg?"

"Not very well."

"Really?" Charles dug a deck from the depths of his enormous portmanteau. "I thought you were good at everything."

"Not if it requires patience. That's my father's forte.

But I never could resist a challenge." Long after the others retired, he and Charles sat in their tent playing cards by candlelight and reminiscing about their days at Eton.

Eventually the talk turned to the Steam Man again, then to steam-powered devices in general, then to the *Flash* in particular. "To be honest," said Charles, "I never imagined she would make it this far."

"To be even more honest," said Harry, "I never imagined *you* would make it this far."

"It hasn't been easy," Charles admitted. "But I can't back out."

"I understand," said Harry. "I know what it's like to have a father who . . . Well, believe me, I do understand."

Charles idly shuffled the deck of cards. "While we're being truthful, Fogg, I must say, I'm a bit surprised *you've* stuck with it this long."

"Are you?"

"Well, as you said, you're not exactly known for your patience and perseverance, are you?"

"You have a point." Harry scratched his head thoughtfully. "I suppose it's just that I've never tackled anything before that was quite so important to me."

"Six thousand pounds is a good deal of money."

"There's much more at stake than money."

"Such as?"

"Such as proving once and for all that the motorcar is not just some overgrown mechanical toy." Harry shrugged. "And perhaps . . ."

"What?"

"Nothing."

After a lengthy silence, Charles spoke. "When I say I can't back out, it's not because of my father. I've disappointed him so many times, once more would scarcely matter. But this time I'm determined to show him what I'm capable of—and perhaps prove it to myself, as well. I suspect you feel the same way. Am I right?"

Harry gazed at him for a moment, then took the deck and shuffled it briskly. "I thought we were playing cards, Hardiman, not having a philosophical discussion."

From the neighboring tent came a drowsy, sarcastic voice. "Whatever you're doing, could you please do it more quietly? *Some* of us would like to sleep."

### Wednesday, August 26

*A mere ten days remain before the steamer departs San Francisco for Hong Kong. Fogg seems to consider that ample time. I do not. I cannot trust to blind luck, nor do I share his utter faith in the reliability of his motorcar; all it would take is a broken axle or ruptured steam pipe, and his ill-considered wager would be as good as lost.*

*I wish that we had not played cards until such a late hour—or should I say an early hour? Elizabeth*

*was up with the sun and bustling about so industri-*
*ously and so noisily that we found it impossible to*
*sleep—getting her revenge on us, I suppose, for*
*keeping her awake last night.*

*We were on the road by seven. As I write this,*
*I notice for the first time a distant, jagged line of*
*blue on the horizon—the fabled Rocky Mountains,*
*if I am not mistaken, though at this distance they*
*look less like mountains than like whitecapped*
*waves about to break over the land. The sight of*
*them gives me an odd feeling in the pit of my*
*stomach. I have seen mountains before, of course;*
*I have even hiked in the Alps. But hiking in the*
*mountains is quite a different proposition from*
*driving a motorcar across —————*

The *Flash* abruptly swerved sideways, sending
Charles's fountain pen skidding across the page. "What's
wrong?" he demanded.

"Oh, nothing," Harry replied nonchalantly. "I was
just looking at the mountains rather than at the road."
He glanced at Johnny, whose last-second yank on the
steering wheel had saved them from a ditch. "Thanks,
lad."

"You're not dozing off, are you?" teased Elizabeth.
"You didn't get much sleep last night."

"Oh, I don't need much," said Harry. "Never have.
Two or three hours, that's all, and I'm ready to go
again."

On the outskirts of Cheyenne, three cowboys on horseback rode toward them, firing their pistols in the air. At first, the intrepid young motorists mistook the men for outlaws, but then realized they were being challenged to a race. After half a mile of pushing their horses to the limit, the cowboys saw that they stood no chance of outrunning the *Flash*.

A grocer in Cheyenne sold them bread, cheese, and bottles of sarsaparilla, plus half his small supply of kerosene. This time Harry strained it carefully through a cloth before putting it in the fuel tank.

Since leaving North Platte, Nebraska, they had seldom been out of sight of the Union Pacific Railroad; now they were running right next to it. As they climbed into the mountains, the wagon road grew so narrow and bumpy that Harry took to the tracks again.

"You know, Fogg," said Charles, "I really don't think this is a good idea. Have you forgotten what happened before? We nearly—"

Harry held up a hand. "Be quiet!"

Charles broke off and listened, eyes wide with alarm. "What is it?" he whispered. "Is there a train coming?"

"No," said Harry. "I just wanted you to be quiet."

In the course of the afternoon, they did encounter two trains, one from each direction, but there was plenty of time to pull off the tracks. The ascent was so gradual, the motorists scarcely noticed how high they had climbed until they saw the patches of pitted snow that lingered in sheltered spots.

"Can you reach my coat, Hardiman?" said Harry. "I think it's in the large leather bag."

"Thank goodness," said Elizabeth. "I'm not the only one who's cold. I've been freezing for half an hour."

"Why didn't you say something?" asked Charles.

"I didn't want to be thought a delicate Miss Mollycoddle." She dug a Mother Hubbard cloak from her carpetbag and wrapped it around her shivering frame.

"The cold doesn't usually faze me much," said Harry. "Perhaps I'm coming down with something."

"Or perhaps you're just human," said Elizabeth, "like the rest of us, and not some clever mechanical invention, like What-His-Name's Steam Man."

"I wish I did run on steam," said Harry. "At least I'd be warm." Though he had packed a heavy woolen overcoat, it didn't help much. It seemed only to weigh him down; after a time, he could barely keep his grip on the steering wheel. With an effort, he reached for the gear stick. "You'll have to drive, Johnny." His words sounded faint and slurred.

"What's wrong?" asked Johnny. He had never known his friend to look anything but hale and hearty; certainly he had never seen him so drooping and pale.

"I'm not . . . I don't . . ." Harry slumped down in the seat.

"I say," put in Charles. "Is he all right?"

"I think he's sick," said Johnny helplessly.

## TWENTY

*In which*

## JOHNNY GETS AN IDEA AND CHARLES GETS INTO TROUBLE

After only a moment's hesitation, Elizabeth sized up the situation and took command. "Well, we can't sit here and wait to be run over by a train. Can you drive the *Flash*, Johnny?"

"If I have to."

"All right, then. Put Harry back here. Charles, you go up front."

Johnny lifted his friend effortlessly and laid him in the backseat with his head in Elizabeth's lap. Then he got them rolling again. Elizabeth put a hand on Harry's forehead. "He's burning with fever. We'd better get him to a doctor. What's the nearest town?"

Charles unfolded his map. "Rawlins, I believe."

Rawlins didn't amount to much. The town owed

its whole existence to the coal mines in the area. The roads, which had to carry heavy mine carts, were well made. The buildings were not; in addition, they were weathered and grimy.

But one of them housed a company doctor, who was also rather weathered and grimy. After examining Harry for thirty seconds or so, he delivered his diagnosis: "Rocky Mountain fever. See it all the time. Nothing I can do for him. Just keep him comfortable until it runs its course."

The town did boast a respectable hotel, built for the benefit of visiting railway and mining magnates. "We'll put him up there," said Elizabeth.

Ordinarily, Johnny would not have dreamed of disagreeing with her, but he felt he had to speak for Harry, since his friend couldn't speak for himself. "He won't want that," he murmured. "He'll want to go on."

She patted Johnny's hand. "Of course he will. But we both know that Harry does not always do the most sensible thing. You'd like him to get well, wouldn't you?"

Johnny nodded.

"In order to do that," said Elizabeth, "he needs rest; he needs to be kept warm; he needs nourishing food. We can't provide any of those things properly on the road. The doctor said he would recover in a few days; surely we can spare a day or two?"

"I suppose," said Johnny uncertainly.

He parked the *Flash* behind the hotel and set about

checking every square inch of the motorcar for signs of wear or trouble. It was holding up remarkably well, considering the rough ride it had had over the railroad ties.

Since he could do nothing to help Harry, he did his best to find something on the car that needed work, so he wouldn't feel so useless. He replaced a few questionable-looking bolts and a brake cable, greased the wheel bearings—though they didn't need it—flushed out the water tank, and changed the filter in the water line. That should have satisfied him, but he couldn't shake the feeling that there was still something amiss.

That evening, as Johnny cleaned several days' worth of dirt off the *Flash*, Elizabeth turned up with sandwiches and a cold bottle of beer. Too self-conscious to eat in front of her, Johnny set the food aside and went on with the washing.

"I thought you'd be hungry," said Elizabeth.

He shrugged. "How's Harry?"

"Sleeping peacefully at the moment. An hour ago, he was tossing about like a dervish and babbling all sorts of nonsense about keeping the car afloat. Apparently he thinks we're going to drive across the ocean, instead of taking a ship. It's just the fever, of course." She moved up next to him, making him shift about uncomfortably. "Listen, Johnny," she said, softly. "There's something I need to tell you. It's about Charles."

"What?"

"Well, I—I hesitate to say this, because I don't want

to accuse him without good reason. But if I were you, I'd keep an eye on him. I have a feeling he may be planning to . . . to do something to the *Flash*."

Johnny glanced at her in alarm. "Damage her, you mean?"

"I don't have any proof, really, just something I overheard. I left him with Harry while I went to supper; as I was returning to the room, I heard him speaking to Harry. I couldn't make it all out, but it sounded as though he said, 'You may think I know nothing about motorcars, old chap, but I know how to fix one, and fix it properly.' I'm sure he did not mean 'fix' as in 'repair.' Harry didn't hear a word of it, of course."

She leaned in even closer. "I slipped into Charles's room, then, and took a quick look through his diary, to see whether he'd written anything incriminating."

"Did he?"

"Only one line. I copied it down: 'I suppose it is in my best interests—or at least my father's best interests—to see this venture fail.'"

"Harry don't trust him. He said that all along." Johnny twisted his cleaning rag nervously in his huge hands. "Wish Harry wasn't sick. He'd know what to do."

"I don't think there's much we can do at this point. We can't prove anything unless we catch Charles redhanded. But I wouldn't let him near the car." Elizabeth put a hand on his sleeve. "You know, as a reporter, I've become rather good at getting the truth out of people. And I think Charles likes me. Perhaps if I play my cards right, I can get him to confess. I'll go now and let you have your supper."

Ever since the accident, Johnny's mind had worked differently. For days at a time he might go about in a sort of fog, doing things by rote like a mechanical man; then, as though a switch had been turned on, some unanticipated thought or idea would appear, fully formed, in his brain.

Sometimes it was a solution to a problem he had been grappling with. Other times it bore no relation to anything else; it was as though, like Newton's famous apple, it simply dropped on him from above. The idea for wrapping the boiler with piano wire had come to him in that fashion.

Not all these flashes of inspiration were so useful. He had also been struck by the notion that, if you could take the wetness out of water, it could be burned as a fuel. He hadn't worked out the details of that one yet.

As he made a bed for himself in the *Flash*, one of these insights occurred to him. Elizabeth had said they must catch Charles red-handed. Well, if Hardiman really was up to no good, all they had to do was make him think they'd left the *Flash* unguarded and he'd show his hand.

Johnny glanced up at the window of Charles's room. The curtains were drawn. Snatching up his bedding,

Johnny slipped inside a dilapidated storage shed. Leaving the door ajar, he folded one of his blankets into a pad and sat down to wait.

He sank into one of his fogs and had no concept of how much time passed before he heard someone call his name. He shook his head hard; the pain brought him wide awake.

"Johnny?" There it was again.

He peered through the crack of the shed door. It was fully dark outside, but Johnny could make out a figure coming down the alley, carrying a lantern. Johnny couldn't see the face, but he recognized the voice. "Hardiman!" he breathed.

"I say, Johnny. Are you here?" To himself, Charles muttered, "Wonder where the deuce he is. It's not like him to leave the *Flash* unguarded." Holding the lantern aloft, he peered into the front and rear seats. "Not there."

Johnny heard the click and creak of the door to the boiler compartment, followed by a clank of metal against metal. He rose and crept into the alley. Charles held the lantern in one hand; the other was stuck in the innards of the car, groping about.

"What are you doing?" Johnny demanded.

Charles jumped in surprise, banging his head against the compartment door. "Ouch! What are *you* doing, creeping up on a fellow that way?" He withdrew his hand and rubbed the back of his head. "I was trying to find my fountain pen, actually. It must have fallen through a crack or something."

"You're lying!"

Charles held up the lantern to get a look at Johnny's face, which was set in a menacing scowl. "Why would I lie? What other possible reason could I have for stumbling about in the dark?" Then, anticipating the answer, he groaned. "Oh, no, not you as well. Look, I'm tired. I'll just search for it in the morning, all right?" He tried to detour around Johnny's imposing frame, but was seized by the lapels.

"No," growled Johnny. "I caught you red-handed. You might as well confess."

Charles pushed ineffectually at the hand that was nearly lifting him off the ground. "There's nothing *to* confess. I lost my pen. I was trying to find it. That's all."

"Tell the truth!" said Johnny. "Or I'll knock it out of you!"

It was clear that Johnny was deadly serious and that there was no reasoning with him. Feeling a sudden flush of panic, Charles swung the lantern at his captor's head. Johnny deflected it easily with his free arm; it crashed to the ground, casting them into near-total darkness.

Charles was not nearly as helpless as he sometimes seemed. He had studied more than just the classics at Eton; he had also learned a bit about the science of boxing. In fact he had fought a few bouts with fellow students and acquitted himself pretty well. He called upon that expertise now, to deliver a nasty uppercut to Johnny's chin. The bigger boy loosed his grip and staggered backward, as much with surprise as with pain.

Charles took the prescribed boxing stance: feet wide apart, fists curled. He landed a few telling blows but they had little effect, except to make his opponent even angrier. There was nothing scientific about Johnny's stance or his punches. He relied solely on strength, and there was no way Charles could hold him off. A fist like a blacksmith's hammer smashed into his chest and he went down, gasping for breath.

For a moment Charles feared the fellow might finish him off with a kick or two. But all Johnny gave him was an ultimatum: "In the morning, you be gone."

Johnny spent the rest of the night in the rear seat of the *Flash*. If he hung his feet over the side, he could get almost comfortable. Just before he fell asleep, another of those notions came from out of the blue; if he built seats that folded down, they could be transformed into satisfactory beds—something to keep in mind if they ever drove around the world again.

When Johnny looked in on Harry the next morning, Elizabeth was sitting at the patient's bedside, spooning runny porridge into his mouth. "Hullo," said Harry, with a feeble grin.

Tongue-tied as always in Elizabeth's presence, Johnny merely nodded, then adjusted his cap.

"Have you seen Charles?" Elizabeth asked him. "He wasn't at breakfast."

"I think he's gone."

"Gone?" echoed Harry.

"I caught him red-handed. I told him to leave."

"He was trying to sabotage the *Flash*, then," said Elizabeth.

Johnny nodded again.

"Hang me," said Harry weakly. "Just when I was beginning to think he was all right."

"Stop talking, now," said Elizabeth. "Just rest."

"I can't." Harry struggled to sit up. "We've got to get going."

"You're not going anywhere for another day at least, if I have to sabotage the *Flash* myself."

Harry sighed. "What day is it?"

"The twenty-sixth, I think. I was depending upon Charles to keep track."

"That leaves us . . . what, ten days before the steamer leaves for Hong Kong? How many miles to San Francisco?"

"I don't know. Charles has the maps, as well."

According to the desk clerk, Charles had checked out early that morning and caught the eight o'clock train to San Francisco. "Well, Johnny," said Elizabeth, "you certainly scared him off. What did you do to him?"

"Not much."

Elizabeth turned Johnny's face to the light. A sizable

bruise decorated his jaw. "He didn't do much to you, either, I see."

Johnny smiled slightly, lopsidedly. "More than I expected."

"Why do you suppose he went on to San Francisco, and not back to New York?"

Johnny shrugged.

"Well," said Elizabeth, "he'll have to face his father when he gets home; perhaps he wants to postpone it as long as possible."

## TWENTY-ONE

*Showing that*

# HARRY HAS NO CORNER ON BEING RECKLESS

**H**arry spent half the day sleeping and the other half fretting about the time they were wasting. He didn't mind facing any obstacle or danger, as long as he could *do* something about it. But simply lying about this way, waiting for the problem to pass, was maddening.

By the next morning, he had improved enough that Elizabeth consented to let him ride in the *Flash*, provided Johnny did the driving. Harry had to admit that it was rather pleasant to stretch out in the rear seat—which fit him better than it did Johnny—and watch the vast sky unfold. Though the thin air was hard on his lungs, it gave free passage to the sun's rays, which warmed him despite the morning chill. Soothed by the soft, breathlike chuffing of the steam engine beneath him, he dozed off.

A few minutes later—or was it hours?—he was jarred awake by a sudden lurch of the motorcar and the sickening sound of metal being twisted and tortured. Harry raised his head and looked around, dazed and disoriented. He had been thrown from the seat and was lying on the floorboards. "What the deuce happened?"

There was no reply. By clinging to the seat back, Harry managed to get to his knees. Johnny was slumped forward, holding his head. Elizabeth was rubbing her chest, as though something had struck her. It took Harry a moment to realize that there was something wrong with the seating arrangement. Johnny was in the passenger seat; Elizabeth was behind the wheel. "What happened?" Harry repeated.

"We hit something," muttered Johnny. He dabbed at his forehead with his bandanna. It came away spotted with blood.

Grimacing in pain, Elizabeth climbed from the car and surveyed the situation. "Now where did *that* come from?"

"What?" said Harry.

"It's a rather large boulder. I never even saw it."

"Pardon me for asking, but why the devil were you *driving*?"

She shot him a fierce look. "Don't shout at me!"

"I wasn't shouting. I was merely asking. And I'll ask again: Why were you driving?"

"Because I wanted to, all right? I thought it might be fun and exciting."

"Ah," said Harry. "Well. I trust you weren't disappointed." He turned to Johnny. "Let me see your forehead, lad."

"Don't go chiding Johnny for letting me drive," said Elizabeth. "He tried to talk me out of it."

"I'm not blaming him."

"Good. It was entirely my fault. I take full responsibility."

"So you'll be repairing all the damage, then?"

She gave Harry a perturbed glance. "You know I can't do that. But I'll gladly pay for the repairs."

"Wonderful. Now all we have to do is find a machine shop." He gazed around at the desolate landscape. "Hmm. Surely there's one around here somewhere."

"Don't be sarcastic."

"At least I'm not shouting."

Johnny climbed out and examined the crumpled front end of the *Flash*.

"How does she look?" asked Harry.

Johnny merely shook his head.

Elizabeth fetched the medical kit and set about bandaging Johnny's wound. "I'm very sorry you hit your head. You were right about it being hard to handle. I should have listened." She attempted to lift Johnny's cap. With a small grunt of panic, he knocked her hand aside and pulled the cap down around his ears.

"Let me do that," said Harry.

"I was only trying to help."

"If you want to help, why don't you back the *Flash* away from that boulder?"

"I didn't think you'd want me to."

"What more can you do? Run her over a cliff?" He showed her how to put the car in reverse and she backed it up a few yards.

Johnny crawled beneath the *Flash* to assess the damage. When he reappeared, his face was grim. "Condenser's caved in. Steering rod's bent."

"Will she make it to the next town?" asked Harry.

"If a team of horses pulls her."

"We can't do that. She has to go the whole way under her own power. Can you fix her well enough so she can be driven?"

"I can try."

"Take a rest first, lad. You don't look well."

Johnny ignored him. "We'll need a fire."

"I can manage that, I think, if Elizabeth will gather the wood."

"Don't talk about me as if I'm not here," said Elizabeth. "I said I was sorry."

"No, you didn't."

"Yes, I did."

"You said you were sorry Johnny hurt his head."

"All right, then, I . . . I apologize for wrecking your motorcar. There. Are you satisfied?"

"More or less," said Harry. "You know how important this is to me."

"Yes, yes," she replied, impatiently. "You've six thousand pounds riding on it."

"It's more than that."

"*More* than six thousand pounds?"

"No, I mean it's not just the money that's at stake."

"Really."

"Yes, really. Why don't you gather some wood while I get a fire started?"

When the wood had burned down to charcoal, Johnny buried the bent steering rod in it; using a small bellows, he heated the metal until it glowed, then carefully pounded it straight. "Good work, Johnny," said Harry. "I don't suppose the condenser can be fixed?"

"Not here. I unhooked it."

"We'll have to vent the steam, then, which means we'll run out of water pretty quickly."

"How quickly?" asked Elizabeth.

"The water tank holds thirty gallons. That might get us forty or fifty miles." Harry sighed. "I suppose we'd better wait until morning. It's nearly dark."

While Johnny set up the tents, Elizabeth prepared a stew from bully beef and dried vegetables. All Harry could manage was to sit on the running board of the *Flash* and watch. "The fire feels good," said Elizabeth. Harry didn't reply. "You're angry with me, aren't you?"

"No."

"Yes, you are, and I don't blame you. I shouldn't have insisted on driving. It's just that . . . well, frankly, I resented the implication that only men can drive motorcars. I wanted to show you—and myself, I suppose—that it wasn't so."

Harry laughed weakly. "It seems we all have something to prove, on this trip."

Elizabeth held her hands up to the fire. The heat made her fingers, which hadn't healed yet, throb painfully. She thought about how gently Harry had bandaged the burn for her. She would never have guessed that he was capable of doing anything so carefully. "What you said before, about there being more at stake than just the money. What did you mean?" Harry didn't answer. "I know you want prove what motorcars can do. Is that what you meant?"

"Partly."

"What else is at stake? Harry? What else?"

"I made a bargain," he said. "With my father."

"A bargain? What sort of bargain?"

"I promised that, if I lose the wager, I'll stop messing about with motorcars and take up some . . . *respectable* profession."

"Something suitable for a gentleman, is that it?"

Harry nodded glumly.

"I've always hated it," said Elizabeth, "when people told me I should behave more like a lady. I never considered the fact that men are expected to behave in a certain fashion as well." She rested her back against the door of the *Flash*. The aluminum was warm from the fire. "So if you win, you'll just go on . . . how did you put it? Messing about?"

"I can't think of any career I could bear to be stuck in."

"Well, if the *Flash* makes it around the world, everyone will want a vehicle just like her. You could always make a career out of building motorcars."

"I'm no businessman. And all I know about machinery is what I've learned from working alongside Johnny on the *Flash*."

"That's what engineering schools are for, Harry."

"School? I wouldn't have the patience for it. I couldn't even make it through Eton."

Elizabeth gazed at him curiously. "This isn't the Harry Fogg I know. I've never heard you sound anything but cocksure and confident."

"I'm just being realistic. I'm not very good at sticking with things."

"Well, then, I suppose you'll just have to go on messing about, won't you? Unless, of course, you lose the wager."

"I won't lose."

Elizabeth gave him an arch look. "That's what you said when you took on the electric motorcar."

Ordinarily Elizabeth didn't hesitate to give herself a leading role in her newspaper stories, but in her account of the auto accident, she neglected for once to mention the major part she played:

**Ogden, Utah, August 28** —————————

Our long-suffering motorcar has suffered a blow that, for a time, seemed likely to be fatal. As we drove along a narrow road through the mountains, a boulder tumbled from the steep slope beside us and collided with the car, bending the steering rod and crushing the condenser. (For those readers unfamiliar with automotive terminology, the condenser is a device that captures steam and returns it to the engine in liquid form.)

Our marvelous mechanic, Mr. Shaugnessey, made temporary repairs that allowed us to limp into Rock Springs—too small a town, unfortunately, to have a decent machine shop. After taking on water and kerosene, we set off again. In the course of the day we crossed three small rivers; each time we topped up the water tank.

By the next day we were in Utah Territory. We followed the railroad into Ogden, a prosperous city with the tools and materials needed to make more repairs to the unfortunate *Flash*, which has come to seem less like a mere machine than like a courageous companion.

Elizabeth tried to convince Harry, who was still far from well, to take a hotel room, but he refused. "We'll need the money later on," he said. His pride wouldn't let him tell her—or Johnny—the whole truth: Even if he didn't spend another dime between Ogden and San Francisco, he would be hard-pressed to pay for their passage across the Pacific. If they traveled steerage, he might just be able to manage it—for all the good it would do. They could hardly expect to get through all of Asia and Europe with no money at all.

That was the worst part about being idle: all the problems that he had been so carefully ignoring now had a chance to rear their heads. One of the things he had ignored, in his rush to rack up the miles, was his mother. He had promised to wire her from time to time, to let her know he was still alive and well.

Elizabeth would have welcomed a cozy, clean hotel room, no matter what the cost. But she felt obliged to share the livery stable with the others, to demonstrate once again that she was no Miss Mollycoddle. After she had made herself more presentable, she announced, "I'm going to see whether the telegraph office is still open."

"Would you mind sending a wire for me?" said Harry.

"If you're sure you trust me to do it properly."

Harry grinned. "Just don't drive there, all right?"

Elizabeth couldn't suppress a smile. She drew out her notepad. "To whom shall I send it?"

"Aouda Fogg, Number Seven, Savile Row, London."

She paused and gave him a curious glance. "Your mother? That's very thoughtful of you."

"Are you being sarcastic?"

"Believe me, if I were being sarcastic, you'd know. What message would you like me to send?"

"I don't know. Something on the order of 'Flash is holding up well, so am I, more later.'"

"Are you sure that's not too emotional? It may bring her to tears."

"*Now* you're being sarcastic."

"Just a little, perhaps."

"Well, I don't know what to say. You're the writer; you think of something."

The telegram she sent on his behalf read AM IN FINE HEALTH AND SPIRITS EXCEPT FOR MISSING YOU DEAR MOTHER YOUR LOVING SON HARI and it did, in fact, bring Aouda Fogg to tears.

Harry considered asking his mother to wire him a few hundred pounds. But he didn't want to give the impression that he was in trouble. Somehow or other he would come up with the money, he was certain of it. It was a pity Charles had turned out to be such a rotter. If he had stayed, he might have been persuaded to keep them in kerosene, at least.

Though Harry didn't like to admit it, he missed having Charles to keep track of all those niggling little details such as mileage and dates and the like. Harry was not good with details. He was, at least, fairly certain of the date. Back in Rawlins, they had determined that it was the twenty-sixth of August. That would make today the twenty-eighth, which gave them an entire week to reach San Francisco.

Unfortunately the repairs to the *Flash* ate up two of those seven days. By the second day, Harry was feeling like himself again—that is to say, so impatient that he could hardly bear it. To keep himself occupied, he removed the rear seat and set about cleaning the engine. Though Johnny had cast and machined all the parts with the utmost care, a little oil inevitably seeped from around the valves, and dust became caked on the cylinders.

As he wiped out the engine compartment, an object caught in the rag. Harry untangled the thing and examined it. "Johnny. Have a look at this."

Johnny slid out from beneath the car. "What is it?"

"A fountain pen. Wonder how it got there." Harry couldn't help noticing the guilty look on Johnny's lopsided face. "Do you know?"

Johnny nodded. "Hardiman said he lost it. I didn't believe him."

"Ah. So when you caught him 'red-handed,' he may not have been sabotaging the car at all? He may merely have been looking for his pen?"

"Maybe." Johnny gave him an anxious glance. "Are you angry, Harry?"

Harry put a hand on friend's shoulder. "No, lad, no. You were only trying to protect the *Flash.* I'd have done the same thing. Poor Hardiman. It appears we may have been wrong about him. Now he'll have to try to explain to his father why he quit. I don't envy him." Harry could imagine all too well how a chap might feel, returning to London without having proven a thing, either to himself or to his father.

# A TRAVELER AND A DAY
# ARE LOST

**T**he following morning they left Ogden behind at last, but Harry continued to cling close to the railroad. According to the owner of the livery stable, the land that lay between here and San Francisco was mostly desert, with nothing resembling a real town, only a few gold-mining camps. If they ran into trouble, the railroad would be their only lifeline.

They had loaded the motorcar down with extra cans of kerosene and water. Though they were within sight of the Great Salt Lake for most of the day, they couldn't draw water from it; the high concentration of salt would have played havoc with the boiler and the pipes.

The land was almost completely barren. They passed at least a dozen bleached skeletons of horses and mules and oxen that had perished trying to haul some gold seeker's wagon to California or Nevada. To block the sun, they raised the leather rain hood of the *Flash*, but it turned the interior of the car into an oven.

Harry handed the wheel over to Johnny and caught a few hours of fitful, sweaty sleep. Around dusk, he took over and drove through the night, stopping only once to take on water from a railroad storage tank. Late the next day, they reached the Humboldt River. It wasn't much compared with the broad Platte, which they had followed through Nebraska; still, after three hundred miles of parched land it was a welcome sight. Since they were nearly out of kerosene, they filled the storage box with birch and juniper twigs for fuel.

Harry considered driving through the night again, but the carbide for the lamps was running low, too; so was his energy. With only four days left before the ship sailed for Hong Kong, he couldn't afford to fall sick again. They camped by the Humboldt and in the morning followed the river westward. After another night spent in the wild, they reached Reno, a busy mining town at the foot of the Sierra Nevadas. The mountains promised to be a bit of a struggle, but after that it should be a quick and easy run to San Francisco. According to Harry's reckoning they still had two days to get there.

They had their first decent meal in days, and Elizabeth filed her first dispatch since leaving Ogden, then they climbed aboard the *Flash* again. As in the Appalachians and the Rockies, the only practical route over the Sierras was the one laid out by the railroad. They passed through a landscape of such rugged, breath-stopping beauty that Elizabeth exclaimed, "Oh, look!" at least once every ten minutes. Harry couldn't look for long, lest he drive off the railroad ties.

Trains were scarcer out here than in the Eastern states—luckily, since the roadbed was seldom wide enough to accommodate both a motorcar and a train. They spent most of their time either bumping along over insubstantial-looking trestles that spanned sickeningly deep gorges or else creeping through incredibly long, dark tunnels carved from solid rock.

Near the summit, the tracks were enclosed by a series of long, low sheds designed to keep the route clear of snow. These shelters created a wooden tunnel that stretched, unbroken, for miles. "Well," said Harry, "here's a poser. If we meet a train inside there, we'll have nowhere to go. And there's no telling when the next one will turn up."

"Of course there is," said Elizabeth. "It's called a timetable."

"Unfortunately, I didn't think to get one."

"Fortunately"—with a flourish, she produced a crumpled railroad schedule from her reticule—"I did."

"Good thinking," said Harry.

Elizabeth shrugged. "I take no credit for it. Charles left it in his room; I merely picked it up."

According to the timetable, the next train wasn't due for two hours. "So unless those sheds stretch on for twenty miles," said Harry, "we should make it through easily."

"Assuming the *Flash* doesn't break down," said Elizabeth.

"There's no reason she should. Is there, Johnny?"

"I—I don't know," murmured the mechanic.

Elizabeth placed a hand on his shoulder. "You're still having that feeling, aren't you? That there's something wrong with the car."

Almost imperceptibly, he nodded.

"Well, if she does plan to break down," said Harry, "I hope she holds off until we're in the open again." Taking a deep breath, he drove forward, into the mouth of the first shelter. A little sun seeped through the cracks between the boards, but not enough to see the tracks clearly. It was hard for Harry to keep the wheels on the ties.

"Can't you go any faster?" said Elizabeth anxiously.

"No!" snapped Harry. His voice echoed from the wooden walls. "Sorry," he said more softly. "I'm doing the best I can."

There didn't seem to be enough air inside the shelters; Harry found himself struggling to catch his breath. The *Flash* seemed to be chuffing more heavily than usual, too, but perhaps it was just due to the echo. When one shed ended, there was a bright gap several feet wide before the next began. Harry stopped in one of these, wiped the cold sweat from his forehead, and asked, "How much time do we have?"

Elizabeth checked her watch. "We've been in here only twenty minutes."

"It seems like an hour," said Harry. "I hope the trains are running on schedule. And I hope your watch is correct." He drove on, peering into the gloom for any hint of a locomotive's headlamp.

At last they emerged from the succession of sheds, squinting in the sunlight like miners surfacing after a long shift underground. The western slope of the Sierras lay spread before them and, in the distance, the broad green Sacramento Valley. "My goodness," said Elizabeth. "Look at this."

"I know, I know," said Harry. "It's beautiful. But I need to keep my eyes on the tracks."

"I wasn't referring to the scenery," said Elizabeth. "I've just glanced at the receipt given me by the telegraph clerk in Reno. I dated my dispatch the third of September."

"So?"

"So, this receipt is dated September fourth."

"Well, I'm sure your editor will forgive you for—" Harry broke off suddenly. "Wait a moment. *This* is the fourth? *Today?*"

"If Western Union is correct."

Harry's stomach lurched, but he tried to remain calm. "Would you please look at the steamship schedule and see when our ship departs for Hong Kong?"

Elizabeth consulted the table on the back of the train schedule. "Let me see. The *City of Peking*, right?

It sets sail at two P.M. on . . . on Saturday, the fifth."
She paused, then added, in a puzzled tone, "But—but
that's—"

Harry nodded grimly. "That's tomorrow."

"Oh, dear."

"If we miss it, how long must we wait for another?"

"The next ship for Hong Kong sails on . . . September twenty-eighth."

Harry gave a tortured groan. "That's more than three
weeks! We can't afford to lose three weeks!"

"But surely we can't make it to San Francisco by two
o'clock tomorrow. Can we?"

Harry took a deep breath, then turned to deliver his
trademark grin. "Well, if you'll pardon my language,"
he said, "we can give it a demmed good try."

Now that they were on the downhill side of the Sierras, Harry abandoned the tracks in favor of the wagon
road. Though it had been impossibly narrow and rocky
all the way through the mountains, the road was gradually becoming wider and smoother.

Harry turned the wheel over to Johnny. "I'd better
get some sleep. We'll have to travel all night."

Elizabeth let him have the rear seat. "Don't worry,"
she said. "I promise I shan't try to drive again."

By the time they reached Sacramento, the sun had
been up for hours. They had plenty of kerosene, so
Harry stopped only long enough to bolt down some
breakfast in the dining room of Ebner's Hotel. "If you
don't mind," said Elizabeth, "I'd like to freshen up a bit."

Harry wasn't sure just what freshening up entailed, but he didn't think it polite to ask. "All right. Ten minutes, no more." As he left the hotel, carrying a plate of food for Johnny, he glanced at the clock behind the desk. Eight-fifteen. "Is that correct?" he asked the clerk.

"Yes, sir."

The steamer for Hong Kong would depart at two o'clock. That gave them almost six hours. "How far to San Francisco?"

"A hundred miles, if you go the long way, around the Bay. If you take the road to Oakland and catch a ferry, you'll cut off a good twenty miles."

Johnny had kept up a good head of steam, so the *Flash* was ready to travel the moment Elizabeth turned up. But the ten minutes she had been granted turned into fifteen, then twenty, and still she did not appear. "Where the deuce can she be?" said Harry. "It can't possibly take *that* long to freshen up, can it?"

"I don't know," said Johnny.

When another ten minutes went by, Harry could bear it no longer. "I'm going to look for her. If she comes back here in the meantime, give a blast on the whistle."

No one in the hotel had seen her since she left the dining room. A maid checked the women's lounge; it was empty. Baffled, Harry returned to the car. "No sign of her?" Johnny shook his head. "The devil take it!" said Harry. "What do we do now?"

"We can't leave her."

"We can't miss that ship, either!" Harry paced back and forth, clenching and unclenching his fists. "She said she'd be no hindrance. She said that if she was, we could go on without her. That's what she said. So. If she doesn't show within the next ten minutes, we're going. She can catch up by train."

"But what if . . . what if she's in trouble?"

"Johnny, she went to freshen up! What could possibly happen? She got a tangle in her hair? One of her buttons fell off?"

When Elizabeth failed to meet her second deadline, Harry said, "We should go."

Johnny made no reply.

"We should just leave," said Harry.

No reply.

"We're running out of time!" Despite his protests, Harry was feeling more anxious than angry. What if something *had* happened to Elizabeth? Sacramento was a gold-mining town, after all; it surely had a large contingent of thieves and ruffians—and worse.

As always, a crowd began gathering to gawk at the marvelous machine. And as always, a policeman turned up to see what all the commotion was about. As Harry was about to report Elizabeth's mysterious disappearance, he heard his name called and turned to see her striding toward them, looking distraught. "Here I am! I'm so sorry!"

"Where have you *been*?" demanded Harry.

"Don't be angry," she said breathlessly. "I couldn't help it. Someone stole my handbag." She addressed the policeman. "Officer, a thief snatched my handbag. It contained all my money—several hundred dollars, at least. I pursued him for what seemed like miles, but couldn't manage to catch him. All I managed to do was get lost." She turned to Harry and Johnny again. "I'm sorry, fellows, truly I am. You must have been frantic."

The policeman advised her to come to the station house and file a report, but she refused. "These gentlemen simply must reach San Francisco by two o'clock. I've cost them enough time already. I'm sure there's no hope of recovering the bag, in any case."

"Well, probably not," the officer admitted. "But—"

"Then let's go!" She sprang into the front seat of the *Flash*. "Harry! Johnny!"

Harry gave an exasperated sigh. The woman was impossible. After holding up their departure for nearly an hour, she had the gall to tell *them* to hurry?

Though they did save twenty or thirty miles by heading straight to Oakland, they saved no time. The road was narrow and winding and Harry had to drive at a maddeningly slow pace. Elizabeth repeated at least four or five times how sorry she was for making them lose an hour.

"It wasn't your fault," said Harry at last.

"It was foolish of me to chase the blackguard, I suppose. But as I said, the bag contained all my money."

"Surely the *Graphic* will wire you enough for your passage?"

"I hope so."

Halfway to Oakland, they lost an hour waiting to be ferried across the Sacramento River. The ferry across San Francisco Bay made them wait even longer. By the time Harry drove onto the San Francisco docks, it was nearly two o'clock. "What pier do we want?" he asked Elizabeth.

"Oh, bless me!" She put a hand to her mouth in distress. "The timetable!"

"What?"

"It was in my bag!"

"What was the name of the ship?"

"It was . . . Oh, I can't remember!"

"The *City of Peking*," said Johnny.

"Good lad!" To a passing ship's officer, Harry shouted, "Where do I find the *City of Peking*, bound for Hong Kong?"

"Hong Kong, is it?" The man rubbed pensively at his chin, while Harry squirmed impatiently. "That'll be Pier Thirty or Thirty-One, most likely. Down that way, at any rate. Say, what sort of motorcar is that, anyway?"

"I'd tell you all about it," called Harry over his shoulder, "but we have a ship to catch!" He sped off down the dock, zigzagging between small mountains of crates and barrels, sending longshoremen scuttling for safety.

By the time they located the *City of Peking*, dockworkers were casting off the ship's mooring lines. Harry could hear the huge engines throbbing. "Pardon me, sir!" he called to the first mate, who was leaning over the rail. "Can you possibly take us aboard?"

"I could take the passengers!" shouted the man. "But we can't afford the time to load your vehicle! We're running late already!" The gap between the ship and the dock was quickly growing wider.

Elizabeth stood up on the rear seat of the *Flash*. "Sir! I am a correspondent for the London *Daily Graphic*. And this is the son of the famous Phileas Fogg! He's attempting to circle the globe!"

"You don't say? I've been reading all about you in the newspapers!"

"Then you know he has a deadline! And if you don't let him and his motorcar on board, he won't make it!"

The first mate spread his hands helplessly. "I'm sorry, ma'am! The Pacific Mail Line has a schedule to keep, too!"

"It also has a reputation to keep!" shouted Elizabeth. "And I'll see to it that—" Her words were drowned out by a blast from the *City of Peking*'s steam whistle. She stamped her foot angrily and uttered some epithets that Harry was just as glad he couldn't hear, for he suspected they were not very ladylike.

# THE TRIO AGAIN BECOMES
# A QUARTET

**H**arry slumped wearily onto the running board of the *Flash* and put his head in his hands. Elizabeth brushed at the dirt that caked the board and then sat next to him. "Don't take it so hard, Harry. Surely you can change your plans a bit, sail to some other Chinese port, perhaps."

"I know. It's not that. I was just thinking . . ."

"What?"

"Well, I was thinking about what my father would have done in this situation."

"That's easy. He would have offered the shipping line so much money, they couldn't possibly refuse."

"Exactly. Whereas I may not even be able to pay our fare, unless we travel Chinese steerage."

"That's because he has a fortune, and you don't."
Elizabeth rose and dusted herself off. "You know, I did
a good deal of research on your father, but I never managed to learn how he came by all his money."

"I'm afraid I can't enlighten you. He never speaks of
it to anyone, not even me."

"Do you think he's hiding some dark secret?"

Harry laughed. "My father? Not likely. He's hardly
the sort who murders rich old widows, or embezzles
funds from a bank. I expect it was something as mundane as purchasing the right stock at the right time."
Harry rose, too, and drew a deep breath. "Well. We'd
best get a steamship schedule and see how long we're
likely to be stranded here. Then we'll look for some
very cheap lodgings."

**San Francisco, California, September 5** ────────
We discovered that, on Tuesday the eighth, the
SS *Belgic* departs for Yokohama, Japan. From
there we will be able to catch another steamship
to Shanghai. Though it will mean taking a longer
route through China, it seems our best option.

As we stood about discussing this, the *Flash*
drew its customary crowd of the curious, including a number of confirmed motorcar enthusiasts.
Among these latter was the harbormaster, who
offered to house both us and our vehicle for several days free of charge. His only condition is
that he be permitted to take a turn in the *Flash*.

> Mr. Fogg and Mr. Shaugnessey are amenable, as
> long as he does not insist upon doing the driving.

Elizabeth penned a few more paragraphs, then went in search of the Western Union office. The harbormaster advised her to take Harry along; though San Francisco boasted a high percentage of millionaires and some very posh neighborhoods, other sections of the city were as dreadful and dangerous as any slum in London, and that was saying a lot.

Londoners liked to complain about the noise and the dirt that filled their city's air, but in both respects San Francisco had the English city beat. An acrid, yellow-gray haze hung over the streets, a product of the sulfurous coal that was burned by nearly every householder, factory owner, and steamship captain. And on top of the inevitable clamor of urban life, San Francisco had added a new layer of sound—the clatter and squeal of the dozens of cable cars that labored up the city's steep hills.

Harry found the mechanics of the cable system fascinating. While Elizabeth sent her telegram to the *Graphic*, he stood gawking at the trolleys that rolled down the middle of Market Street. It was a quarter hour or more before Elizabeth emerged from Western Union, looking distraught.

"They didn't wire you any money, did they?" said Harry.

"They sent no reply at all. I don't know what to

think. Perhaps I'll return later and see whether they've responded." She sighed. "I was so hoping to have a decent meal, in a real restaurant."

As usual, Harry's pride got the better of his common sense. "Well, I expect I can afford to buy you dinner," he lied, and proceeded to choose the most elegant eatery on the block. As they waited to be seated, Elizabeth eyed the other women's attire—and, Harry noticed, self-consciously smoothed her own rumpled, dusty traveling outfit. "They're wearing the same fashions as the London ladies," she whispered.

"What did you expect?" said Harry. "Buckskins and wampum beads?"

She gave one of her uninhibited laughs, turning the heads of several diners—including a very familiar blond-haired one. "Good heavens!" gasped Elizabeth. "It's Charles!"

"Hang me," murmured Harry. "So it is." When the hostess came to seat them, Harry told her, "We're joining friends, at that table." He nodded toward Charles and his dinner companion, a jowly, middle-aged fellow with the outmoded style of overgrown sideburns known as dundrearies. Both gentlemen sprang from their chairs when Elizabeth approached the table.

"May we?" said Elizabeth.

"Of course," replied Charles. He introduced them to the older man, whose name was Drummond and who was, it seemed, an old friend and business associate of

Julius Hardiman. "We met at the hotel where I've been staying," Charles explained.

"I should have thought you'd be well on your way to England by now," said Elizabeth.

"No." Clearly uncomfortable, Charles turned the stem of his water glass between his fingers. "As a matter of fact . . ." He paused and cleared his throat. "As a matter of fact, I've been waiting for you three. I've been checking in at the telegraph office, on the assumption that you'd wire your newspaper when you arrived."

"Why?" asked Elizabeth.

"Well, frankly, I was hoping that I might rejoin the *Flash*."

"After you tried to sabotage her?"

"But I didn't, you know. It was all a misunderstanding. I lost my fountain pen and was searching for it, that's all. Johnny thought I was up to no good, and he wouldn't listen to reason. I was hoping that, once you'd all had time to cool down and reconsider . . ."

"We have reconsidered," said Harry. "You see, I found the pen."

Elizabeth gave him an incredulous look. "Why didn't you tell *me* that?"

"Johnny asked me not to. He didn't want you to think him foolish or impetuous, knocking poor Hardiman about for no reason."

"I knocked *him* about a bit, as well," Charles hastened to say.

"I know. You gave him quite a bruise."

"Did I?" Charles sounded rather gratified.

"Listen, Hardiman," said Harry, "if we were mistaken about you, I apologize."

"Well, you *were* mistaken; I assure you, I had no intention of damaging the car."

Harry studied him a moment, then extended a hand, which Charles shook in his customary limp manner.

"Well, now that's settled," said the man named Drummond, "shall we order some dinner? I'm famished."

Like Charles's father, Drummond was a railroad man; in fact he had come to America to explore the feasibility of building a new line through Canada to Alaska. He did not, however, share Julius Hardiman's contempt for horseless carriages. In fact, he agreed with Harry that the motorcar would revolutionize transportation, and he intended to be a part of that revolution.

"What would it take for me to get a look at that machine of yours?" he asked. "Perhaps even take her for a spin?"

"Oh, I'm afraid they never let anyone else drive her," said Elizabeth pointedly.

"Is that so?" Drummond did not look pleased; clearly he was, like Charles's father, accustomed to getting his way.

Harry grinned amiably. "I suppose we might be able to arrange something."

"Excellent!" The man rubbed his pudgy hands together. Elizabeth gave Harry a scathing look that he did his best to ignore.

Drummond was in such good spirits that he insisted on paying for everyone's meal, including the roast beef sandwiches Harry ordered for Johnny. As the foursome left the restaurant, Elizabeth whispered, "You're going to let him drive the *Flash*?"

Harry shrugged. "A short distance, perhaps."

"You wouldn't let *me* drive her!"

"That's different."

"Because he's a man, is that it?"

"No. The difference is, if Drummond wrecks her, he can afford to pay for the damage."

While Charles escorted Elizabeth to the harbormaster's house, Harry took Drummond to the warehouse where Johnny stood guard over the *Flash*. Since it was growing dark, Drummond had to content himself with examining the car and asking a string of questions, some quite technical.

Harry's replies were purposely vague. He knew very well what the man was up to: Drummond meant to find out all he could about the *Flash* and use the information to build a machine of his own. Seeing that he was wasting his time, Drummond gave a tolerant smile. "Well, Mr. Shaugnessey, Mr. Fogg, you've constructed a very impressive machine. I'll return Monday for that drive you promised me."

Johnny shot his friend a glance that clearly said, *You're going to let him drive?*

"If you don't mind," said Harry, "I believe I'll walk with you a way, sir." Over his shoulder he called, "I'll be back to take my turn at guard duty, Johnny."

"Never mind," said Johnny sullenly. "I'll do it."

It felt good to be on foot for a change. They walked to Drummond's hotel on Market Street, discussing motorcars and machines all the way. When they parted, Harry's mind was still so occupied that his sense of direction temporarily deserted him. With night coming on, he found himself in the unsavory section of the city that the locals referred to as "south of the Slot"—the channel in the center of Market Street that contained the trolley tracks.

There were no millionaires' mansions here, only overcrowded tenements; no grand hotels, only seedy rooming houses; no theaters or opera houses, only rowdy music halls; no elegant restaurants, only saloons filled with drunken sailors and the thieves and women of ill repute who competed for the sailors' money.

It did not occur to Harry to turn back. He was certain that, if he kept heading downhill, he would reach the docks soon. He did wish, however, that he had thought to bring along the revolver. Not that he would actually shoot anyone, not unless he was in mortal danger. But the feel of a gun stuck in his waistband would have been reassuring.

A row of gas lamps, like those along Market Street, would have been reassuring, too. But there were none in this neighborhood, only an occasional light at the door of a saloon or music hall. As Harry passed through one of the pools of darkness, he saw the shadows ahead of him shift and heard a guttural voice growl, "Now, don't make trouble for yourself, wog. Just hand over your money."

# HARRY MAKES A PERFECT DELIVERY AND A NEW ACQUAINTANCE

**H**arry flattened against a crumbling brick wall and peered into the blackness. He could barely make out two figures standing perhaps ten yards from him. One was a burly fellow in a dark coat, brandishing some small object—a knife, Harry guessed. The other was tall and slender, with what appeared to be a turban on his head and a satchel of some sort in one hand. Apparently he, not Harry, was the thief's target.

Harry stood still as stone and breathed as softly as he could while he considered his next move. Though he was impulsive, he was not about to throw himself upon a man carrying a knife.

"Let's have the bag!" the thief growled.

"I am sorry," said the other man, in a surprisingly

calm voice, "but I cannot do that." He set the satchel on the cobblestones, removed his frock coat, folded it carefully, and placed it atop the satchel.

"All right," said the thief. "If that's the way you want it, wog." He shuffled forward, waving the knife as though he relished the prospect of using it.

Instead of retreating, the turbaned fellow took up a defensive position, one unlike any Harry had ever seen. Crouching low, the man raised his front leg and thrust his arms to one side, the elbows bent, the fingers curled.

Harry did not wait to see what would happen next. He snatched up a chunk of broken brick and went into a stance of his own—that of a crack cricket bowler. He swung his arm in a circle and let the brick fly; it caught the burly man square in the center of the chest. With a hoarse cry that was equal parts pain and astonishment, he staggered backward; his knife clattered onto the cobbles.

When the thief had disappeared into the darkness, the turbaned man turned and bowed slightly. "Thank you for your assistance, sir." His accent, with its rolled r's and its odd lack of inflection, was quite familiar to Harry; Aouda Fogg's few Indian friends sounded much the same.

"You're welcome. We should get moving, in case he returns with reinforcements."

The man seemed in no hurry. He donned his coat in

a leisurely fashion, then picked up his satchel. "Would you happen to know where I might find inexpensive lodgings?"

"I'm sorry; I've been here only a few hours myself." Harry laughed. "If I knew the city, I'd have known to avoid this neighborhood." They headed downhill, toward the harbor. "You didn't seem particularly afraid back there," said Harry.

"No. Though I truly am grateful to you, I could have defended myself."

"If you don't mind my asking, how exactly would you have done that?"

"I am a student of *kalarippayattu*."

"Who?"

"It is not a person. It is a traditional Indian martial art."

"The unusual stance you took is part of it, then?"

"It is called the *asvavadivu*—also known, more crudely, as the horse posture."

"You could actually have disarmed the thief?"

"And disabled him if necessary. Thanks to you, it was not necessary. You have an excellent throwing arm. Do you by any chance play cricket?"

"I used to do, at Eton. And you?"

"At the Institute of Mechanical and Electrical Engineering. We did not have much of a team, but as good as one might expect from students of the sciences."

They launched into a spirited discussion of various

cricket teams and players and, before they knew it, had reached the well-lighted area of wharves and warehouses. The stranger gazed at Harry with frank curiosity. "I assumed from your speech that you were English. I see now that you are not."

"My mother is from India."

"But she has raised you to be a proper British gentleman."

"She's tried. I'm not certain it's worked out."

The man laughed. "Fortunately for me. Few British gentlemen would have risked their own lives to save that of a foreigner. It would be gentlemanly of us, I suppose, to introduce ourselves. My name is Dhiren Ramesh."

He was a good-looking, athletic fellow of perhaps thirty. Though his well-tailored gray suit and cream-colored waistcoat were like those worn by any professional man in New York or London, no one would have mistaken him for an Englishman or an American. And the red turban he wore made it clear that he did not wish to be mistaken for one.

"I have been studying America's railroads," he said, "and I am now on my way to Russia to help plan a railway across Siberia." He raised his leather satchel. "Had the thief taken this, he would have been quite disappointed. It contains mainly sketches and notes and mathematical calculations."

They shook hands; the man's grip was strong, almost painful. "Harry Fogg. I'm traveling around the world in a motorcar."

Ramesh smiled broadly. "It is a great pleasure to meet you. I have been following your progress in the newspapers. How is your vehicle holding up?"

Harry stopped before the warehouse. "See for yourself, if you like."

"I would like that very much, but it is late. Another day, perhaps. Will you be in San Francisco long?"

"Only two more days, I hope. We plan to sail on Tuesday, on the *Belgic*."

"In that case, there will be many opportunities for me to see your motorcar. I have a cabin on the *Belgic* as well."

Early on Monday, Harry and Elizabeth returned to the Western Union office. When she emerged, the look on her face told Harry that she had heard no word from the *Daily Graphic*.

"I don't understand it. They seemed to like my stories. Why would they cut me off this way?" Her blue eyes threatened to fill with tears. She swallowed hard, then took a deep, slightly shaky breath. "Well. If I don't hear from them soon, you may have to continue without me."

Harry scratched his head. "See here, Elizabeth; I know you're quite capable of taking care of yourself and all that, but we can't just *leave* you here."

Elizabeth smiled faintly. "Thank you, but I've caused you enough delays already; I can't let you risk losing your wager on my account. If necessary, I can find work and earn the money for my passage home."

"No," said Harry. "No. I'll find some way out of this, I promise you."

That afternoon, both the harbormaster and Drummond, the railroad man, turned up to hold Harry to his promise. After showing them how handily the *Flash* climbed San Francisco's steep grades, he gave Drummond a turn at the wheel. The man would have run them into a stack of spice crates had Harry not yanked on the hand brake just in time. Despite the near-disaster, Drummond clearly found the experience exhilarating. "I must get myself one of these machines!" he boomed.

Around four Johnny returned from escorting Elizabeth to the telegraph office; the *Daily Graphic* was still ignoring her. "We can't leave her," Johnny said. "Maybe Hardiman would pay her way."

"She's far too proud to ask him." Harry patted his friend's shoulder reassuringly. "But don't worry, lad. I've been mulling it over, and I think I've come up with a plan to raise the money for her and for us."

"I knew you would. What's the plan?"

"I'll tell you later," said Harry, "once I've seen whether or not it works." He hurried away, leaving Johnny to guard the *Flash* again. Johnny had already made every conceivable adjustment and repair to the motorcar, including replacing the broken windscreen at last. All he could do was sit and stare into space.

After an hour or so, Elizabeth arrived bearing food and drink and a copy of *Under Two Flags*. "I thought you might be bored, so I brought you something to read."

Johnny pulled his cap down over his ears. "Thanks," he murmured. He set the book and the food aside and pretended to be cleaning the brass housing of the acetylene lamps.

Elizabeth realized for the first time that, despite all his cleverness, Johnny might not know his letters. "If you like," she said softly, "I could read aloud while you have your supper." When he didn't reply, she retrieved the book and sat on a packing crate. "I'll have to turn away from you, I'm afraid, in order to catch the light from the window. Will you be able to hear me all right?"

"Yes," said Johnny, gratefully.

Elizabeth was a fine reader, dramatic and subtle by turns, and surprisingly adept at mimicking men's voices. As Johnny listened, he lost all awareness of his actual surroundings and drifted into the world created by the words. As fond as he was of Harry, when his friend returned and broke the spell, Johnny almost wished he had stayed away awhile longer.

Harry was brandishing several pieces of paper. "I've got them!" he announced triumphantly.

Elizabeth looked up from the book, a bit put out at being interrupted. "I assume you mean the steamship tickets."

"Yes!" He waved one of the documents in front of Johnny's face. "And here I have a bill of lading for the *Flash!*"

"Wonderful," said Elizabeth.

Harry plunked down on the packing crate next to her. "You might show a bit more enthusiasm. After all . . ." He dangled another of the papers before her nose. "I've a ticket for you as well."

Elizabeth's well-formed mouth fell open. "How on earth did you manage *that*?"

Harry's grin faded just a little. "Never mind how I managed it. The important thing is, we sail for Yokohama in the morning!"

# TWENTY-FIVE

## *In which*

# A REMEDY IS FOUND FOR HARRY'S IMPATIENCE

They were not forced to travel Chinese steerage, after all. Harry had actually taken two cabins in second class—one for himself and Johnny, and another for Elizabeth. Charles, of course, made his own arrangements; to Harry's surprise, the usually fussy fellow contented himself with a "cramped and dreary" second-class cabin as well.

As Harry and Elizabeth stood at the rail watching San Francisco disappear behind its sulfurous haze, Harry said, "When do we reach Yokohama?"

Elizabeth consulted her schedule. "They don't give a specific date. The steward says the crossing can take anywhere from a fortnight to sixteen days, depending upon the weather."

"And of course we lose a day when we cross the date line," said Harry.

"Still, we'll be in Shanghai by the end of September. That leaves us a month and a half to cross Asia and Europe."

"Right," said Harry cheerfully. "More than enough time."

Elizabeth stared silently at the water for a minute or two. "You really needn't have paid for my passage, you know."

"Is that your way of saying thank you?"

"I'm grateful, Harry, truly I am. But it must have used up every bit of money you had. How will you purchase supplies and fuel for the rest of the trip?"

"Don't worry about it, all right? I have plenty of money."

"I don't see how, after— Oh. I think I understand. You wired your father. That's it, isn't it?" Harry didn't reply. She laid a hand on his arm. "That must have been a bitter pill to swallow. I'm sorry. When I signed on, I promised I wouldn't cause you any trouble, and it's all I've done."

"Oh, I don't know. On the whole, I'd say you've been more of an asset than a liability."

She made a disparaging sound. "Oh, yes. I crashed the car into a boulder; I made you miss the steamer for Hong Kong . . ."

"You also helped us outrun a prairie fire," he said,

"and you looked after me when I was ill. Not to mention putting Charles in his place a time or two." This elicited a laugh from Elizabeth. "But the best thing you've done," Harry went on, more seriously, "is to treat Johnny with kindness and consideration. He's had precious little of that in his life."

For once, Elizabeth seemed at a loss for words. She put her chin in her hands and gazed at the froth churned up by the steamship's propellers. Harry was lost in thought, too. Now that he had taken care of the money problem, his main concern was how he would keep himself from going mad during the interminable two weeks that lay ahead.

The evenings went by quickly enough. Harry and Charles occupied themselves with games of bezique or écarté. Sometimes Elizabeth joined them for a few hands of whist; other evenings she sat on deck reading to Johnny, whom she actually coaxed out of his cabin and into a deck chair.

The days were more trying. Whatever the weather, Harry strode up and down the deck like a dog on a treadmill or stood in the bow, staring out over the ocean as if hoping that Yokohama might appear on the horizon a week or two ahead of schedule. This was where Dhiren Ramesh found him. "Mr. Fogg. It is a pleasure to see you. I hoped we might meet again, but I was not certain in which class you would be traveling."

The genuine warmth of the man's greeting took Harry by surprise. The fellows at Eton and at the Reform Club could put on a show of well-met-old-chap heartiness, but it often felt forced, superficial; you were left wondering whether they truly were glad to see you or were just going through the motions expected of a gentleman. With Ramesh, there was no doubt. It was both refreshing and a bit disconcerting.

They resumed their conversation as if they had spoken a few hours earlier, and not a few days ago. When Harry expressed his impatience, Ramesh smiled. "I believe I have just the remedy for that. We shall organize a cricket match."

There were enough enthusiastic Englishmen aboard, plus a couple of Indian men, to make up two sides. Ramesh had a bat and ball in his luggage; folded-up deck chairs served as their wickets.

They quickly discovered one major drawback of playing aboard a ship: There was nothing to stop the ball from flying into the ocean. They substituted apples from the bowls in the dining room.

Harry was accustomed to playing all out; his first time up, he struck the ball so hard it exploded into applesauce. "Sorry! I suppose that should count as an out." After that, he was more restrained, and began to enjoy the game for what it was—not a serious contest, just a bit of a lark.

Passengers gathered to watch the match, including Charles. "Why don't you join us, Hardiman?" called Harry.

"No, no," Charles protested. "I'm no cricketer."

"Then you're in the same boat as the rest of us duffers," said one of Harry's teammates. "Come on, there's a good fellow."

Elizabeth leaned into Charles and said softly, "If you don't, I will." He handed her his jacket and strode onto the field, which had been marked out on the deck with chalk. As luck would have it, the very next shot came rolling right at him; to his surprise and Harry's, he scooped it up easily.

"Throw it at their wicket!" Harry told him.

Charles flung the apple at the upended deck chair; it toppled over, to cries of "Good arm!" and "Way, oh!" Later that afternoon, Charles managed to score a run when the juice-slick ball shot from a fielder's hands and over the rail. "Well done, old chap!" Harry pounded him on the back. Charles responded with a rare grin.

Though his side ultimately lost, Harry took it quite philosophically. Charles did not. "We'll get them next time!" he vowed.

Ramesh seemed amused by his grim resolve. "The *Bhagavad Gita* teaches that we should be indifferent to success or failure. One should simply do one's part as cheerfully and as competently as possible, without thinking of the outcome."

Harry laughed. "The English have a similar saying. 'It's not whether you win or lose, it's how you play the game.'"

"In my experience," said Ramesh, "few Englishmen

live by that rule. For most of them, winning seems to be of the utmost importance."

"It may be true that we like to win," replied Charles, "but only if it's done fairly and honorably."

Ramesh raised an eyebrow. "If you have studied the history of India, you know that the conduct of your countrymen there has been neither fair nor honorable."

"And I suppose the conduct of your countrymen *has* been? My uncle served in India, and he has told me stories of how the sepoys butchered English women and children."

"You are right, of course. There have been unspeakable, unforgivable atrocities on both sides. But I am sure you agree that none of them would have occurred had the British not insisted upon ruling India."

Though Ramesh remained calm and reasonable, Charles had grown more and more agitated. Finally he spun about and stalked off. The Indian man sighed. "Perhaps I should not have spoken so frankly. I did not mean to anger him. It is just that I grow a bit weary of Englishmen and their attitude toward our country— which of course they regard as *their* country. The jewel in England's crown, I have heard it called."

When Ramesh said "our country," Harry felt that he was included. He wanted to protest that India was not his country, that he knew practically nothing about it, just the little his mother had told him. They had studied the country's history briefly at Eton, but Harry had not really been paying attention.

And yet, though he couldn't call himself an Indian, he knew he would never be considered a proper Englishman, either; it had been made clear to him many times, most recently by Julius Hardiman and his cronies.

That night, over a game of cards, Charles said, "That Indian fellow. Is he a friend of yours?"

"What if he is?"

"That's your business, of course. I just think that the stuff he was saying earlier was a lot of rubbish. I'd like to see what India would amount to without us English."

"Yes," said Harry, thoughtfully. "So would I."

# THE SHORTEST ROUTE IS NOT NECESSARILY THE QUICKEST

At breakfast the next morning, Harry found Ramesh sitting by himself. They fell easily into conversation again. Harry mentioned that he was looking forward to driving across India, since he knew so little about his mother's homeland. He didn't mention the fact that Aouda's in-laws might wish to kidnap him.

Ramesh gave him a puzzled glance. "Surely you will not pass through India?"

"The plan is to land in Shanghai, then cut across southern China and Burma. I've been told it's the shortest route."

"Only if you do not count the distance traveled up and down."

"There are a lot of hills, then?"

"Not hills, my friend—mountains. Very high, very

steep mountains. I would not want the task of putting a railroad through them, I promise you that. In fact, I would not care to attempt them even on the most sure-footed of donkeys, and no one has ever called me faint of heart."

Harry frowned and picked at his eggs. "I didn't know about the mountains. I wonder whether Julius Hardiman did. He was the one who suggested I take that route."

"Perhaps he knows southern China only from a map. If he had actually crossed it, he would certainly not advise anyone else to try."

"Unless . . ." said Harry.

"Unless what?"

"Unless he wanted them to fail."

Ramesh's job as a railway engineer had taken him throughout eastern Asia, and he knew of only one feasible route: the so-called Great Russian Post Road. Patched together by the Russian government from a series of existing wagon roads, it led from the port of Vladivostok all the way across Siberia to Moscow. "I traveled it once, years ago; this time I will explore it more closely, to determine whether it is suitable for the railroad."

"Surely there are mountains there, too?"

"Of course; but not like those in China and Burma. Let me fetch my topographical maps and show you."

A look at the maps convinced Harry that they were

better off going through Siberia, even though it meant adding five hundred miles. "I'll be sorry to miss seeing India, though."

Ramesh slid a map of his country from his chart case and gazed at it wistfully. "I shall miss it, too. I have been nearly six months in America, and will likely spend an entire year in Russia. It is a long time to be away from a place one loves."

Harry was struck by the sadness in Ramesh's voice. If it had not been for the wager, Harry would have been in no hurry to return to London. There were so many other places to see. Though he had covered a lot of territory, and would cover a good deal more, he wasn't really experiencing it, only passing through.

Ramesh placed a finger on the southern tip of India. "Here is my home."

"Kerala. It must be very beautiful."

"It is a fertile region, full of rice fields and spice gardens and coconut groves. The weather is always warm there." He gave a small shudder. "I shall have to purchase a fur coat in Vladivostok." With a laugh, he added, "And an extra-large fur cap, to fit over my turban."

In the days that followed, Ramesh told him many things about India: the astonishing variety of its landscape and climate; the advanced civilizations that had flourished there for over four thousand years; its rich legacy of literature and art; all the races and languages and religious beliefs that coexisted there; the changes wrought by its various "conquerors"—of whom Britain was only the latest.

"I feel as though I should apologize," Harry said, "for what my country has done to yours."

"You will be apologizing to yourself, then, for you belong to both worlds."

Harry stared at the man. He had always thought of himself as belonging to neither.

"In any case," Ramesh said, "the English will not rule us forever. Countries, like individuals, are continually reborn."

"Reborn? You believe in reincarnation, then?"

"Of course. We call it *samsara*. Those who imagine that we have only this one life tend to become impatient and impulsive, always feeling that their time is running out."

"But now I know the cure for impatience," said Harry. "Are you up for another cricket match this afternoon?"

Ramesh smiled. "Does Ganesha have an elephant's head?"

"Who is Ganesha?"

"A Hindu deity."

"And *does* he have an elephant's head?"

"He certainly does."

At the first opportunity, Harry discussed the Russian route with Johnny, who agreed that it made more sense.

Elizabeth was not so sure. "According to the *Graphic*'s Moscow correspondent, Siberia is in rather a sorry state these days. There are severe food shortages, and an alarming number of outlaw bands who prey upon travelers. Not to mention man-eating tigers."

"Well," said Harry, "China has its share of bandits and tigers, as far as that goes. In any case, we're not helpless. We have a couple of rifles and a revolver. We'll make it through all right, I'm sure of it."

Charles was even more negative. "If my father advised you to go by way of China, he must have had a good reason."

"That's what I'm afraid of," said Harry.

"See here, Fogg. I've told you, he would never resort to such underhanded tactics. As I said before, we English may play to win, but we play it fair and square."

"You may be right," said Harry. "Perhaps he didn't deliberately mislead me; he may simply have been mistaken."

"So you prefer to believe what your Indian friend tells you?"

"Frankly, yes."

Charles nodded sourly. "Well, it's your decision. I'm only an observer. But if you run into trouble in the frozen wastes of Siberia, don't blame me or my father."

Harry couldn't help smiling at Charles's melodramatic tone. "I don't imagine the wastes will be frozen just yet. It's only the sixteenth of September."

"The seventeenth," said Charles smugly. "We passed

over the international date line a few hours ago."

The following day, the *Belgic* sailed into a typhoon really worthy of the name; the deck was deluged by wind-driven rain and drenched by such enormous waves that they might have been traveling beneath the surface of the sea, like Captain Nemo. Passengers confined themselves to their cabins or to the lounge or smoking room. A few gathered in the dining room at mealtime, but most were too nauseated to bother.

Harry had never been subject to seasickness. He had been told that he was a born sailor, and perhaps there was some truth in that; Phileas Fogg had revealed once, in a rare unguarded moment, that as a young man he had gone to sea. But when the big ship wallowed in the waves, even the unflappable Harry had some uncomfortable moments.

Ramesh seemed oblivious to the ship's acrobatics, thanks to something he called *yoga*. "It is ancient discipline," he explained, "which enables one to control—to some extent, at least—the functioning of both the body and the mind."

"Would it enable me to be more patient?" asked Harry. "Now that we can't play cricket, I'm champing at the bit."

Since the dining room was so empty, he and Ramesh were seated at the main table, across from the captain, an imposing man of sixty or so, with skin like tanned leather and a neatly trimmed gray beard that didn't quite conceal a livid scar on one cheek. "You're the chaps who organized the cricket matches, then?" he said.

"Yes, sir," admitted Harry. "I'm afraid we spoiled quite a lot of apples."

The captain laughed. "No matter. It's kept the passengers happy." He thrust out a callused hand. "I'm Captain Keough, by the by."

"Harry Fogg. And this is my friend Dhiren Ramesh."

The captain raised a bushy eyebrow. "Fogg? Any relation to Phileas Fogg?"

Harry groaned inwardly. "He's my father."

"The devil take me. I don't suppose Phileas has ever mentioned me? William Keough?"

"No, sir, not that I recall."

"I'm not surprised." Keough stroked his beard thoughtfully, as if there was something on his mind but he was uncertain whether or not to bring it up. "The fact is," he went on, in a low voice, "many years ago, your father and I were business partners."

Harry leaned forward eagerly. At last, a chance to write something upon the blank slate that was his father's past. "Business partners? What sort of business?"

"Well, it's rather a long story."

Ramesh rose from the table. "If you will pardon me, gentlemen, it is time for my yoga exercises." It was clearly an excuse; Harry knew his friend didn't wish to intrude.

The captain drew a tankard of dark beer for himself and one for Harry, then began his story.

## TWENTY-SEVEN

### *In which*

# LONG-BURIED SECRETS
# ARE DUG UP

**W**hen they were little more than boys, he and Phileas Fogg had been deckhands aboard the same whaling vessel. For Keough it was a way of escaping a brief, brutal life in the slums of London. Fogg, by contrast, came from a family that was once quite wealthy but had fallen on hard times. He was determined to restore their fortunes.

A quick learner and a hard worker, Fogg soon advanced to the position of first mate on a shabby schooner that plied the Irish Sea, carrying manufactured items to isolated islands and ports. It was not a profitable business, and the shipping company constantly teetered on the brink of bankruptcy.

But in time Fogg and Keough managed to buy a ship of their own and establish a flourishing trade in the West Indies, which gave them the capital to build a second ship, then a third and a fourth. Fogg handled the finances; Keough outfitted the ships and hired the crews.

Eventually they had a falling-out and Keough sold his share in the business to his partner for a tidy sum—which Keough proceeded to squander on a series of ill-advised ventures. Fogg, meanwhile, built the shipping company into an extremely valuable enterprise; at the age of thirty-five, he sold it for an astonishing amount of money and moved to London.

Keough clearly still resented the way things had worked out. Speaking of it seemed to leave a bad taste in his mouth. He took a swig from the tankard of beer, which he gripped with both hands so the ship's erratic motion would not send it flying.

"Thank you for telling me all this," said Harry. "There's one thing I don't understand, though. If the company you worked for at first was so hard up, how did you ever save enough for a ship of your own?"

The captain's scarred, weathered face took on a sardonic smile. "Well, that's another story—one I'm not sure your father would want you to hear." He drained the tankard, then wiped his mouth and beard carefully with his napkin. "On the other hand, I don't much care what Phileas Fogg wants or doesn't want."

Keough proceeded to fill in the missing portion of his tale. When the owners of the failing shipping company saw how eager Fogg was to advance himself, they approached him with a proposition: They would insure the schooner's cargo—mainly flour and sugar and tools and such—for far more than it was worth. Its new captain, Fogg, would then deliberately run her aground on some isolated, rocky coastline. The company would collect the insurance money and split it with him and his first mate, Keough.

Though Fogg disliked the shady nature of the deal, Keough convinced him it was a sort of standard business practice, one that harmed nobody except the infernal insurance companies, which could well afford to lose a few thousand pounds.

With a small crew aboard, the two men scuttled the schooner on a reef off the coast of Cornwall. While the sailors rowed ashore in lifeboats, local villagers swarmed out to pick the carcass of the ship clean, as they had done with so many other wrecked vessels.

When Keough finished, Harry sat sober-faced and silent, trying to absorb all that he had heard. The captain cleared his throat uncomfortably. "Perhaps I should have left that part of the story untold. I don't want to turn a man's own son against him. Don't judge him too harshly; he was young and reckless."

"No, no," said Harry. "I'm glad you told me." He cracked a bit of a grin. "It's good to know that he wasn't always the careful, clockwork man he is today. He had desires and ambitions; he took risks; he flouted authority. His methods weren't quite cricket, of course, but he did what he set out to do—he restored his family's fortunes." Harry sipped at the dark, slightly bitter beer. "He seldom speaks of my grandfather and grandmother. I wonder whether he ever revealed to them where the money came from."

The captain grimly shook his head. "He had no chance to, I'm afraid. Both his parents died that same year . . . of a fever they contracted while in debtor's prison."

Harry had not seen Elizabeth since the previous evening, when she left in the middle of dinner. He suspected that she, too, was suffering from mal de mer. He ordered a container of chamomile tea and some slices of dry toast and carried them to Elizabeth's cabin, staggering slightly each time the ship lurched. He knocked softly on her door. When there was no reply, he rapped more forcefully.

"Go away!" groaned a wretched voice.

"It's Harry. May I come in?"

"No. Just go away, will you, and let me die in peace."

"If you don't open the door, I'll be forced to summon the ship's doctor."

There was a long silence. Just as Harry was about to pound again, the door opened a few inches and her pale, haggard face peered out at him. "What do you want?"

"I've brought you some tea and toast."

Elizabeth put a hand to her mouth. "Are you deliberately trying to torture me?"

Harry pushed the door gently open; too weak to resist, Elizabeth retreated and sank onto the bed. "You should drink a little something, at least," said Harry. Putting down the tray, he arranged her pillows to allow her to sit up.

She pulled her housecoat tightly about her and brushed at her hair ineffectually with one limp hand. Normally, she kept her dark tresses braided and coiled atop her head, but now they hung loose and tousled. "I must be a sight."

"You look lovely," said Harry.

"Liar."

The sour smell of vomit permeated the small, stuffy cabin. "I'll open the porthole a bit, shall I?" The moment Harry unfastened the round, brass-framed glass, a gust of wind forced its way in, bringing with it a considerable quantity of salt spray. "Oops."

"It's all right," murmured Elizabeth. "It feels good."

Harry poured a cup of chamomile tea and held it to her lips. "Try some of this."

She raised her hands to guide the cup, but they trembled too much. Closing her eyes, she sipped at the tepid tea. She managed to drink half of it, and at first it seemed as though it might stay down. But after a minute she pushed him urgently aside and, leaning over the edge of her bed, spewed the tea into her bedpan. Harry busied himself at the cabin's fold-down sink, wetting a washcloth with which he wiped her perspiring face.

"You don't need to do this," said Elizabeth weakly.

"You took care of me back in Wyoming. Turnabout is fair play."

"Don't talk to me about fair. If there were any fairness in the world, you'd be as sick as the rest of us. How are the others holding up?"

"Johnny's not doing too badly. He spends most of his time in the cargo hold, with the *Flash*. I don't know about Charles. I should look in on him. I'll be back later, with fresh tea. And a clean bedpan."

Charles was in almost as sorry a state. Harry spent all that day and the next tending to him and Elizabeth by turns. Finally, after two full days of being tossed about like a medicine ball, the *Belgic* sailed into calmer waters.

# THE MOTORISTS ARE ONCE
# AGAIN ON SOLID GROUND

**T**o Harry's delight, the next day the cricketers continued their game. Though it did not exactly make the days fly, it kept him from losing his mind. Sensing Harry's restlessness, Ramesh asked whether he had ever considered meditation.

"Medication?" said Harry. "Something on the order of laudanum, you mean?"

"No, no, medi*ta*tion. It is a means of relaxing and clearing one's mind."

"I could certainly use that," said Harry. "Does it take long to learn?"

Ramesh gave a hearty laugh.

"What?" said Harry.

"Pardon my amusement, my friend; it is just that

you seem so impatient to learn patience. The truth is, one never really masters meditation, any more than one masters the martial arts. All we can hope is to become better students."

"I'm afraid I'm not much of a student." Harry was silent for a moment, then said, "You indicated that you studied engineering. I suppose if a chap wanted to know more about machines and motorcars and such, that would be the best way?"

"It would help. You don't seem to relish the prospect."

"I've nothing against learning; I just don't know that I'm cut out for it. I mean, it seems to demand so much time and effort."

Ramesh shrugged. "No more than, say, driving a motorcar around the world."

"That's different."

"Is it?"

"Yes. It's like cricket or rugby; it requires physical effort, not mental."

"It also requires persistence. And that is all one really needs in order to learn a discipline, whether it is *kalarippayattu* or engineering."

"Or meditation?"

"Or meditation."

Under Ramesh's tutelage, Harry worked hard at meditating. He failed miserably at first, but he persisted, and by the time the *Belgic* reached Yokohama, he could clear his brain for a good ten seconds at a time.

They docked on the twenty-third of September; that gave the intrepid motorists and Dhiren Ramesh just enough time to obtain visas from the Russian consul and book berths on the SS *Longmoon*, which sailed for Vladivostok the following afternoon. Elizabeth, meanwhile, wired the *Daily Graphic* yet again. When she returned from the telegraph office, she thrust a wad of pound notes into his hand. "That should pay for my passage on both the *Belgic* and the *Longmoon*."

"You finally got a reply, I take it."

"Yes. And I sent them a rather lengthy story, including a riveting first-person account of what it's like to be horribly seasick." She played with the handles of the ornate Japanese handbag she had bought. "I also told my readers how you took care of me. I . . . I never thanked you for that."

Harry knew it was as close as she was likely to come to actually expressing gratitude. "You're welcome."

"I put in something about the new route as well. I hope that was all right."

"Of course. I doubt that we'll be mobbed by Siberian peasants who have been eagerly following our progress in the newspapers."

She laughed. "No, I suppose not. I only hope we're not *robbed* by Siberian peasants. Or by bandits."

"Or eaten by tigers," said Harry with a grin.

Harry had expected Yokohama to be pleasantly strange and exotic but, thanks to the influence of European traders and merchants, it looked little different from Bristol or Liverpool. He was not sorry to leave.

It was a mere five or six hundred miles to Vladivostok as the crow flies. Unfortunately, the *Longmoon* couldn't fly; it had to sail around the end of the long, narrow island of Honshu. The trip took them three full days.

There were no cricket matches this time. Harry was sure most of the passengers hadn't even heard of the game. To help the time pass, he practiced the meditation techniques he'd learned from Ramesh, so diligently that he sometimes turned up late for his card games.

When Charles complained, Harry said calmly, "You need to learn to be more patient, my friend."

Charles gave him an odd look. "I say, Fogg; what's come over you?"

"I've just been doing a bit of meditation."

"Well, if you ask me," said Charles, "you need to take a smaller dose."

Vladivostok proved even less exotic and attractive than Yokohama. It was populated mainly by Russian soldiers and sailors, by Korean and Chinese laborers who had recently begun laying track for the Trans-Siberian Railway, and by European merchants who supplied their needs. The streets were unpaved, and each gust of wind filled the air with grit and dust. A good deal of it decorated the sides of the square, ugly buildings.

Harry could only imagine how bleak the place must appear to someone accustomed to a lush tropical landscape. Ramesh took it all in, then sighed in resignation and held out his hand. "I am afraid we must say farewell for a while, Hari. I am confident, though, that our paths will cross again."

"I still hope to make it to India someday."

"I have no doubt you will," said Ramesh. "When the time is right." Picking up his satchel, he headed off down the boardwalk. His bright red turban was one of the few spots of color in the gloomy scene. Harry watched it, bobbing above the heads of the townspeople, until it was lost from sight. Then he turned to the other intrepid young motorists.

"Well," he said, rubbing his hands together, partly from anticipation and partly because of the chill in the air. "We still have a few hours of daylight left. Let's get the *Flash* rolling, shall we?"

### Somewhere west of Vladivostok, Siberia, September 27 ————————————————

The round-the-world racers have now passed the halfway point in terms of the time allotted them. Forty-eight days remain in which to reach London. We have traveled well over half the distance—some 15,000 miles so far—but much of it was done aboard a ship. Every mile of the 10,000 that remain must be traversed the hard way.

We did not remain in Vladivostok long enough to cable a dispatch; it will have to wait until we reach the next sizable city—if there is such a thing in Siberia. We had stocked up on tinned food and carbide pellets and other necessities back in San Francisco, so the sole supplies we took on were ten gallons of very expensive kerosene and a traveler's guidebook, after which we set out upon the Great Russian Post Road.

Though it is only nominally a Road, and certainly far from Great, it is at least dry. There is little need for a map, for the route is well delineated by telegraph poles and by the black-and-white posts that serve as mile markers—or, to be perfectly accurate, *verst* markers. According to the guidebook, a *verst* is roughly two-thirds of a mile.

Every twenty or thirty *versts* there is a way station where the postal service drivers, or *yemschiks*, may exchange their weary steeds for fresh ones. Apparently some of these stations also offer accommodations to travelers, but the guidebook's author does not recommended availing oneself of them unless one is equipped with some sure-fire method of killing lice, fleas, and bedbugs. Your humble reporter did, in fact, pack something called Keating's Powder, which is guaranteed to repel insects of every sort. But one cannot help questioning its efficacy; it has proven to be no use at all against mosquitoes.

Though the *Graphic*'s Moscow correspondent issued warnings about man-eating tigers, he failed to mention the dangers of man-eating mosquitoes (which, unfortunately, do not discriminate against women). Each time the *Flash* slows to negotiate a rough spot in the road, the nasty pests (mosquitoes, not tigers) descend upon us in droves. Our sole defense is to raise the leather rain roof and lower the side curtains. We did discover that if Mr. Shaugnessey lights his pipe and fills the car with pungent tobacco smoke, it discourages the buzzing blackguards a bit. It also sends the other passengers into uncontrollable fits of coughing.

Another look at the guidebook informs one that the number of inhabitants in all of Siberia is less than the population of London. It is not difficult to believe. Aside from the post-houses there are few dwellings along the way and no villages at all, only *verst* after *verst* of trees, mostly evergreens, with a smattering of oaks and maples whose leaves are just beginning to turn.

After driving for several hours we did encounter another vehicle, one of the carriages used by the post drivers. We braked at once and pulled over, to avoid frightening the three-horse team. The *yemschik* slowed, too, and gaped at our motorcar, then shouted something that none of us could understand. Considering the man's hostile tone, it was probably just as well.

These post carriages, which are called *tarantasses*, are unlovely, utilitarian vehicles, little more than a box on wheels, with no suspension of any sort. Though their primary purpose is, of course, to carry letters and packages, we discovered that there was a passenger within this one, for he lifted the leather side curtain to peer at us.

There seemed to be no seating of any sort; the man was perched upon his luggage. He looked quite uncomfortable and very envious of our motorcar. When the driver cracked his whip, the carriage lurched forward, sending the passenger tumbling from his suitcase seat. From now on, when this reporter is tempted to complain about the cramped accommodations aboard the *Flash*, she will try to remember to thank her lucky stars that she is not crossing Siberia in a *tarantass*.

Elizabeth did not mention that the guidebook she referenced so frequently was, in fact, purchased by Charles, and that it was Charles who brought all those facts and Russian terms to her attention. Elizabeth tended to rely more on her own opinions and observations than on reading or research. Still, she didn't mind sounding knowledgeable when she got the chance.

By dusk, the *Flash* had covered more than sixty miles,

but had reached nothing resembling a settlement. The crew hastily set up the tents and built a fire, throwing on green boughs to create a smoke screen that foiled the mosquitoes—more or less.

"Unfortunately," said Charles, gloomily, "if there are bandits, the fire will lead them right to us."

They took turns standing sentry—sitting, actually— throughout the night. Elizabeth insisted upon doing her share of guard duty. Harry was still not entirely certain that he could trust Charles; just to be on the safe side, he slept in the backseat of the *Flash*.

# THE TRAVELERS DECIDE TO CROSS CHINA AFTER ALL

**A**round noon the next day, they came upon a town that consisted of half a dozen houses, a small whitewashed church, and an army barracks, all built of logs. The sight of their motorcar brought peasants, soldiers, and clergy swarming from their respective buildings, openmouthed in astonishment.

An officer who spoke a little English invited them to his quarters to share what passed for luncheon in Siberia—tea, salt fish, and heavy black bread that was ostensibly made from rye flour but featured some other ingredient that tasted rather like powdered pine bark—which, in fact, it was. To make tea, the man hacked a chunk from a large brick of grayish stuff and boiled it for a quarter of an hour. These bricks were called *kerpichni chai*, and consisted of the dust and twigs and crushed leaves that were swept up off the floor of tea merchants'.

"I am sorry we cannot offer you something better," said the officer.

"No, no, this is fine," said Harry. "Far better than the tinned beef we've been eating."

"It's very filling," put in Elizabeth, forcing a smile. She pushed her chipped china plate aside. "In fact, I don't think I could possibly eat another bite."

Charles quickly changed the subject. "We were surprised at how solid and dry the roads are here. In America, we had to fight our way through knee-deep mud at times."

The Russian officer nodded gravely. "There is a reason why the roads are so dry and the rivers so shallow. We have had five months of . . . what is the English word?"

"Drought?" said Elizabeth.

"Yes. Drought. The grain harvest this year was very poor. And the people cannot plant their winter crop in such dry ground." He took a bottle of clear liquid from a shelf and poured a shot for each of them. "Fortunately, vodka may be made without grain. *Nostrovia.*"

"Cheers," said Harry. Though it had little flavor, the vodka took the taste of pine bark and tea dust out of their mouths. "What is it made of, then?"

"Sugar beets." The officer downed another shot and shook his head. "I do not know what will become of the people here. If the government does not send aid, I do not see how they will survive. Some, I regret to say, have left their farms and taken up robbery. We spend much of our time chasing after these outlaws."

But apparently the bandits they really needed to fear were the Chungese, nomads who lived in northern Manchuria. "Oh, well," said Harry, "we won't be passing through China."

"You cannot avoid it, unless you go a thousand *versts* out of your way."

"But we don't have Chinese visas," said Charles.

The soldier shrugged. "No matter. We control the province of Manchuria—for now, at any rate. You will find several garrisons of our soldiers, who will assist you if you need it. Since we are a hospitable people, they will no doubt feed you, as well."

"Oh, good!" said Elizabeth brightly, picking a bit of pine bark from her teeth.

When they emerged from the barracks, they found the *Flash* surrounded by villagers—more of them than it seemed the little settlement could possibly contain. The men were all dressed more or less alike, in blue shirts, brown trousers, and bearskin caps; the women wore faded print dresses, the children patched hand-me-downs. Though the men had boots, the women and children were barefoot, despite the chill.

Johnny sat slumped in the front seat, looking so much like a cornered animal that Harry couldn't help laughing, though he hid it well. Luckily, none of the townsfolk were attempting to touch the car. In fact, they seemed a little afraid of it. Then one boy of ten or eleven, so thin that he seemed all knees and elbows, crept cautiously forward and touched the metal; he gave a triumphant shout, as though he had survived some ordeal.

"You want to take a ride in her?" said Harry. He held open the driver's door and gestured to the boy. "Go on, get in. We'll give you a ride." Though the boy obviously knew no English, he grasped Harry's meaning. Ignoring the protests of his mother, he climbed in. "It's all right," Harry assured the woman. "It's perfectly safe."

"She thinks we're kidnapping him," said Elizabeth. "I'll stay here as hostage until you come back."

They drove a few yards up the road, with the boy laughing in delight, then returned. The other children pressed forward, pleading for a ride. "Now you've done it," said Charles.

Harry shook his head. "I'm sorry," he told the children. "No more rides. We have to be on our way." The disappointment in their faces was heartbreaking. Harry dug through their supplies, came up with a bag of desiccated pineapple he had bought in San Francisco, and handed it to the boy who had ridden with him. "Here. Pass that around, will you?" While the children were distracted, Harry took Elizabeth's arm. "Let's go!"

As they headed out of the village with yapping dogs and shouting children in their wake, Harry said, "Sorry to leave you at the mercy of the crowd, Johnny. I'll stay with the car next time."

"I don't mind staying with it," said Charles.

"You two are just trying to avoid the twig tea and pine-bark bread," said Elizabeth. "Next time, *I'll* stay with the car."

Harry laughed. "We'll take turns, all right?" After a time, he said, more soberly, "I wish I could have given them more than just bag of pineapple."

"We can't supply every village in Siberia," said Elizabeth. "Besides, there may be a better way to help them. I'll tell my readers how truly desperate the situation is here; surely it will motivate someone to organize a relief effort."

"That's a good idea," said Harry.

"I do have one from time to time," Elizabeth replied brusquely, as though he had insulted rather than complimented her. Perhaps, Harry thought, she was as unaccustomed to praise as the rest of them were.

That evening, as he and Elizabeth sat throwing green branches on the campfire and dodging the clouds of smoke, Harry said quietly, "You promised to tell me about yourself and your family."

"I said I *might*. Eventually."

"That was a month ago. Do you plan to wait until we're back to England?"

"I have no particular plans. I've just been waiting for the right time."

"Oh. Well, I was curious about your father, that's all."

"What about him?"

"I wondered whether he was as distant and as difficult to please as mine."

She considered the question for a moment. "No. I expect he's nothing at all like your father."

"I see."

"I doubt that you do."

"Well, you haven't given me much to go on."

She tossed another limb on the fire. "My father . . . My father has been less fortunate than yours. He once had a well-paying position and a good reputation. But then, a year or two after I was born, he . . . he committed a single foolish act, and lost it all. My mother was so distressed by this change in their fortunes that her health declined drastically. Naturally, we could not afford proper care for her. When I was six, she died."

"I'm sorry. It must have been very difficult for you."

"Yes," she said, her voice thick with emotion. She cleared her throat and raised her chin resolutely. "But it also made me strong. And resourceful. And determined to succeed."

"Actually, my father had much the same experience. His parents, too, lost everything they had. From the time he was my age, he was forced to make his own way in the world."

"I didn't know that."

"Nor did I, until recently." Harry stretched and yawned. "I believe I'll call it a day." He headed for the

*Flash*, but turned back to say, "I'm glad you talked me into letting you come, Elizabeth. I hope it brings you that success you're after. I hope your newspaper stories are a sensation, and make your name—whatever it is— into a household word."

Elizabeth could find no words to reply. She sat gazing thoughtfully into the fire and sipping strong tea, brewed from the last of the tea leaves she had brought, to keep herself awake. It worked so well that, when it was time to rouse Johnny for his turn at guard duty, she let him sleep.

# FOR A CHANGE,
# NOTHING UNFORTUNATE
# BEFALLS OUR PROTAGONISTS

**W**hen Charles rejoined the crew, he had also resumed his journal entries.

### Tuesday, September 29

*Fifty-four days gone; forty-six remaining. Early this morning, we left the post road and crossed the border into Manchuria. Though there is a large Russian presence in the province and the landscape is much the same as in Siberia—rolling grassland broken by the occasional river valley—the moment we entered a town it was clear that we were in China.*

*The houses are better built and more ornate, decorated with porcelain figures and carved dragons. The signs hanging on the shops are painted with Chinese symbols. The streets are filled with*

*small carriage-like vehicles pulled by humans, not
horses. There are no women to be seen. The men
wear loose smocks of white or blue, and their faces
are mostly hairless; even their heads are shaved, save
for a single long braid that hangs down their backs
or is curled into a sort of bun.*

*Strangely, they display no curiosity at all about
the Flash. It's as though the whole notion of a mo-
torized car is so alien to them, they do not even acknowledge its existence. The people and the town
seem more prosperous than those in Russia, but
they lack three things upon which we have come to
rely—railroads, a telegraph system, and a source of
kerosene.*

*To my astonishment, Fogg has consented to stop
at a roadside inn for refreshments. Unfortunately,
the tea here is, if possible, even more vile than
that given us by the Russian soldiers. The wheaten
bread, however, is quite edible—which, in a way, is
rather a pity; if they had that pine-bark stuff, we
could have used it for fuel.*

As it was, the motorists were forced to burn tree bark
and dead limbs in the firebox. It was hard to keep
the steam pressure constant, and their speed suffered
because of it. Still, in only two days they traveled the
five hundred miles from Valdivostok to the sizable city
of Kharbin, where they could sleep without fear of being attacked by bandits.

Harry began to suspect that the outlaw situation had been somewhat overstated. Because Japan threatened to take over Manchuria, the Russians had strengthened their military might in the province. The troops of mounted Cossacks that patrolled the roads did more than just keep the bandits at bay; when the *Flash* bogged down fording a stream, they pulled it free. Harry didn't have the heart to refuse their offer of food and drink, though he and his companions suffered for it.

A day west of Kharbin the travelers encountered a range of mountains, but they weren't much of a challenge compared with the Rockies or the Sierras. By the third of October they were back in Siberia, where they resumed travel on the post road, with its familiar telegraph poles and its black-and-white *verst* markers.

From time to time they passed a large heap of stones with a tree limb sticking from it, decorated with strips of ribbon and paper that fluttered in the breeze. The purpose of these baffled the companions. Just before they reached Tchita, the mystery was solved when they encountered a caravan of Buryats, the nomadic herders who had occupied the area for centuries.

The group consisted of perhaps a dozen blue-clad men on horseback, four wagons, and several hundred head of cattle. As they passed one of the stone piles, a horseman stopped, said a brief prayer, and tied a strip of yellow cloth to the tree branches. "It's a shrine," said Charles. "Buddhists, I expect."

"My goodness!" whispered Elizabeth. "I just realized that half those horsemen are actually women. And they're riding astride their mounts, not sidesaddle. In some ways they're more civilized than we are."

Tchita, the capital of the province, was an attractive city with a good supply of kerosene and even a passable hotel where Charles took a room for the night. Harry and Johnny shared a stable with the motorcar. Though Elizabeth chose the relative luxury of the hotel, she did not mention the fact in her dispatch, not wanting to seem less than intrepid.

### Tchita, Siberia, October 5 ————————

Over a meal in the dining room of the Hotel Grand, we learned from a French-speaking fellow diner that the majority of Tchita's residents are convicted criminals, but not of the desperate sort. No, their only crime was that they dared to speak out against the Czarist government or against the Church. As punishment, they were exiled here. Since many of these men and women are well educated and skilled, they have made the town into something of a cultural oasis in the midst of the desolate steppes.

Not all the "criminals" sent here are religious or political dissidents, of course. The more dangerous convicts are put to work in the gold mines —except for the ones who escape, and apparently there have been thousands. A fair number of these *varnaks*, as they are called, have made their way back to Europe, armed with passports that are either forged or taken from some unlucky citizen, along with his life.

Not all escapees are so clever or so lucky. After enduring a month or two of the Siberian winter, some give themselves up; others die before they have the chance. A few actually manage to survive in the wild by hunting or trapping—or preying upon townsfolk and travelers. (This reporter, for one, would have been just as happy not knowing that latter piece of information.) Since the greater part of the Russian army is stationed in Manchuria, protecting it from invasion by the Japanese, there are not nearly enough soldiers in Siberia to keep these rogue *varnaks* in check.

In the days that followed, though the intrepid young motorists kept their rifles and revolver at the ready, they saw no sign of bandits. And, though the skin of an enormous Siberian tiger had decorated the wall of the Grand Hotel's dining room, the travelers spotted no wildlife more threatening than a small pack of wolves, which kept its distance from the smoke-belching machine.

The steppes gave way to forested hills and valleys with scattered farms. Four days west of Tchita, they topped a rise and found stretched out below them a lake so blue that it hurt the eyes and so extensive that they could not see the upper end of it. "Lake Baikal," Charles informed them.

"And I expect you have some fascinating facts about it to share with us," said Elizabeth drily.

"As a matter of fact, I do. It is the world's deepest lake, and one of the largest. According to the guidebook, it is longer than the whole of England. It is also the only freshwater lake in the world where seals can be found."

"Really?" said Elizabeth. "That actually is rather fascinating. Do you mind if I include it in my next dispatch?"

Johnny pointed toward the middle of the lake. "There's a ferry."

"If we take that," said Harry, "it'll save us a good deal of driving."

To his frustration, they missed the ferry by minutes; the next wasn't due for eight hours. They set up a temporary camp and, purchasing a salmon from a local fisherman, cooked an unusually sumptuous supper that included fried potatoes and the remains of a spice cake they had bought in Tchita.

After the meal, Harry had a long nap. When, at four in the morning, they finally reached the far bank of Lake Baikal, he was chipper and cheerful and ready to set off again. The temperature was near-freezing, but once they raised the rain hood and fired up the boiler, it became so cozy inside the car that everyone except Harry dozed off.

Just outside Irkutsk, the right front wheel of the *Flash* dropped into a large sinkhole, unseen in the faint light of the acetylene lamps. The shock rattled Harry's teeth. The passengers groaned and stirred. "What was that?" muttered Johnny.

"Oh, nothing much." Harry backed up and detoured around the spot. "Just the world's deepest hole. Deeper than all of England, in point of fact."

"Any damage?"

"No, no, everything's fine. Go back to sleep."

A few minutes later, Harry heard a faint but alarming clunk from beneath the car, then another. But when several miles went by and the sound didn't recur, he shrugged and dismissed it. Probably just a stone caught in the wheel, he thought.

If Charles and Elizabeth had been awake when they reached Irkutsk, they would surely have requested a brief layover for food and freshening up. But since they were dead to the world, Harry drove through without stopping, relishing the fact that he had put one over on them.

It was not the wisest thing he might have done. In fact, in Harry's long history of impulsive, ill-advised actions, this would take its place among those he regretted most.

# AS WITH THE PROVERBIAL LOST HORSESHOE, A SINGLE NAIL CAUSES A DISASTER

**W**est of Irkutsk the landscape changed gradually from grassland that resembled the American prairies to a thick forest of pines, firs, and birches that the Russians called taiga. Though the sun was nearly up, within the deep woods it remained dark as night.

The road was changing, too. It was no longer narrow and rutted, but relatively smooth and solid and nearly wide enough for two vehicles side by side.

One thing that had not changed was the vast emptiness. Harry met only one other vehicle, a postal *tarantass*, and the only dwellings were two shabby post stations. Ordinarily he wasted no time worrying about what might happen, but he couldn't help thinking that this would be a desolate place to break down.

He pushed the thought from his mind. The *Flash* had proven even more reliable than they hoped. There was no reason to suppose it would suddenly suffer some major malfunction—no reason except for that nagging feeling of Johnny's, the feeling that something was not quite right.

Unable to shake his sense of unease, Harry tried the meditation techniques he'd learned: carefully controlling his breathing, mentally focusing on some simple object—he chose a cricket wicket—and intoning the syllable *om*.

His concentration was broken by a grinding sound from beneath the rear seat of the *Flash*. Johnny sat up abruptly, clutching his head, knocking his workman's cap askew. "Stop the car, Harry! Stop the car!"

Harry pushed in the throttle and disengaged the gears. The grinding sound immediately stopped. He and Johnny traded fearful looks. "It's the differential," said Harry. "Isn't it?"

Johnny nodded grimly.

Elizabeth and Charles were awake now, too, and leaning over the back of the seat. "Is that bad?" asked Charles.

Johnny pulled his cap down over his ears. "Couldn't be much worse."

"I didn't think to bring replacement gears," said Harry. "I never imagined we'd need them. You said these would last forever."

"They should've," said Johnny.

Uncharacteristically, Elizabeth had not said a single word. Her blue eyes were wide and her face looked pale and drawn. "Are you all right?" Harry asked.

She nodded and shrank back in her seat. "This is going to set you back several days, at least, isn't it?"

"Probably. We'll just have to make it up by driving faster." Harry took a deep breath and clapped his hands together. "Well. Let's get at it, shall we?"

Johnny started to climb from the car but halted halfway and put his head in his hands.

Elizabeth came alive at last. "Oh, Johnny, you're having one of your headaches, aren't you?" She sprang from the car, retrieved the bottle of Dr. Pemberton's Syrup, and gave Johnny a large dose. "You just lie back, now, until you feel better. I'll give Harry a hand."

"No, I'll do it," said Charles. "You don't look well, either."

Elizabeth gave him a wan smile. "Thank you." After downing two capfuls of the syrup herself, she walked several yards into the woods and sat down on a fallen birch.

"Watch out for man-eating tigers!" Harry called to her.

"I say, Fogg," said Charles, "you shouldn't rag her that way. She's not feeling well."

"I was trying to cheer her up. Besides, who put you in charge of her welfare?"

"Someone needs to be, and you certainly don't seem inclined."

"How terribly old-fashioned of you, Hardiman. I

think she's pretty well proven that she can look out for herself."

"I do not consider it old-fashioned," Charles said haughtily, "to behave as a gentleman." His tone implied that Harry couldn't be expected to understand.

Harry chose, in the interests of keeping the peace, to ignore the implication. "Does it say anywhere in the *Gentleman's Behaviour Manual* that you can't help jack up a motorcar?"

Once they had the chassis raised and securely supported by chunks of wood, Harry set about removing the cover of the differential. Though the light was still poor, he could see that the gears had been badly damaged. The grease in the differential was filled with bits of broken metal. Most were the size of bread crumbs, but one larger piece projected from among the gears. Using his handkerchief, Harry wiggled it free and examined it. When he emerged from beneath the *Flash*, his face was set in an angry scowl.

"What is it?" asked Charles. "What's wrong?" Harry extended the handkerchief. In the center lay a grease-covered object. "It looks like a nail," said Charles.

"It *is* a nail. The question is, how did it *get* there?"

"Are you asking me? Or are you accusing me?"

"Both."

Charles glared at him. "I've told you twice that I am *not* trying to damage your machine! I shan't tell you again!"

"Who else could have put this there?" demanded Harry, thrusting the greasy nail in the other boy's face.

Charles knocked his hand aside, sending the evidence flying. Furious, Harry shoved him backward, but Charles quickly regained his balance and lashed out with his right fist, catching Harry on the side of the head. More blows were struck on both sides. Though Harry was the stronger of the two, Charles's boxing experience gave him the upper hand. He landed a punch in his opponent's ribs that totally took the wind out of Harry, who sagged down onto the running board of the car, grimacing and cradling his aching side. The anger had been knocked out of him, too. Through gritted teeth, he managed to murmur, "Good hit, old chap."

Elizabeth hurried up to them. "What on earth has gotten into you two?"

Charles had fished out his own handkerchief and was dabbing at the blood that trickled from his lip. "He accused me again of sabotaging the car. I've had about enough of that."

"Sabotaging it? How?"

Charles retrieved Harry's greasy handkerchief and, picking off the pine needles, displayed the nail, which was still stuck to the cloth. "He found this in the differential."

"Oh, dear," said Elizabeth.

Charles sat next to Harry on the running board. "I didn't want to mention this, Fogg, but have you considered the possibility that . . . well, that your father is behind this sabotage business?"

Harry stared at him. "My *father*? Why would he ruin my chances of winning this wager? He's the one who'll have pay up."

"Perhaps it's worth it to him." Charles wadded up his bloody handkerchief. "I know about your agreement with him, Harry—that you'll give up motorcars if you lose. Some of the men at the Reform Club overheard your conversation, and naturally they didn't keep it to themselves."

Harry gazed down at the ground, feeling dizzy and disoriented. Was Phileas Fogg actually capable of such a thing? He really had no idea. The sad truth was, Harry didn't know the man well enough to know what he was capable of. Who would have imagined he could be so unscrupulous as to scuttle a ship? And yet, if Captain Keough's story was true, he had done just that.

Despite his uncertainty, Harry felt obliged to defend his father. "But he *couldn't* have done it. We changed the grease back in Des Moines, remember? We saw no sign of the nail then."

Johnny sat up and adjusted his cap. "Could've been in back, out of sight."

"Then it would have damaged the gears long ago, not waited until now."

"What if it was stuck?" said Charles. "It may have needed a hard jolt, like the one earlier, to jar it loose.

Besides, your father needn't have done it in person. He could have hired someone—perhaps the same someone who messed about with the car in Philadelphia."

Elizabeth, who had stood silently by, now spoke up. "I think you're all being very unfair! I can't believe that any man would do such a thing to his own son!" Thrusting the greasy handkerchief into Charles's hands, she stalked off into the woods.

Harry was taken aback by her fierce defense of his father; until now, Elizabeth had seemed to regard Phileas Fogg as a scoundrel who kidnapped women and won wagers by underhanded means. With a groan, he got to his feet. "Well, there's no way we can know anything for certain until we get home. All we can do now is try to fix the damage." He turned to Johnny. "You can fix it, right?"

"Can't cast a new set of gears."

Harry looked up and down the road, scratching his head. "Irkutsk is about three hours' drive back that way—say, seventy or eighty miles. It's sure to have a decent machine shop. If I walk back to the post station, I'm sure I can hire a horse. We can't wait until the next *tarantass* comes along; it could be half a day or more."

"I'll go," said Johnny. "I know what's wanted."

"I just thought . . . well, I thought perhaps you'd rather not."

Johnny shrugged. "I'll manage."

"Do you need to take the old gears?"

"No. I've got everything I need." He tapped his head. "Up here."

"All right, then, while you're gone I'll remove all the broken stuff." He grinned and nudged Johnny. "Don't forget to take along some tins of bully beef, in case you get hungry."

Elizabeth insisted on accompanying Johnny. "I need to send a story to the *Graphic*. It's been nearly a week since I last wired them."

"Then I'd better come as well," said Charles.

"No. Thank you, Charles, but it's really not necessary. Besides, Harry will need someone to stand guard while he works. And, contrary to what he would have us believe, he does need to sleep occasionally."

"If there actually are bandits skulking about," said Harry, "they're just as likely to attack you as they are me."

"We'll take the revolver, then."

Harry sighed. "All right, all right, do as you like." He and Charles traded glances that said, *She will in any case.*

It took Elizabeth and Johnny two hours to walk back to the post station. Though Johnny was shy and awkward in her presence, he managed to say a few words. "I don't think Harry's da did it."

"Nor do I. But I don't believe Charles did, either." They strode along in silence for a time, then Elizabeth said, "This won't ruin your chances to win the wager, will it?"

"I hope not. Harry says . . . Harry says we could make more motorcars."

"Really? You mean actually go into the business of building them?"

Johnny nodded. "If we lose, we won't have the money."

"No, I suppose not. But perhaps you could find investors."

He made a scoffing noise. "Who'd give money to a blacksmith and a tinkerer?"

Elizabeth either had no answer or was too out of breath to offer it.

The post station did have horses for hire, at the exorbitant rate of ten rubles per day. The days were growing short, so the pair made it only halfway to Irkutsk before darkness fell. They spent the night at another post station, a dismal log hut whose only furnishings were a flimsy table and chairs and several benches that served as beds. Their supper consisted of bowls of boiled millet and glasses of hot water; though she understood almost nothing the stationmaster's wife said, Elizabeth gathered that travelers were expected to provide their own tea.

There was no bedding as such, only a pile of mangy-looking fur rugs infested with lice and fleas. Johnny wrapped himself in one, but Elizabeth covered herself only with her Mother Hubbard. By morning she was so chilled that she feared she might never get warm again. But perhaps it was better than the unbearable itching that plagued Johnny.

At dusk the following day, exhausted and aching from the long ride, they reached Irkutsk. Though Johnny insisted on staying in the stable with the horses, Elizabeth gratefully took a room—and a warm bath—at a surprisingly modern hotel.

After several tries, the machine shop managed to cast and grind a set of gears that satisfied Johnny. By the time they were ready to head back, it was the fourteenth of October; they had wasted four days, and the return trip on horseback would take another two. "Harry won't be happy," said Johnny.

"Well," said Elizabeth, with a forced smile, "luckily I have some news that will cheer him up. I'm not rejoining the *Flash*."

Johnny gaped at her. "But . . . but why?"

"I have my reasons." From her reporter's notebook, she tore a sheet of paper that was covered with her small, precise handwriting. She folded the note and, taking one of Johnny's large hands in hers, she placed the paper in his palm and closed his fingers around it. "That will help to explain, I hope."

"I can't read it," said Johnny.

"I know. If Harry wishes to read it to you, I can't prevent him, but I've asked him not to."

"Why?"

"Because." Elizabeth paused and swallowed hard. "Because I want you to go on thinking well of me."

"I will," said Johnny. "I will, no matter what."

"I wish that were so." With her lace-edged handkerchief, she dabbed furtively at her eyes. "I'd better go now, before I make some sort of scene."

"But *where* will you go?"

"I've made some inquiries. Apparently there's a steamboat that takes passengers down the Angara River to some city with an unpronounceable name; from there, one travels by coach to the Ob River and takes another boat down it, to the eastern terminus of the railroad." She gave a half hearted smile. "It sounds very scenic."

"You'll not write about our trip anymore?"

"No." She gave a sharp, bitter laugh. "Unless I make something up. I'm quite good at that."

"You'll meet us in London, though?"

She took his rough hand again, for just a moment. "Perhaps. But don't count on it. Good-bye, Johnny."

If Harry had been there, he would have known what to do, what to say to keep her from leaving. All Johnny could do was watch helplessly as she walked away.

Certain that his friend would be seething with impatience, Johnny did not stop at the station where he and Elizabeth had spent such a miserable night. He rode straight through, hunched against the cold, dozing in the saddle, switching mounts occasionally to give each horse a rest. Traveling after dark was an open invitation to bandits, but he was too downcast to care.

Early the next afternoon he reached the station where he had hired the horses. He left them there and walked on, his legs so cramped and sore that he nearly fell. A few hours later he spotted the *Flash*, which Harry and Charles had pushed off the road. A short distance away, they had set up one of the tents. Johnny broke into a trot. "Harry?" he called. There was no reply.

Johnny peered through one of the *Flash*'s isinglass windows. The car was empty. "Harry!" he shouted again. He felt an anxious prickle of pain in his damaged skull. Filled with a sense of foreboding, he circled the cold remains of the campfire and lifted the flap of the tent. Inside, his friends had set up one of the wooden supply boxes to serve as a card table. Cards were strewn about on it.

Of the cardplayers themselves, however, there was no sign.

# THIRTY-TWO

*Showing what*

## BECAME OF
## HARRY AND CHARLES

**F**or the first several days after the group split up, Harry and Charles were quite vigilant. Harry spent the dwindling daylight hours beneath the *Flash*, removing the ruined gears, while Charles did sentry duty, a book in one hand and a rifle in the other.

Knowing Johnny wouldn't return for several days, Harry forced himself to work slowly and carefully, cleaning out every trace of broken metal. Then he went over the rest of the car thoroughly, checking and tightening, greasing and oiling.

Each night after dinner, they played écarté and bezique and a two-handed version of whist they had invented. It was growing too chilly to sit comfortably about the campfire, so they pitched one of the tents close to the fire pit and tied back the flaps to capture the heat. With the open front facing the road, they could keep an eye out for anyone approaching.

In the space of three days, the total traffic consisted of three postal *tarantasses*, a woodcutter, a traveling peddler, a band of colorfully clad Gypsies, a small contingent of Cossacks, and a hundred or so chained prisoners guarded by soldiers with bayonets. These were followed by half a dozen wagons that carried political exiles, half of them women and children.

"This won't be a country for exiles much longer," said Charles. "My father says that once they complete the railway, settlers will pour into Siberia by the tens of thousands. It'll soon be as civilized as Europe."

"For better or worse," said Harry.

"What does that mean?"

"I was just wondering what will become of those nomadic people who've lived here for centuries."

Charles shrugged. "That's the way of the world, Harry. It's called progress."

"That's what it's called by the people who come in and take over. I expect the ones being displaced and downtrodden have another word for it."

"Oh, don't be such a bleeding heart. You're as much in favor of progress as anyone. If you have your way, those nomads will be using motorcars to herd their cattle." They resumed their card game, and Charles took the final trick of the hand. "One odd trick; that gives me a total of five points."

"Are you sure?"

"Quite."

"Only I thought it was four."

Charles glared at him. "Are you accusing me of cheating?"

"Of course not. I just wondered whether you counted properly."

"You're the one who has trouble with figures, not I!"

"All right, all right, there's no need to fly off the handle, old chap. Perhaps I wasn't paying attention."

Charles looked a bit sheepish. "Sorry. I suppose I'm tired of being accused of things, that's—"

Harry held up a hand to silence him. "Sshh! Did you hear that?"

"No," said Charles. But a moment later, he did hear something—a twig snapping outside the tent. He and Harry dived for the rifle simultaneously. Harry came up with it and scrambled through the door of the tent.

At first he saw nothing, only the shadows cast by the firelight. But then the shadows closed in and became three-dimensional figures. Harry raised the rifle, then realized there was no use. As the intruders entered the circle of light, he saw that there were more than a dozen, and all of them were armed.

Some wore Cossack garb—long embroidered tunics, sheepskin hats, knee-high boots—and for a moment Harry believed they were soldiers. Forcing a smile, he said, *"Drasti!"* The simple greeting was one of the few Russian words he had learned.

A tall, incredibly ugly man in a bearskin coat stepped

forward. He was not smiling. *"Cu da?"* he demanded.

"I beg your pardon?"

"I believe he wants to know where we're from," said Charles, his voice unsteady.

"England, actually," Harry replied. *"Anglija."*

Now the man did smile, and Harry rather wished he hadn't. Aside from the rotten teeth, there was something truly unpleasant about that smile; it was far more menacing than an angry scowl. The man said something that made his companions laugh, but the laughter was no more reassuring than the smile.

Harry whispered to Charles, "What did he say?"

"No idea."

The ugly man reached out and yanked Harry's rifle from his grasp. Harry didn't bother to resist. When the man seized his arm, he did put up a struggle and, for his trouble, received a blow on the head that left his ears ringing. Two outlaws took hold of Charles and half carried him along.

The group plunged into the black depths of the forest. Disoriented, unable to see, Harry felt as though he'd been thrust underwater; he found himself gasping for air. He twisted his head to look behind him; already the trees were blocking out the firelight. A few moments more, and he lost sight of everything that had provided some measure of comfort and familiarity in this unfamiliar land—the tent, the fire, the *Flash*, the post road.

When his eyes adjusted to the gloom, he saw a new

set of shadowy shapes—the outlaws' horses. The leader indicated that they should mount up. When Harry was in the saddle—an uncomfortable affair made of leather stuffed with horsehair—his hands were bound together, then tied to the saddle frame. "Charles?" Harry called. "Are you all right?"

"Smashing," came the dry response. "Do you suppose if we gave them all our money, they'd let us go?"

"If that were all they wanted, they'd have taken it by now."

"What's their game, then? You think they mean to hold us for ransom?"

"*Zatknis, durac!*" growled the ugly man. Though the words were foreign, the meaning was clear. They were to keep their mouths shut.

They traveled for a good hour—actually, an extremely miserable hour—staying well away from the post road. At last they emerged from the taiga and onto a sloping meadow where more horses grazed. Below them lay a small lake half choked with reeds. At one end was a cluster of crude log cabins roofed with dirt and chinked with moss. A haze of wood smoke hung in the air.

The outlaws unsaddled their horses and led their captives to the largest hut. From the outside it looked rather ramshackle, but the interior proved surprisingly neat and comfortable, if a bit Spartan. There were bunks and a table and chairs, all fashioned from logs—not elegant, but sturdy and serviceable. In the center was a circular stone fireplace; a trapdoor in the roof allowed the smoke to escape . . . eventually. The light from the fire was supplemented by a kerosene lamp.

The only piece of factory-made furniture was a maple rocking chair. Seated in it was a striking fellow of indeterminate age; though his hair and mustache were completely gray and his face lined and weathered, his frame was trim and muscular. When his dark eyes met Harry's, their gaze was both curious and calculating. He spoke a few words in Russian. The ugly man and his companions nodded and left the hut. The man in the rocker motioned Harry and Charles to sit.

"Do you speak English?" Harry asked.

The man shrugged. "A few words, only. *Parlez-vous français?*"

"*Oui, un peu.*"

The conversation continued in French—fluent on the Russian's side, halting on Harry's. "I know your names, of course," said the man. "Mine is Grigory Annekov."

Harry automatically shook the outstretched hand; Charles ignored it. "Why is it you have taken us here, Mr. Annekov?" asked Harry.

"You seem like intelligent lads. I'm sure you've figured it out by now."

"You desire to have money for us."

"Perhaps I should do the talking," put in Charles, in English. "No offense, but your French is execrable."

Harry grinned wryly. "That bad, eh?"

Charles nodded and said in flawless French, "You intend to hold us for ransom, I would imagine."

"Not exactly," said Annekov.

"What, then?"

"Well, in Mr. Fogg's case, it is not a ransom so much as a reward. And we will be holding him only a few days."

"And after that?" asked Harry, who was constitutionally unable to sit silently by.

"After that, my men will deliver you to the gentleman who is offering the reward."

Charles turned to Harry with a baffled look. "What is he talking about?" he asked in English. "Why on earth would anyone be offering a reward for you?"

Harry didn't answer. "This gentleman you mention. Is he by any chance from India?"

"Ah," said Annekov with a smile. "I see that I was not mistaken about your intelligence."

# A FAMILIAR FACE UNEXPECTEDLY REAPPEARS

Charles shook his friend's arm. "Harry? Harry, what's this all about? There's something you haven't told me, isn't there?"

Harry sighed. "It's rather a long story, I'm afraid."

"Well, just summarize it, then!"

Harry briefly recounted what his mother had told him about the rajah's fanatical relatives. "I didn't realize just how fanatical they actually were. I could imagine them trying to kidnap me if I'd gone by way of India. But to hire someone in *Siberia* to do it for them . . ." He shook his head incredulously. "How much money do they give you?" he asked Annekov.

"Enough. Far more than we can make robbing towns and travelers, certainly."

"But . . . but how did they even manage to contact you?" asked Charles.

Annekov shrugged. "The same way your father contacts his business associates. By telegraph, of course. And to learn your whereabouts, all we had to do was read the newspapers. Ah, these modern inventions—they've even improved the lives of outlaws. I can scarcely wait until we're able to trade in our horses for motorcars. And when the railroad comes through—" He clucked his tongue. "Just think of the possibilities."

"This Indian man, he not wants . . ." Harry was beginning to understand how Johnny felt, having to search for the right word to express himself. "He does not want Charles. Let Charles go."

"My men were instructed to capture you, Mr. Fogg, no one else. But I am not one to look a gift horse in the mouth. According to the newspaper stories, Mr. Hardiman, your father is president of a railway. I suspect he would pay a few thousand pounds to make certain his son returns home safely."

Charles laughed humorlessly. "You don't know my father."

"No? Well, we shall see. Once Mr. Fogg is disposed of, I'll wire your father. Until then, consider yourselves my guests. My house is yours."

Charles glanced around distastefully. "If it were mine," he said, "I'd burn it down."

Annekov gave him a look so withering that Charles

regretted his words. "I assure you, Mr. Hardiman, this is not the sort of accommodation I am accustomed to, either. I was not always an outlaw, you know. For nearly fifteen years I was a respected professor at St. Petersburg University. But then—" His voice took on an ominous tone that was clearly ironic. "Then I fell in with a 'bad crowd,' a group of unsavory criminals known as the *Narodniki*."

"Socialists?" said Charles.

Annekov nodded. "We wanted only to make life better for the common man. But we were deemed a threat to the established order, so several comrades and I were sent here—not as exiles, mind you, but as actual convicts, sentenced to eight years' hard labor in the mines. I escaped—obviously—and . . . and found other employment." The Russian rose from his rocking chair and stretched. "Well. My working day is just beginning, but I am sure you gentlemen are exhausted. You'll find the beds quite tolerable, I think. The mattresses are stuffed with wool." He donned his fur coat and hat and started out the door, but turned back to say, "If it is any consolation, a share of the reward and the ransom—should your father pay one—will go to aid other political dissidents."

"Oh, well, in that case," muttered Charles, "we don't mind at all being kidnapped and held prisoner."

Harry knew well enough that the door would be barred, but his optimistic nature compelled him to try it anyway. "It's barred," he said.

Charles peered out through the single small window. "What's more, there's an armed chap just outside, standing guard."

Harry yawned. "Well, we may as well get some sleep, then."

"How can you think about sleeping, at a time like this?"

"I'm not thinking about it." Harry stretched out on one of the bunks; the wool-filled mattress was a bit lumpy, but soft. "I'm just doing it."

Over the next days they were confined to the hut, except for visits to the privy, while Annekov made arrangements by telegraph with Aouda Fogg's former in-laws. It was agreed that Annekov's men would transport Harry to the city of Verniy, eight or nine hundred miles to the southwest, where the dead prince's relatives would take possession of the prisoner.

As always, the enforced idleness kept Harry in a constant state of frustration. He tried playing cards with Charles but couldn't keep his mind on the game. Since the room was too small to permit much restless pacing, he resorted to other means of quelling his impatience.

As he sat cross-legged on the floor with his eyes closed, taking measured breaths and softly intoning "Ommmm," he heard Charles speaking, as if from a great distance: "I say, Fogg. Are you all right?"

"Sshh," whispered Harry. "I'm meditating."

"On what?"

"Nothing. Just meditating. You should try it."

"You look deuced silly, you know."

"Silence, my friend. I need silence." Though Charles grudgingly obliged, Harry could not get his own brain to cooperate. It persisted in dwelling upon their predicament.

Harry had lost track of what day it was, and, without the aid of his diary, so had Charles. In any case, Johnny would certainly have returned to the site of the breakdown long ago. The poor lad would be utterly bewildered, wondering what had become of his companions and what to do next. Luckily, he would have Elizabeth with him. She was a levelheaded sort; surely she would see that the logical thing to do would be to repair the *Flash* and continue the journey, on the assumption that the missing pair would turn up sooner or later.

This was, of course, a rather questionable assumption. It was beginning to look as if they might never rejoin the others. But as far as the wager was concerned, it didn't really matter. No one had ever said that, in order for the *Flash* to win, Harry and Charles must be aboard.

That night they were again left under guard while Annekov led a raiding party to obtain supplies and money for the journey to Verniy. "Get a good sleep, Mr. Fogg," advised the outlaw chief. "You have a long trip ahead of you, in the morning."

The situation had begun to seem daunting even to the dauntless Harry. He did not worry about his own fate so much as about the *Flash* and about Johnny, about the outcome of his wager, and about how his mother would feel when she learned of his capture. Though he felt it his duty to find a way out of this mess, he had never been much on planning and scheming. He was the sort to wait for an oppportunity, a chance to act. Some such opportunity might yet present itself. If it did, he would make the most of it. Until then, there was nothing to be done but to lie down on one of the bunks and doze off.

Charles, meanwhile, sat in Annekov's chair, nervouslyrocking and racking his brain. Sometime before dawn he fell asleep, only to be wakened again by a hand gently shaking his shoulder. "What?" he mumbled drowsily. "What is it?"

"Please be very quiet," whispered a voice in his ear. "We do not want to alert anyone."

The oil lamp had gone out, and Charles could see nothing but the glow of embers in the fireplace. "Who on earth—?"

"Be quiet!" the voice repeated softly but urgently. "Where is Harry?"

"What—I don't—Isn't he in the bed?"

There was a slight rustle of clothing, followed by a moment of silence. Then Charles heard Harry's voice, sounding sleepy and surprised. "Is it really you?"

"Get up, please," said the other voice. "We must hurry."

Harry and Charles stumbled about, searching for their coats and shoes. "What happened to the guard?" asked Harry.

"You will trip over him if you are not careful."

"You killed him?"

"There was no need. I brought him inside, so he does not freeze. Come. I have horses waiting."

When they emerged from the hut, the moonlight revealed their rescuer's identity at last. "Ramesh!" breathed Charles.

"Keep moving, please." The Indian man placed a hand on his back and propelled him toward the woods.

Before they reached the trees, a tall form emerged from the shadows to block their path. In one hand he held a lantern, in the other the reins of Ramesh's horses. He raised the lantern, revealing his face, which was unmistakable in its ugliness. "You might have made it," he said, in French, "had your horses not been so skittish. On my way to the privy, I heard them snuffling and prancing about."

"Let us pass," said Ramesh, "and you will not be harmed."

"Harmed?" The ugly man gave a derisive laugh that showed his rotted teeth. "You have no weapon."

"Nor have you."

"Ah, that is where you are wrong." Letting the reins drop, the man pulled aside his bearskin coat to show a revolver stuck in his sash. "I go nowhere without this, not even to the privy."

As the man reached for his pistol, Ramesh's right foot lashed out, so swiftly it could scarcely be seen. The toe of his boot struck the man's thigh. The Russian's leg collapsed beneath him. Ramesh delivered another quick blow, this time with the stiffened fingers of one hand. Harry did not even see where it landed; all he saw was its effect. It left the ugly man sprawled upon the ground, gaping in astonishment, unable to move.

Harry was so surprised that, for a moment, he couldn't move, either. Then Ramesh's voice brought him to his senses. "Get the horses, gentlemen."

But Ramesh made no move to mount up. Instead he knelt, picked up the revolver, and flung it into a patch of brush. Then he bent over his victim and opened the man's tunic.

"What are you doing?" demanded Charles. "Let's go!"

"I injured him. It is my responsibility to undo the damage." With his fingers, Ramesh prodded several spots on the Russian's chest and neck. The ugly man groaned and stirred. "Do not worry," Ramesh told him. "You will recover in a day or two." At last he rose, walked calmly to his horse, and swung into the saddle.

As they guided their mounts into the forest, Charles said, "You shouldn't have helped him. Now he'll rouse the others."

"Not before we're well out of reach."

But apparently Ramesh underestimated the Russian's strength of body and of will. Before five minutes passed, they heard faint shouts behind them, and several gunshots. "They're after us!" cried Charles.

The three urged their horses into a trot, or as near to it as the animals could manage through the dense taiga, with its maze of fallen trees. "Do you have any idea where we're going?" Harry asked.

"In all modesty," said Ramesh, "I have an excellent sense of direction."

"So do I. But it was dark when they brought us here, and we took a roundabout route."

"I know. I followed your trail."

"How do you happen to be here? And how did you know we were in trouble?"

"I was surveying the land west of Irkutsk and found Johnny repairing your motorcar. He was quite distraught and quite baffled by your disappearance."

"And you weren't?"

Ramesh shrugged. "The tracks and other signs made it clear what had happened."

"Thank you for rescuing us, my friend."

"It was my pleasure."

Harry grinned. "I'm afraid Annekov won't be very pleased."

"The outlaw chief? He hoped to ransom you, I suppose?"

"Um. Not exactly." Harry gave Ramesh the same summary Charles had gotten a few days earlier.

"I have heard that the rulers of Bundelkund can be ruthless," said Ramesh. "I am ashamed to call them my countrymen." They rode on in silence for a time. Then Ramesh said, "There is something I have not told you. Elizabeth was not with the *Flash*. According to Johnny, she has returned to England by another route."

Before Harry could ask why, he was interrupted by more shots. A bullet clipped a tree branch above their heads.

"They've spotted us!" shouted Charles, and dug his heels into his mount's ribs.

"Careful, old chap!" called Harry. "If your horse breaks a leg, the game's up!" Then, despite the gravity of the situation, he gave a sharp laugh. He couldn't recall ever warning anyone else to be careful; ordinarily he was the one being warned.

"We're almost to the post road," said Ramesh. "We can put on some speed then." Minutes later they burst from the forest and onto the road. Now that they were in the open, Harry saw to his surprise that it was nearly daylight. Charles's horse reared as he reined it in. "Which way?"

Ramesh pointed, and they set off at a gallop. "Wait!" shouted Harry. "We're heading back toward the *Flash*! We should be leading them *away* from her!"

"We have guns there!" replied Charles. "At least we'll be able to defend ourselves!" He glanced over his shoulder. "Besides, we can't very well turn round, can we?"

Harry twisted about in the saddle. Their pursuers had emerged from the woods and were thundering down the road after them. There were at least half a dozen outlaws, and several were such skilled horsemen that they could simultaneously ride and shoot—not very accurately, but it was only a matter of time before one of their bullets found a target.

# THE TRUTH ABOUT ELIZABETH IS AT LAST REVEALED

**R**amesh's horses were used to carrying packs, not riders; they didn't have the speed or stamina of the Siberian ponies the outlaws rode. Already Harry felt his mount beginning to falter. He fervently wished they had the *Flash* in working order. It could have outrun the horsemen with ease.

To his astonishment, a moment later the motorcar appeared in the distance, speeding toward them, throwing up an enormous cloud of dust. Immediately, Harry regretted his wish. Before they were able to climb into the *Flash* and turn her around, their pursuers would be upon them. Not only would the outlaws recapture Harry and Charles, they'd have Ramesh and Johnny. Perhaps worst of all, any hope of winning the wager would be lost.

"Go back!" Harry waved both hands at Johnny so vehemently that he nearly fell out of the saddle. "Turn around!" Apparently mistaking his gestures for a greeting, Johnny waved back. "No, no!" groaned Harry. "Get out of here, Johnny! Go!" But the *Flash* kept coming.

As it drew nearer, Harry saw that the billows of dust hanging in the car's wake had been concealing something. He let out a whoop and burst into exuberant laughter.

Charles cast him a dumbfounded glance. "Have you gone mad?"

"Yes! But it's a good sort of mad! Look what's following the *Flash*!"

Charles squinted at the road ahead. Just then a gust of wind swept the curtain of dust aside, revealing a band of mounted Cossacks, brandishing pistols and sabers.

"You've brought the cavalry!" Harry called as Johnny pulled the *Flash* up alongside them. The three riders guided their mounts off the road and the Cossacks galloped past, uttering savage, high-pitched cries that made them sound less like a troop of soldiers than like a horde of devils.

The outlaws wasted no time firing on the Cossacks. They wheeled their horses and headed back the way they had come. Half the soldiers pursued them; the other half joined the intrepid motorists and their vehicle. A Cossack officer addressed them in French. "I doubt that the *varnaks* will bother you again. But to be certain, we will escort you as far as our garrison at Zima. You will be our guests this evening. We will share a glass of vodka. You will tell us of your adventures, and we will tell you the proud history of the Cossack people."

"We will be delighted," said Harry.

"No, we won't," muttered Charles, in English.

Ramesh retrieved his surveying equipment and supplies from the car. "I must take my leave now, gentlemen. I have work to do."

"You've done a good day's work already," said Charles. "You saved our lives."

"Not really. I saved your fathers some ransom money, perhaps."

"You may well have saved *my* life," said Harry. "The old rajah's relatives tried to kill my mother. Who knows what they had in mind for me?" He grasped Ramesh's hand, but when he tried to express his gratitude, his friend silenced him.

"No, Hari. Do not thank me now. You will come to India one day and discover the other half of yourself. Then you will truly have cause to thank me."

Harry laughed. "So will the rajah's relatives, if I walk right into their hands."

"If you are there as the guest of another Hindu family, they would not dare to harm you."

"Well, you know," said Harry, "when Johnny and I develop our new, improved model of the *Flash*, we will need to road test it."

"Excellent!"

"If I do come to India, will you teach me *kalarippayattu*? The way you dispatched that ugly chap was nothing short of astounding."

Ramesh smiled. "There are a number of other things you need to learn first, my friend."

"I know, I know. Patience and caution, right?"

"Perhaps. I believe, though, that the most important quality one can learn is good judgment. It is possible, after all, to be *too* cautious. There are times when one must act quickly. But, as the master who taught me was fond of saying, there is a difference between acting quickly and acting rashly."

"I shall try to remember that."

"And I shall look forward to the time when we meet again." Placing his palms together, Ramesh bowed his head slightly. *"Namaste."*

Harry mirrored the gesture. *"Namaste."*

As they drove away, Charles said, "You don't really intend to take the Cossacks up on their offer, I hope. I don't think I can bear any more black bread and *kerpichni chai.*"

"Well," said Harry, "as you know, I'm no expert on 'gentlemanly behaviour,' but wouldn't it be rude to refuse their hospitality?"

Charles sighed. "I suppose so. Now I know why Elizabeth left—so she wouldn't have to endure any more Russian hospitality."

"If that's meant to be a joke," said Harry, "it's not very amusing."

"Sorry."

Harry turned to Johnny. "Did Elizabeth tell you why she was leaving?"

"Oh. I forgot." Johnny dug the folded sheet of notebook paper from the pocket of his coat. "She said to give you this."

Holding the note close to his chest, Harry read the small, neat handwriting:

*Dear Harry,*

*I sincerely hope that you will repair the* Flash *and reach London in time to win your wager.*

*I never imagined that I would find myself wishing such a thing. In fact, my main object in joining you was not to write about your journey, but to make certain you did not complete it. That may be difficult for you to believe, but perhaps less so when I tell you my full name, which I have so far withheld from you. It is Elizabeth Ann Stuart.*

*My father is Andrew Stuart. As you may know, the bet he made with your father twenty years ago cost him dearly, both in money and in pride. He never recovered from the loss; nor, as I have told you, did my mother. For years he kept the details of the matter a secret from me. When he finally revealed them, I swore that I would find some way to get* back at your father, who I believed had won the wager unfairly.

I found work as a reporter and used my position to uncover what I could of Phileas Fogg's past, hoping to find something I could use against him, with little success. Then I learned of the wager you had made and saw it as the perfect chance to exact— Revenge is too strong a word. Justice?

As you have no doubt guessed, it was I who damaged the steam line in Philadelphia and, I am now ashamed to say, it was I who placed the nail in the differential. I could not bear to have you suspect your father. Whatever else he may have done, he does not deserve the blame for that. Nor do you deserve to suffer for his sins.

While I am in the confessional, I may as well confess that my collision with the boulder was no accident, and the theft of my handbag was no theft, only a ploy to delay you further. I do not expect you to forgive me. My only hope now is that you will be able to undo the damage I have done, and will still reach London by the specified date.

I know I have no right to ask anything of you, but if you feel any sympathy at all toward me, you will not reveal the contents of this letter to Johnny or Charles. I would prefer not to utterly destroy their good opinion of me. I am confident that you will think of some plausible explanation for my depar-

*ture; when you put your mind to it, you are nearly
as good a liar as I am.*

*Bon voyage,*
*Elizabeth*


*PS One thing I am not good at is apologizing, but
perhaps I can write it. I am sorry. There.*


A lump had formed in Harry's throat, so bitter that it
stung. Though he felt many things—betrayed, disappointed, angry—curiously enough he did not feel surprised. The fact was, the signs had been there all along;
he had just refused to see them. As always, he had been
too trusting. He carefully folded the note again. Then
he raised the side curtain and tossed the small square
of paper into the road.

"What did it say?" asked Johnny.

It took Harry a moment to gather his wits and to
find his voice. "The *Daily Graphic* gave her a different
assignment, a more important one."

"Really?" said Charles. "Where did they send her?"

"Germany," said Harry. It was the first thing that
came into his head. "She's covering the European whist
championships." He didn't care much whether or not
the others believed him. He owed her nothing.

"The *whist* championships?" said Charles. "They
consider that more important than a motorcar journey
around the world?"

"Perhaps they've written us off as a lost cause."

"But we're not," said Johnny.

Harry managed a smile. "No, we're not, thanks to you. You replaced the gears with no problem, eh?" Johnny nodded. "Good lad," said Harry. After a moment, he added, "By the way, Hardiman, I meant to say, you were a real brick about the whole kidnapping business. You've more grit than I gave you credit for."

"Well. Thank you."

"Don't mention it," said Harry. "Oh, one other thing."

"What?"

"I'm sorry I accused you of trying to sabotage the *Flash*."

"Apology accepted. What made you change your mind?"

"Nothing in particular. I just don't think you did."

"Good. Because I didn't, you know."

"I know."

It was frustrating, being forced to hold back the *Flash* in order to keep pace with the Cossack cavalrymen. They didn't reach Zima until late that afternoon. Exhausted from the events of the previous night, Harry and Charles accepted the soldiers' offer of a meal and a bed, both of which proved better than expected. Since Johnny was still infested with lice and fleas from his stay at the post station, Harry insisted that he scrub himself and his clothing in a zinc tub belonging to one of the officers.

## Sunday, October 18

*73 days gone, 27 remaining. Last night, for the first time in months, it rained; not a slow, soaking rain that would have enabled the farmers to plant their winter wheat, but a fierce, brief downpour that turned the fields to mud, and of course the roads as well. Before we could set out this morning, we had to jack up the Flash and install the cleated rear wheels.*

*After eight hours of wallowing through the mire, we reached the Tchuma River, to find it so swollen with rain that it has flooded the plains for half a mile on either side. Telegraph poles and verst markers project from the water like dead trees in a swamp. Even worse, the raging waters have swept away the ferryboat, which is the only means of crossing the river.*

*We are forced to spend a cramped, damp night in the Flash; I sit awake, staring longingly at the lights of Nijni-Udinsk across the river.*

## Monday, October 19

*This morning a small army, or rather navy, of curious townsfolk poled their boats across the turbulent river, eager to get a look at our machine. Using a bit of awkward sign language, abetted by the occasional word of English, French, or Russian, we asked whether the boatmen could construct a makeshift ferry, using their boats as pontoons. One of them* assured us that it was quite possible, for a price. Fogg gave the man ten rubles, with the promise of ten more plus a ride in the motorcar, when and if we reach the far side safely.

I am in favor of waiting for a day or two, until the river is more manageable, but Fogg insists that we cannot afford to. He has a point, unfortunately. It has been three weeks since we left Vladivostok, and we have covered barely two thousand miles. At that rate, we will not reach England until the middle of December, far too late for Fogg to win the wager.

Johnny, of course, thinks his friend can do no wrong, and is willing to do whatever Fogg suggests. I am afraid I cannot be quite so trusting. The chap has done too many foolish and impulsive things. I still feel there is something not quite right about the way he suddenly came up with the money he needed to continue the journey.

### Later the same day

We and the moujiks, as the townsmen are called, spent several hours cutting down trees and lashing them to the gunwales of the boats to form a raft. When Fogg drove the Flash onto the raft, the weight caused the boats to sink to an alarming degree. By the time all the boatmen climbed aboard, our improvised ferry was riding so low that water threatened to pour into the pontoons. This did not seem to worry the moujiks in the least. In fact, they were in high spirits, as though it were just some jolly outing on the river, to be followed by a picnic and games.

It took us an hour to cross the flooded plain, partly because the men plied their poles so half-heartedly and partly because we kept running into trees and telegraph poles. When we reached the middle of the river, however, the Russians put their backs into their work. After a frightening passage, in which the raft bucked and spun about sickeningly, we entered another calm stretch—none too soon, for the boats had taken on so much water that we were in imminent danger of sinking.

By the time we entered Nijni-Udinsk, it was so dark that even Fogg was reluctant to risk driving on the roads, which are still far from dry. We purchased food and kerosene and some space in a livery stable. Though I am still keyed up after our wild ride, I must get some sleep, for we are to set off again before dawn.

# THIRTY-FIVE

## *In which*

# THE MOTORISTS AGAIN BECOME PRISONERS

In the days that followed, Harry, determined to make up the time they had lost, began to resemble Johnny Brainerd's Steam Man, a sort of automaton with a single purpose—to cover as many miles as possible in as short a time as possible. He kept his eyes and his mind on the road, spoke little, and seldom laughed. They stopped only when absolutely necessary—to relieve themselves, to refill the fuel and water tanks, to remove the cleated wheels and install the regular ones, to catch a few hours of exhausted sleep.

They had taken to reckoning time not by the calendar date, but by how many days remained until the fourteenth of November, which Johnny insisted on referring to as Doomsday. Harry would have preferred a more optimistic term, such as Victory Day, but Johnny's name was the one that stuck.

On Doomsday Minus Twenty-Three, they reached the broad valley of the Yenisei, the largest river in Siberia. Beyond the Yenisei, the gloomy taiga gave way again to the treeless, rolling grasslands known as the steppes. The farther west they traveled, the larger and more closely spaced the towns became—for all the good it did the travelers. Often they were in and out of a town so quickly that Charles, to his frustration, was unable to even learn the name of the place. His diary entries had become rather sketchy and repetitive:

**Friday, October 23**
*Doomsday Minus Twenty-Two. Stopped in an unidentified town just long enough for a meal of eggs, bread, and tea. Now camped alongside an unidentified river. I stand watch while the others sleep. We have not played cards for some time. Harry seems to have no interest in whist or bezique, or in much of anything except putting the miles behind us. I wish Elizabeth were still with us.*

**Saturday, October 24**
*Doomsday Minus Twenty-One. Bought kerosene in an unidentified town. Dined on bread, eggs, and tea. Tried in vain to find a map, to get some sense*

of where we actually are and how far we have
to go. Will no doubt camp on the steppes again
tonight.

### Sunday, October 25
*Doomsday Minus Twenty. Stayed the night in
an actual hotel! I even learned the name of the
city—Tomsk. It is home to the sole institution of
higher learning in Siberia, Tomsk Imperial University, which was opened a mere three years ago,
and which I of course did not have time to see.
It prompted Fogg to inquire whether I meant to
attend university. When I replied that I did, he
said, to my surprise, that he had been considering
the possibility himself. With his academic record,
I doubt any reputable school would take him. But
perhaps he could give Tomsk University a try.*

*Crossed the Tom River on a curious sort of
ferry, powered by a cable attached to an anchor. A
small boat went ahead of us, carrying the anchor,
dropped it in the river, then the other end of the
cable was reeled onto a winch or capstan turned by
a long-suffering horse.*

### Monday, October 26
*Doomsday Minus Nineteen. Camped on the steppes
last night, nearly froze. The mosquitoes seem to be
done with, at least. Drove through two unidentified towns without stopping. Passed by a settlement*

*of Ostiaks, another of those tribes whose way of life is disappearing the face of progress. I cannot imagine they will miss it much. They live in birch-bark wigwams, dress in clothing made of pounded birch bark, and eat from bowls made of birch bark. I could not tell what they were eating. Birch bark, I expect.*

### Tuesday, October 27
*Doomsday Minus Eighteen. We are in perhaps the largest, most appealing, most prosperous city I have seen since leaving San Francisco and, ironically, I find myself wishing that, as we have done with so many other towns, we had passed through without stopping.*

*I am writing this entry from a gaol cell. We have had a stroke of bad luck.*

Charles was being kind. In truth, their misfortune was due less to bad luck than to a mistake on Harry's part—not a large mistake, nor a foolish one, just an ordinary oversight. But sometimes small errors can lead to serious consequences.

Omsk was, as Charles indicated, a well-populated, busy metropolis—far too busy to suit Harry. The streets were filled with wagons and carriages and people on foot who stopped to gawk at the marvelous machine. Harry was forced to slow the *Flash* to a crawl, which only made matters worse, since now the gawkers gathered around the car for a closer look. A man in a European-style suit called to them, "You are the English motorists, yes?"

"*Da!*" replied Harry.

To his fellow Omskites, the man shouted something that included the words *aftomobil* and "Fogg." The people responded with cheers. "It looks as though they've heard of us," said Harry with his trademark grin, which had been seen so seldom of late.

Johnny groaned and, sliding down in his seat, pulled his cap over his ears.

Thanks to the growing crowd of well-wishers, the already-choked thoroughfare became nearly impassable. Harry had to halt frequently and suddenly; he was continually applying or releasing the hand brake, pushing the throttle in and out, engaging and disengaging the gears. So occupied was he with avoiding collisions that he neglected to lower the flame on the burner, and Johnny, upset by all the people and the noise, failed to notice. At last the boiler built up such a head of pressure that the safety valve blew, sending steam shooting from the smokestack.

The alarmed townsfolk scattered, some crying out in fright; the commotion, in turn, startled several horses, including one harnessed to a cart full of clay pottery. The animal reared into the air, dumping its load onto the pavement and shattering half the pots. The driver, who was also thrown from the cart, stormed up to the motorcar, limping and spouting a stream of what Harry could only assume were invectives and imprecations.

Harry shut down the burner and did his best to apologize in his limited French, but the man would not be mollified. He began shouting, *"Policija! Policija!"* Two policemen pushed their way through the spectators, who had recovered from their fear and reassembled.

Brandishing their batons, the officers herded the motorists and the injured party toward the station house. Johnny had to be pried away from the *Flash*. "Harry?" he pleaded.

"It'll be all right, lad." Harry spoke to the officers in French. "What about our carriage without horse? She cannot stop in the center of the street!"

"Don't worry," said one of the policemen. "Someone will move it."

"Yes," said Harry. "That is what worries me."

"No one will steal it, if that's what you mean," said the man, rather crossly. "This is a law-abiding town. Now get moving."

Though it galled him to do it, Harry resorted to the tactic his father had so often used on his fabled journey: He offered to pay the cart driver double what the pots were worth if he would drop the charges against them. "You Englishmen and your money," said the policeman. "You think you can buy your way out of this? I've told you, this is a law-abiding town. You must go before the magistrate."

"And when will the magistrate be here?"

"Tomorrow."

They spent the next twenty-four hours in a badly heated jail cell so small that Harry could not even pace about. He sat cross-legged on a bunk and meditated and, for a change, it actually seemed to help. Charles passed the time by playing solitaire and writing in his diary. Johnny curled up in his bunk like some hibernating animal waiting for spring.

The following afternoon they were brought before the magistrate, who quickly scanned the police report, then glanced up with an eager look on his face. "You are Harry Fogg?" he said, in English.

"Yes, sir."

"I have been following your adventures in the Moscow newspaper. But there has been nothing for at least a fortnight; I wondered what had become of you. You managed to repair your motorcar, I take it?"

"Yes, sir, we did. We also escaped a band of outlaws and crossed the Tchuma River in full flood. The only tight spot we have not managed to extricate ourselves from is the Omsk jail."

"I am sorry for the inconvenience," said the magistrate. "I hope it has not cost you too much time."

"An entire day, actually."

"How many days remain before you must be back in England?"

Harry turned to Charles, who said, "Seventeen, Your Honor."

"Seventeen days? To cross all of Europe? Then why on earth are you standing here? It is clear that the whole incident was merely an accident!" The magistrate shouted something in Russian. Whatever he said, it had a profound effect. The three motorists were ushered from the room—not roughly, like prisoners, but respectfully, like visiting dignitaries. "Good luck to you, gentlemen!" the magistrate called after them.

The police escorted them to the spot where they had left the *Flash*. "You see," said Harry cheerfully, "I told you it would be all right."

"Except that we lost an entire day," said Charles.

"Not to worry. We'll make up for it. As long as the *Flash* holds up, we're—" He broke off and halted in his tracks, staring at their motorcar, which someone had pushed out of the street and onto the wooden sidewalk.

"What is it?" said Charles. "What's wrong?"

"We've been robbed," said Johnny.

# THIRTY-SIX

*In which*

## THE TRAVELERS CHANGE
## CONTINENTS

**E**very bit of their equipment and supplies had been carried off, including their heavy coats, their bedding, the tents, the canned goods—even Johnny's tools. What's more, the acetylene lamps had been removed from the fenders, and there were gaping holes in the rain hood where someone had cut away numerous squares of the leather.

"I thought you said this was a law-abiding town!" cried Charles.

"This is not the work of criminals," said the policeman. "I suspect it was ordinary townsfolk who wanted a souvenir from the famous globe-circling motorcar."

"Oh, well," said Charles, "when we're freezing and starving to death out there on the steppes, we'll console ourselves with the knowledge that it was all just a bit of harmless fun!"

"Calm down, Charles," said Harry. "We can buy more supplies. Let's just consider ourselves lucky we're not still sitting in that jail cell."

"I could easily arrest you again," said the policeman, "for showing disrespect to an officer of the law."

"The magistrate would only release us," said Charles smugly.

"Perhaps." The policeman sounded even more smug. "But it could take some time to schedule another hearing for you—possibly as much as a week."

Charles grudgingly let the matter drop. It took the rest of the afternoon to replace the stolen supplies— not all of them, by any means, only the most essential items. As Harry and Charles stood in a mercantile store, selecting woolen blankets, Harry unexpectedly let out a laugh. "I'm glad you find the situation so amusing," said Charles.

"I was just thinking about how you told off that policeman. Not very gentlemanly of you, old chap."

"I was angry. I still am."

"I know. And you must admit, that in itself is rather amusing."

"In what way?" demanded Charles.

"Well, you sounded so indignant, so . . . proprietary, as though the thieves had done you some grave personal injury. But most of the supplies were ours; all you lost was a portmanteau with a couple of changes of clothing. And I noticed that, earlier, you said 'we lost an entire day'—not *they*, but *we*. You seem to consider yourself an actual part of this expedition, not just an observer."

"Haven't I earned that right?"

"Of course you have. But isn't that conflict of interest, or something? I mean, your father is betting two thousand pounds that we'll lose, and yet you seem determined to have us win."

Charles fingered one of the blankets thoughtfully. "When we started out, you know, I thought the whole idea was ludicrous. I was certain we'd break down before we got out of England. But this trip has convinced me that motorcars are just as practical as locomotives— more so, in fact, because you can go anywhere you like with one, not just along a set of tracks. Someday soon they're going to replace the railroads. If we can make my father understand that, it's worth a lot more than two thousand pounds."

"I agree," said Harry. "Now, we'd better pay for all this and get on the road; we have a lot of miles to make up."

"Right. But see here, Harry. Perhaps you'd better let me take care of this. You can't have much money left."

"Thanks for the thought, my friend, but I can't have your father accusing me of cheating—accepting aid and comfort from the enemy, as it were."

"It's not his money; it's mine."

"All the same, I'd rather not. Besides, I have more than enough to cover it."

"I don't mean to be rude, but how the deuce did you manage that? I saw your bankroll after you lost that race to Morrison. You were running low even then."

Harry scratched his head and shifted about uncomfortably.

"Never mind," said Charles. "I suppose it's none of my business."

"No, no, the fact is, I'm tired of keeping it to myself. Just promise me one thing—you won't breathe a word about this to Johnny."

"All right. I promise."

"You remember your father's friend, Drummond, whom we met in San Francisco?"

"Of course. What about him?"

"Well, I . . . The thing is, I . . . I sold him the *Flash*."

"You're joking."

"No, unfortunately, I'm not. I was nearly out of money, and it was the only way I could think of to raise enough for the rest of the trip. I certainly couldn't ask my father for more."

Charles shook his head incredulously. "That was a deuced stupid thing to do, Harry. I see why you didn't want me to tell Johnny. But you know, he'll find out eventually, and he's going to be extremely upset."

"Ah, but that's where you're wrong. You see, I wasn't

nearly as stupid as you think. I didn't sell Drummond the *Flash* outright. I made a deal with him: He gets the car only if we lose. If we win, I give him back his money, and we keep the *Flash*. So Johnny never needs to know."

"Provided we win the wager, that is."

"Oh, we'll win—" Harry started to say, but at that moment Johnny came through the door of the mercantile.

"Aren't you done?" asked Johnny.

Harry gave Charles a warning glance, then forced a smile. "Almost. Did you get the tools you needed?" Johnny held up a box full of clanking metal items. "Good lad," said Harry. "Better return to the *Flash*, now, before the policeman gets tired of guarding it."

By the time they left Omsk, it was nearly dark. They hadn't had time to go hunting for acetylene lamps to replace the stolen ones. The best Harry could do was an ordinary kerosene lantern. He hung it on the end of a pole that projected several feet in front of the car. It didn't shed much light on the road, but it was better than nothing.

Though he was weary after their uncomfortable night in jail, there was little chance he would fall asleep at the wheel; the cold air that rushed through the gaps in the leather hood kept him wide awake. By dawn, when he handed the wheel over to Johnny, they were nearly two hundred miles closer to England. Charles had gotten his hands on a map at last and, according to his calculations, they had roughly six thousand miles to go.

After a few hours' sleep, Harry took over again. "No offense, Johnny," he said, "but you drive too slowly."

"If I go fast," said Johnny, "it hurts when I hit the bumps."

"It hurts you, or it hurts the *Flash*?"

"Both."

"I won't hurt her," said Harry. "I promise."

But later that afternoon, as Harry was trying to drink from their canteen with one hand and steer with the other, he let the car drift too far to the right. The shoulder of the road had washed away, leaving an abyss into which the front wheel dropped with a painful thud and the sickening sound of cracking wood. "The devil take me," said Harry.

When they attempted to lift the car out of the hole, they discovered that the souvenir hunters of Omsk had even taken their jack. With a stout tree trunk and a good deal of groaning, they levered up the *Flash* and slid the front end onto solid ground, then replaced the broken wheel with one of the cleated ones. It made for a bumpy ride, and the cleats chewed up the gravel, but it got them to Tiumen, where, for a change, they had a leisurely dinner while the wheel was repaired.

"I'm sorry, Johnny," said Harry. "I should have been more careful."

Johnny shrugged. "Lucky they lasted this long. Should've used steel ones."

"That's one of the improvements we'll make," said Harry, "before we set out on our next journey."

Charles laughed. "Once you've traveled round the world, where is there left to go?"

"Oh, I don't know," said Harry. "What about the North Pole?"

Though the Trans-Siberian Railway would not reach Vladivostok for many years yet, it had made it east as far as Tiumen. There was no longer any need, however, for the intrepid motorists to drive on the tracks. The post road had at last become a highway worthy of the name, broad and level and surfaced with crushed stone. Over the next two days they made better time than they had since beginning the journey.

On the evening of Doomsday Minus Fourteen, they entered Ekaterinburg. According to Charles's map, the Ural Mountains lay just beyond the city. "Perhaps we should wait for daylight to cross the mountains," he suggested.

Harry reluctantly agreed. "It looks like rain, in any case. We should probably fix the holes in our hood."

They rented space in a livery stable and set about repairing the hood, securing the patches with both glue and stitching, to be certain they held. For a change, Charles did his share without being asked. For even more of a change, he did not insist on finding a hotel; he supped on cheese sandwiches and beer and slept on a bed of straw alongside the others.

They set out the next morning before sunrise. The rain had turned to a light drizzle. Still, they were glad to have a sound roof over their heads. Though they were slowly gaining altitude, they saw no sign of any actual mountains. "Are you sure you read the map properly?" asked Harry.

"Quite sure," replied Charles indignantly.

"There's a marker." Johnny pointed to a marble pillar alongside the road.

Harry stopped and climbed out to see what was inscribed on the pillar. When he returned, he was laughing.

"What?" demanded Charles. "What does it say?"

"Well, on one side it says 'Asia.' On the other side it says 'Europe.'"

"That means we're at the summit of the Urals. How did that happen, without our even noticing?"

"Very gradually, apparently." Harry felt around beneath the seat and came up with a bottle of champagne. "Aha. The thieves in Omsk didn't clean us out completely." He untwisted the wire bail and popped the cork. "I bought this back in Vladivostok, lads, to be opened when we reached European soil." Since they had no drinking glasses, they passed the bottle around.

"To victory!" Charles took a sizable swig, then gave a subdued burp. "Pardon me."

"Oh, no," said Harry. "You will not be pardoned until you produce a proper belch." Snatching the bottle, he proceeded to demonstrate.

"I can top that." Johnny took a great gulp of the

bubbly and uttered a sound like a small explosion.

Charles claimed the bottle again. "All right, I'll show you lot." He downed so much so fast that, when he burped, champagne spurted from his nose. Harry and Johnny howled with laughter; despite the burning in his nostrils, Charles couldn't help joining in.

The smile faded from Johnny's face and he said forlornly, "I wish Elizabeth was here."

"So do I," said Charles. "She deserves to be part of this celebration." He raised the bottle. "To Elizabeth." He took a drink and handed the champagne to Harry, who shook his head and passed the bottle to Johnny. "What's wrong?" asked Charles.

"It must be a poor vintage," said Harry. "It's left a bad taste in my mouth."

## THIRTY-SEVEN

*In which*

# CHARLES LEARNS
# A THING OR TWO

After the incident in Omsk, even Charles had to agree that it was best to get through towns and cities as quickly as possible. They were lucky enough to hit Perm just before dawn on Doomsday Minus Twelve. Two days later, at around midnight, they rolled quietly through Kazan. At 2:00 A.M. on Doomsday Minus Eight, they navigated the empty streets of Nizhni-Novgorod unnoticed—or so they thought.

Unfortunately this put them on the outskirts of Moscow late in the afternoon of that same day. As they sat alongside the road discussing whether to lie low for a few hours or to risk running the gauntlet that lay ahead, Johnny said, "Somebody's coming."

A horse-drawn hackney pulled up directly in front of them. A small, slender fellow in a bowler hat sprang from the cab and approached, smiling broadly. "Harry Fogg, I presume?"

"That's right."

"Daniel Bennett, Moscow correspondent for the London *Daily Graphic*." They shook hands. "Elizabeth has just been telling me all about you gentlemen and your marvelous motorcar."

"Elizabeth is here?" asked Johnny eagerly.

"No, no, she left this morning, on the train. There was also a good deal she did *not* tell me. I was hoping you might consent to a brief interview."

Harry shook his head. "We can't afford to stop for that long, I'm afraid."

"Oh, no need to. I'll ride with you." Bennett signaled to the cabman, who drove off. Without waiting for an invitation, the reporter swung nimbly into the rear seat of the car. "You'll want to avoid the main thoroughfares. They'll be packed with people wanting a look at you."

"How on earth," asked Charles, "did they know when to expect us?"

"The Moscow *News* has been posting bulletins regularly in its front window, tracking your progress. They receive telegrams, you see, from all the cities you've passed through. One came in from Nizhni-Novgorod early this morning. Everyone is eager to welcome you to Moscow. I'm told the mayor is even planning to throw a banquet in your honor."

Harry groaned. "We don't have time for banquets, or for adoring crowds."

"Not to worry," said Bennett. "We'll take the backstreets. Turn here." As he guided them through the fringes of the city, he kept up a barrage of questions—including the usual ones concerning Phileas Fogg, which Harry, as usual, declined to answer. After half an hour of this, Bennett said, "You'll be out of danger soon. Just one last question—and this is off the record: Can you tell me why Elizabeth left the expedition?"

Harry glanced warily over his shoulder at the reporter. "She didn't explain it to you?"

"Actually, she did. But I want to hear your side of the story."

"There are no sides to the story. The *Graphic* gave her another assignment, that's all."

Bennett gave a rather unpleasant laugh. "Is that what she told you?"

"Apparently she told you something quite different."

"Well, she seemed rather reluctant to speak about it. I expect she was a bit embarrassed about the whole thing."

Harry tried desperately to think of some way to stop Bennett from revealing the truth, without giving anything away to Johnny and Charles. The best he could do was to yank on the hand brake; the car skidded to a halt, sending everyone lurching forward.

"What's wrong?" Johnny demanded, rubbing his head, which had bounced off the windscreen.

"A dog," said Harry. "Didn't you see it?" He turned to the reporter, who was retrieving his lost bowler hat. "Sorry. While we're stopped, Mr. Bennett, you may as well get out."

"Yes, all right," said Bennett grumpily. He climbed from the *Flash*, but remained perched on the running board. "Oh, about Elizabeth . . ." Harry pulled out the throttle and the car surged ahead, dumping the reporter unceremoniously into the street.

That evening Harry and Charles took dinner at a small inn, leaving Johnny to guard the motorcar. The food, like the roads, had improved considerably since they entered Europe. Over a cup of genuine tea, Charles said, "What do you suppose Elizabeth told that reporter?"

"Heaven only knows," said Harry. "She is accustomed to say whatever suits her purpose at the moment."

"But why wouldn't she just tell him the truth—that she had another assignment?"

Harry didn't reply.

"Oh," said Charles. "Because it wasn't the truth. That's it, isn't it?"

Harry still said nothing.

"Why did she really leave, Harry?"

"I can't answer that. I'm afraid you'll have to ask her."

"Very well, I shall. Assuming we ever hear from her again."

Harry gave a wry smile. "Oh, I have no doubt that we will hear from her. She is determined to be a famous reporter and, as you know, she has a way of getting what she wants."

The main highway out of Moscow led northwest, to the capital city of St. Petersburg. But according to Charles and his map, they could save three hundred miles by heading directly west, through Minsk and Warsaw. The route to Minsk was far less traveled, which meant there were fewer horses and bicyclists to startle. It also meant that the road was not maintained very well.

Harry and Johnny took turns driving through the night, but with only the kerosene lantern to illuminate the rutted road, they barely crept along. Late in the afternoon of Doomsday Minus Seven, they stopped for a couple of hours' rest and a cold meal, then set out on another all-night motoring marathon. They didn't arrive in Minsk until the wee hours of Doomsday Minus Six, far too early to purchase a new lamp for the *Flash*. A few hours' sleep and they were off to Warsaw.

The newspapers had apparently lost track of them, for there were no crowds waiting to welcome them in the former Polish capital, which was now in Russian territory. By parking the car out of sight in an alley, they managed to have a decent meal, buy acetylene lamps and kerosene, and be on their way before anyone knew they were there.

Johnny could drive no more than a few hours before his head began to throb so badly that he couldn't see. Most of the burden fell on Harry. He often went eight or ten hours without a break, slept for three or four, then took the wheel again. The strain was beginning to show. He looked wan and haggard and, since he rarely took the time to shave or to eat properly, somewhat thin and scruffy as well.

On Doomsday Minus Four, as they sat at the border between Russia and Germany, waiting for their passports to be visaed, Charles said, "See here, Harry. You look as though you're ready to drop. Surely we can afford a few hours' rest."

"I can rest when we reach London," said Harry.

"Then suppose I drive for a bit." Harry didn't reply. "I'm not a simpleton, you know," said Charles. "And it's not exactly complicated, is it?" Still no reply. "I've been watching you two operate the car for three months now. I think I've grasped the basic principles involved."

Johnny, who was slumped in his seat with his cap tipped over his eyes to block the light, murmured, "Let him try, Harry."

"What if he runs her off the road?"

"You did," said Johnny.

Harry grinned wearily. "Good point." He sighed and climbed into the rear seat. "All right, old fellow. Give it a go, then. Just be careful, will you?"

For several moments, Charles didn't move. He hadn't actually expected Harry to agree. Now that he'd been given permission to drive, he suddenly felt very unsure of his ability to do so.

"I don't believe you can reach the controls from here," said Harry. "You'll have to sit up front."

"I know that," replied Charles irritably. But Harry's good-natured needling had stirred him into action. He put on his eyeglasses—which he had always been too vain to wear in front of Elizabeth—squeezed between the seats, and plunked down behind the wheel. *I can do this, I can do this*, he repeated silently. He had driven a four-horse team, he reminded himself. He had piloted one of his father's locomotives. Surely he could handle a motorcar.

When the border guard returned with their passports, Charles let off the hand brake, engaged the gears, and gingerly pulled out the throttle. The *Flash* leaped forward, nearly mowing down the guard, who was raising the barrier. "Sorry!" Charles called over his shoulder.

"Watch the road," said Harry.

"I'm watching, I'm watching." Gripping the wheel with one sweaty hand, Charles pushed in the throttle slightly with the other. The *Flash* struck a small depression in the road, nearly wrenching the steering wheel from his hand. "The devil take it!" he said softly, between clenched teeth.

Harry had to clench his teeth, too, to keep from

shouting, "That's enough! Stop the car!" Though he did his best to appear calm, he was far from it, and though he didn't really mean to watch Charles's every move like a cat watching a robin, he couldn't help himself. But after half an hour or so, when it seemed that Charles was getting the feel of the car and the road, Harry began to relax a little. Eventually, exhaustion overcame him and he drifted off.

Sometime later, he was jolted rudely awake. The car had stopped moving and was listing alarmingly to one side. Harry sat up, groaning and rubbing his eyes. "Oh, bollocks!" he said, under his breath. "I knew it! I should never have let him drive!"

# THIRTY-EIGHT

## *In which*

## THE MOTORISTS ENCOUNTER A SEEMINGLY INSURMOUNTABLE OBSTACLE

Charles and Johnny were crouched by the left rear wheel, gazing at it glumly. Harry leaned over the side of the car. "What did you do?"

"Nothing!" snapped Charles.

"'Tis not his fault," said Johnny. "'Tis a bad bearing."

"Oh. My mistake, old chap. Sorry."

Even without a proper jack, it was a quick job to replace the faulty wheel. Getting it repaired was a more lengthy matter. They were stuck in Berlin much of the afternoon of Doomsday Minus Three—ample time for word to get around that the intrepid young motorists and their marvelous machine were in town. By the time they were ready to leave, the wheelwright's shop was surrounded.

Most of the spectators were merely curious, but

some had apparently laid wagers on the outcome of the contest. Those who had money riding on the *Flash* urged the wheelwright to make haste. Those who had bet against it laughed and told him not to bother, for the car couldn't possibly reach London in the three days that remained.

There were horseless carriage enthusiasts in the crowd, too, including a man named Benz who offered to show them a vehicle he had built, powered by a gasoline engine. Harry even spotted a small contingent of New Luddites, or their German equivalent, shouting antitechnology slogans; they were booed down by the motorcar fanciers.

The crew of the *Flash* climbed into the car. Harry stood on the driver's seat and called, "Ladies and gentlemen, please clear a path, so we may be on our way!" A few people moved aside, but the gap was filled at once by other eager onlookers.

"Put her in gear," said Charles. "They'll move."

*Act quickly*, Harry reminded himself, *but do not act rashly*. "What if they don't move?" he said. "I don't want to hit anyone."

Johnny, slumped in his seat, tapped his friend on the leg. "Remember what happened in Omsk?"

Harry grinned. "Good thinking, lad!" he said softly. "Turn up the burner!" The moment Johnny increased the flow of kerosene, the pressure in the boiler began to climb. When it reached 600 psi, Harry shouted, "Look out, everyone! She's going to blow!" A moment later, the safety valve let go a gush of steam. Magically, like the Red Sea parting, an avenue opened up before them.

As the car pulled away, one of the New Luddites raised a length of iron pipe and brought it down on the right rear fender, caving it in so badly that the wheel scraped against it. After only a moment's hesitation, Charles leaned over the side of the car. Grabbing the aluminum in both hands, he gave a prodigious yank that nearly sent him tumbling from the car but straightened the fender enough to let the wheel turn freely.

"Good work, old man!" called Harry.

"My driving was good, too!" said Charles. "Admit it!"

Harry laughed. "All right, all right, I admit it! You're a very capable driver!" And in fact, later that day he let Charles take the wheel for several hours while he caught a much-needed nap.

Though the highway from Berlin to Paris was an excellent one, it was so congested with carriages and wagons that they were forced to creep along at a horse's pace—sometimes even less, for the other drivers slowed to get a good look at the horseless carriage. To keep from bursting like an overheated boiler, Harry sang medleys of music-hall tunes at the top of his voice. Charles contributed his wavering tenor to the cause. Occasionally they even heard Johnny tunelessly mumbling the words.

"Well," said Harry, "we needn't worry about startling the horses. If they can tolerate our singing, our motorcar won't even faze them."

They didn't cross into France until the morning of Doomsday Minus One. They avoided Paris entirely by turning north at Reims. From that point on, they had no need of a map. Harry had been here on holiday more than once; so had Charles. Thanks to the railroads and the cross-Channel ferries, one could leave London at eight in the morning and be in Paris for afternoon tea.

By early evening, they were on the docks at Calais, the departure point for the paddle-wheel steamers that plied the English Channel. "Well, lads," said Harry, "Dover is only a two-hour ferry ride away. After that, it's an easy drive to London. If all goes well, when the members of the Reform Club arrive for breakfast tomorrow morning, we'll be there waiting."

But, as the Scottish poet Robert Burns pointed out, the best-laid schemes have a way of going agley. There was one rather large problem that none of them had anticipated. The Channel steamers were designed with foot passengers in mind; they weren't equipped to carry anything as large and cumbersome as a motorcar.

As an off-duty ferry captain—a fellow Englishman appropriately named Shipley—explained, "There's no room on deck, and they have no cargo holds to speak of. All large freight has to be shipped from a deepwater port."

"Where is the closest deepwater port?" asked Charles.

"Le Havre."

"That must be two hundred miles from here!"

"Nearly. And those big cargo vessels can't put in at Dover, either. You'd have to go to Bristol or Liverpool."

"But we don't have that much time," said Harry, trying hard to remain calm. "We must be in London by ten-fifteen tomorrow morning, or we lose six thousand pounds." *And*, he thought but did not say, *we lose the* Flash *as well.*

Captain Shipley stared in astonishment. "You're not—you're not the round-the-world racers?"

"Guilty as charged," said Harry.

"Well, permit me to shake your hands, gentlemen. I have five pounds riding on you. I made the wager with another captain, a Frenchman. He always scoffs at the notion that the English could possibly build a decent motorcar. I knew you'd prove him wrong."

"We haven't yet," said Charles. "And we shan't, either, unless we find some way across the Channel."

Harry, who had been eyeing the half-dozen ferries moored nearby, pointed to a curious catamaran-like vessel made of two hulls joined together, with a paddle wheel in between. "What ship is that?"

"The *Castalia*," said the captain. "She's been taken out of service. Too slow to suit the ferry company. They'll be sending her back to Dover soon, to be dismantled."

Harry turned to his friends. "Are you thinking what I'm thinking?"

"The Tchuma River?" said Charles.

"Exactly. What do you think, Johnny? Could it be done?"

"Don't see why not."

"Could *what* be done?" asked Shipley.

"In Siberia," said Harry, "we crossed the Tchuma River on a raft made by laying logs across the gunwales of several small boats."

"Ah. So you're thinking that, if you jury-rigged a platform between the two bows of the ship . . ."

"There'd be room for the *Flash*," finished Harry. "Any idea how soon the *Castalia* will sail?"

"As soon as the repairs are completed. She's having some engine trouble."

Harry grinned and put an arm around Johnny's broad shoulders. "Well, as it so happens, we have a man here who is an absolute wizard where engines are concerned."

"Is there any chance," asked Charles, "that the captain of the *Castalia* would agree to our plan?"

Shipley smiled. "Oh, he'll agree, all right."

"What makes you so certain?"

"Because," said the captain, "the *Castalia* is my ship."

While Johnny assisted the mechanics in the engine room, his friends oversaw the building of the platform, which was made of thick planks bolted to the railings on both the ship's hulls. The crew also constructed a wooden ramp that led from the dock to the deck.

The captain suggested pulling the motorcar aboard with a winch, but Harry, unwilling to do anything contrary to the rules of the wager, insisted on driving up the ramp. Though he came within an inch of running the *Flash* into the harbor, he finally maneuvered it safely onto the platform, where it was tied down with thick ropes.

Now all that remained was to get the ship's engines running. Not wishing to put any pressure on Johnny, Harry stayed clear of the engine room. Instead, he paced about on deck, glancing at Charles's watch every few minutes and repeatedly checking the *Flash* to make certain it was secure.

To have a reasonable chance of beating the deadline of a quarter past ten, they needed to reach Dover by six in the morning—seven, at the absolute latest. And since the *Castalia* was slower than a single-hulled ferry, they must allow at least three hours for the crossing. That meant they should leave Calais no later than 3:00 A.M.

Midnight came and went, then one o'clock, then two, and still the engines showed no sign of life. At half past three, Johnny emerged from belowdecks, looking utterly exhausted, holding his head with both hands as though it threatened to come apart. Harry fetched the Dr. Pemberton's Syrup, which Elizabeth had left behind, and gave his friend a large dose. "Lie down, lad. Have a good long rest."

Charles drew Harry aside and whispered, "We don't have *time* for him to rest!"

"He can't work if he can't think."

"But it's already—" Charles started to say, then abruptly broke off. "Harry?" he said softly. "Did you hear that?"

"What?"

"A sort of . . . a sort of *chugging* sound?"

Harry listened intently, then broke into a grin. "It's the engines!" He turned to Johnny. "You got them running, lad! Why didn't you say so?"

Johnny gave him a faint, weary smile. "You didn't ask," he said.

## THE *FLASH* NEARS THE FINISH
## LINE—AND THE DEADLINE

**N**ot only had Johnny repaired the engines, he had somehow contrived to make them run more efficiently. With the help of a strong breeze from the southwest, the *Castalia* made the crossing in well under three hours, to the delight of Captain Shipley. "Perhaps," he said, "the company will decide to keep her in service after all."

Though the motorists made as much haste as possible, even firing up the *Flash* well before they docked, by the time they set out on the Great Dover Road it was nearly seven o'clock. Fearful that, like Phileas Fogg, they might have lost track of the date, Harry bought a copy of the Dover *Telegraph* to confirm that it was indeed Doomsday. The newspaper was dated November

14—one hundred days, by the calendar, since they departed London. It seemed more like a thousand.

On the front page was a story saying that, at last report, the marvelous motorcar and its intrepid young crew were crossing the border between Germany and France, and were expected to arrive in England sometime that morning—too late, in the paper's opinion, to win the wager. "It just goes to show you," said Harry, "that you can't believe everything you read."

It had begun to drizzle, now, and the stiff breeze that had helped them across the Channel had grown even stiffer; each gust blew cold rain in around the flapping side curtains of the *Flash*. "'November's sky is chill and drear,'" quoted Charles, shivering.

"Shakespeare?" asked Harry.

"Sir Walter Scott."

"Well, at least the dreary weather is keeping the traffic off the roads." Still, they encountered several dozen carriages and wagons, and each time Harry had to creep along to avoid an accident. When they hit a vacant stretch, he tried to make up for lost time, yet he was careful not to push the *Flash* too hard.

"Won't she go any faster?" asked Charles anxiously.

"Of course she will. But we've come too far and endured too much for me to risk losing the whole match now. Don't worry; we've plenty of time."

Charles checked his watch and scowled. "Oh, yes. If by 'plenty of time' you mean 'barely enough.'" He shook his head. "I don't know when you got so cautious."

Harry grinned. "We seem to be trading roles, don't we? Now you're the impatient one."

In each town they passed through, a few people braved the wind and rain to get a glimpse of the famous *Flash*. As the motorcar cruised by, they waved and cheered. Harry gave a quick toot on the steam whistle.

"The crowds in London will be a good deal larger," said Charles.

"I'm afraid so," said Harry. "I've been thinking that we'd do well to avoid the main thoroughfares—take some route no will expect us to take."

"What about the Vauxhall Bridge?"

"Good idea, old chap. We can go up Bridge Road to Picadilly, then down St. James's Street to Pall Mall. They'll be looking for us to come from the other direction."

At nine o'clock they turned onto the Old Kent Road, which led to the Vauxhall Bridge. "One and a quarter hours left," said Charles. All three motorists were so tense that they had fallen into Johnny's habit of speaking in terse fragments. At nine-twenty they crossed the Thames. By nine-thirty they were heading east on Picadilly. "Almost home," said Harry.

"Don't miss the turn," said Johnny.

"No fear. Lift your curtain, lads, and keep an eye out for St. James's Street."

"Just ahead," sang out Charles.

After a few more minutes of excruciatingly slow and careful driving, they turned onto Pall Mall, the wide avenue on which the Reform Club lay. "Time," said Harry.

"Twenty minutes until ten," replied Charles, smiling broadly.

"Well, lads, it looks as though we've got it—"

"Harry!" interrupted Johnny. "Look there!"

Fifty yards ahead of them, a brewer's cart, piled high with kegs of beer, was pulling out of an alleyway and into the street, obstructing it completely. "Good lord," groaned Harry. It was like a bad dream, in which he would be forced to experience all over again the accident that, some three months earlier, had set into motion this whole chain of events.

But no. This time things were different. This time he was not driving so recklessly. This time he was able to bring the *Flash* to a stop well before he reached the cart. He pushed up the side curtain and leaned out, looking for some sign of the drayman. The wind-driven rain nearly blinded him, but as far as he could tell there was no one about, only the wagon and the horse.

"We'll have to move it ourselves," said Charles, and climbed from the car. But as he reached for the horse's bridle, half a dozen men in mackintoshes and rain hats emerged from the alleyway. They were carrying clubs, axes, and signs that read NO MORE MOTORCARS and DEATH TO THE DEVIL-WAGONS.

Charles spun about and shouted, "Get the car out of here! Now!" Two of the largest Luddites seized him by the arms and held him helpless, ignoring his desperate struggles and his ungentlemanly curses. Harry sprang from the car, ready to rush to his friend's aid, but Charles shouted, "No! Never mind about me! Save the *Flash*!"

Harry hesitated. Act quickly, but not rashly. Concluding that the car was in more danger than Charles, he jumped back into the driver's seat and stomped on the reverse pedal. But Johnny, who was keeping a lookout to the rear, shouted, "Stop!" Harry braked and peered out through the side curtain. Another wagon had pulled up behind them, blocking the way. There was no escape.

"The guns, Harry," said Johnny. "Get the guns."

Harry shook his head in despair. "I can't, lad. They were stolen, remember?"

Grimly, they climbed from the car to face the mob. Harry wished he had had time to learn at least one or two of Ramesh's *kalarippayattu* techniques. The best he could do was to arm himself with a large wrench from the toolbox. He managed to get in a few good blows before one of the men clubbed the makeshift weapon from his hands. Another swung a stick into the backs of his knees, knocking him off his feet.

Johnny's huge fists took a worse toll on their attackers, but it was only a matter of moments before he lay helpless, all but unconscious, on the wet street.

With its defenders disabled, the *Flash* was easy prey for the Luddites. They did not, as Harry expected, rain aimless blows down upon the motorcar; they were more methodical in their destruction. Two of the men unfastened the front of the leather rain cover and folded it back. Two others yanked up the rear seat and flung it aside, revealing the car's wire-wrapped boiler. A hulking man with an ax stepped forward and delivered a fierce blow to the top of the boiler. The thin steel split open, sending a geyser of steam into the air, like a sigh of defeat.

The axeman gave a brisk, satisfied nod. "That should do it," he said. "Let's go."

The men moved off, taking the cart and horse with them. Charles's captors released him and pushed him toward the car almost gently, as though they had no wish to harm him. "You blackguards!" Charles shouted hoarsely, tears of frustration mingling with the rain that streamed down his face. "You won't get away with this! I'll see that you're brought to justice, every last one of you!"

Harry got unsteadily to his feet and was almost knocked off them again by the fierce wind. He shuffled over to Johnny, who had risen no farther than his knees. With Harry's help, Johnny made it to the rear seat of the *Flash*, which had been tossed onto the sidewalk. There he sank down again. "How's the car?" he murmured.

Though Harry knew without looking that it was bad,

he forced himself to examine the damage. There was a ragged rent in the top of the boiler, not unlike the one left in Johnny's head years earlier by the horse's hoof. The hole in the metal could probably be repaired, but not without a welding torch, and certainly not in the half hour that remained before they must be at the front steps of the Reform Club.

Charles kicked at one of the signs the Luddites had tossed aside. "It's hopeless, isn't it?"

"I'm afraid so." Harry sank down on the running board, out of the wind, and put his head in his hands. "We were so close to winning."

"But see here, we're only a quarter mile from the club. Surely we could push her that far?"

"No doubt we could," said Harry. "But the rules state in no uncertain terms that the *Flash* must travel the entire distance under her own power."

"I won't tell anyone."

"They'll *see* us doing it, Charles."

"I suppose you're right. So we're just going to give up, is that it?"

Harry threw up his hands. "I don't *want* to give up, old man! You know how much I have riding on this! But I don't see that we have any choice!"

"The *Flash*'s wheels can still turn," insisted Charles. "There must be *some* way of getting her rolling." He turned his face into the wind, which was blowing from southwest to northeast—the same direction in which Pall Mall ran. "If only we had a sail of some sort."

"A sail," said Harry.

"Yes, you know, like that wind-driven sled you said your father rode on across the prairies."

Harry rose to his feet, impelled by a growing feeling of excitement and hope, like a head of steam slowly building. "Perhaps we do, though. Perhaps we do."

"The tents were stolen. What do we have that—" He followed Harry's gaze. "The rain hood?"

"Of course! We unbolt it and turn it around so it catches the wind!"

"Do you really think—"

"There's no *time* to think, old chap, let's just *do* it!"

# FORTY

*In which*

## THE LONG JOURNEY COMES TO AN END—BUT NOT THE STORY

**W**hen Johnny saw what they were up to, he pushed himself painfully to his feet and lent a hand. He had designed the rain hood to be easily removable. Within ten minutes, they had completely detached it from the car. Though the wind threatened to tear it from their hands, they managed to turn it 180 degrees and fasten it to the windscreen supports with clamps and heavy wire.

The moment they unfolded the hood, the wind caught it, rocking the car forward. "It looks as though it may work," said Harry, "if we can find something to hold it open—a sort of mast, as it were."

Charles scooped up a heavy stick that one of the Luddites had dropped. "Will this do?"

"I think so." Harry grinned. "Ironic, isn't it, us making use of one of their weapons to help propel the car?" While Johnny and Charles struggled to hold the hood open, Harry wired the stick to the metal bars of the frame. They had to stand on the running boards in order to finish the job, because the *Flash* had already begun to move.

Unfortunately, it was heading straight for the sidewalk. "Harry!" shouted Johnny. Without even pausing in his task, Harry calmly thrust out one foot and used it to turn the steering wheel.

At last the stick was wired securely in place. "Got it!" he shouted. "Jump down, lads!" He hopped into the street, too, and walked alongside the car, guiding the steering wheel through the open driver's door. When a particularly strong gust of wind filled the improvised sail, he actually had to break into a trot to keep up. Elated, he burst into song. "Sailing, sailing, over the bounding main, and many a sto-ormy wind shall blow-www . . . ere Jack comes home again!"

Charles jogged up to join him. "If the wind gets any stronger," he said anxiously, "it's going to tear the whole thing apart." At that moment, the breeze died down a bit, and the car slowed. "Oh, no!" said Charles.

Harry laughed. "There's just no pleasing some chaps. Do you want a strong wind or not?"

"I just want to get there."

The clock in the tower of St. James's Palace sounded

the first of ten strokes. "Is that the right time?" asked Harry.

Charles checked his watch. "Mine says two minutes after."

"So we have at least thirteen minutes, then."

"You say that as if it's plenty of time."

Harry grinned. "In a rugby match, it's an eternity." His smile faded. He glanced toward Johnny, who was plodding along some distance behind them, then said softly to Charles, "You know, I've been thinking."

"Really?" said Charles, in mock amazement.

Harry ignored the sarcasm. "It occurs to me that there was something odd about the way those Luddites attacked the *Flash.*"

"How do you mean?"

"Well, they didn't behave as you'd expect machinery-hating fanatics to behave, did they? They obviously had no desire to destroy the car. They wanted only to disable her, and they knew exactly how to do it. I don't believe they actually were Luddites, Charles. I think they were ordinary thugs who were hired to stop us."

"Hired? By whom?"

"Well, whoever it was, he obviously instructed his men not to harm you. They had no qualms about beating up Johnny and me, but I noticed they treated you with kid gloves."

Charles stared at him. "You think—you think it was my father!"

"I didn't say that."

"But you implied it!"

"Well, think about it. What other explanation is there?"

"I don't know!" said Charles. "But I can assure you, my father would never stoop to such tactics!" He had made this same protest before, in nearly the same words, but this time it seemed, even to him, to lack conviction.

Behind them, Johnny called, "Look there!"

Harry faced front. The rain had let up a little and, for the first time, he could see more than a dozen yards ahead. The street before the Reform Club was packed with people, all of them facing east, the direction from which they expected the *Flash* to appear—if they expected it to appear at all.

"I'll clear a path for us," said Charles, and ran ahead, shouting, "Move out of the way, please! Let us through!"

A few spectators turned in his direction, then a few more, until finally everyone had spotted them. A clamor arose from the crowd, composed of cheers, cries of astonishment, and shouts of encouragement. Over the din, Charles's voice could barely be heard, crying, "Get out of the way! Clear the street!"

As the windblown motorcar sailed into the narrow passage between the banks of bodies, Harry hopped into the seat and pulled gently on the hand brake. The *Flash* rolled to a stop directly before the Reform Club steps. "Time!" he shouted. Though he was addressing

Charles, he was answered by a whole host of voices. There was considerable dispute over the precise number of minutes past ten, but there was unanimous accord that they had beaten the ten-fifteen deadline.

Harry and Charles made their way through a throng of well-wishers offering congratulations and handshakes and slaps on the back. Near the top of the stairs, Harry turned and scanned the street in the direction they had come, searching for Johnny. He felt a pang of panic, fearing that perhaps his friend had been hurt worse that he realized, and had collapsed somewhere. Then he noticed a large figure, shoulders hunched against the rain, hurrying away, unable to endure the prospect of facing so many people.

Harry sighed and shook his head. A newspaper reporter forced his way through the crowd of admirers, shouting, "Mr. Fogg! Mr. Fogg! Can you tell me what one factor was most important in accomplishing this amazing feat?"

Harry almost told the truth. He very nearly said, "The mechanical genius of Johnny Shaugnessey." But he knew that he would be doing his friend a disservice, that Johnny would want to remain as far from the limelight as possible. After a moment's thought, Harry said, "There were many factors, of course. But I would have to say that the most important of all was sheer, stupid luck."

Charles tapped his shoulder. "Harry, look. Down there, next to the car."

Though the *Flash* was surrounded by people, Harry's eye was drawn to the one familiar figure among them—a tall young woman in a long coat, bareheaded despite the rain. "Elizabeth," he said, under his breath.

She was gazing up at their makeshift sail, with a faint smile on her face. She shook her head, whether at the crude, slapdash nature of the thing or at the cleverness of it, Harry couldn't tell. Her gaze fell on the ruined boiler, then; she reached out a hand—as someone will reach out in sympathy to a friend who is hurt or distressed—and patted the metal body of the *Flash*.

A well-dressed man stepped forward and, with a small knife, began cutting away a chunk of the leather hood. Elizabeth whirled around, her face flushed with anger, and said something to the souvenir seeker that Harry could not hear. Whatever it was, it sent the man scurrying away, his head down.

"I'm going to go speak to her," said Charles.

Harry took his arm. "I wouldn't. You'll only embarrass her, old chum. Besides, you're needed inside the Club. You're the expedition's official observer, remember?" Harry beckoned to one of the policemen who stood nearby. "Do you suppose you could go down there and keep an eye on our motorcar until we return? If you don't, I'm afraid there'll be nothing left."

The peeler touched the brim of his helmet. "Be 'appy to, sir. And congratulations."

Just outside the front doors of the Club, Aouda

Fogg stood waiting patiently to greet her prodigal son. Though public displays of affection were not considered ladylike, she couldn't help wrapping her arms about him. Then, standing on tiptoe, she raised her veil and gave him a kiss on each cheek. "I am very happy to see you, Hari. But, oh, you look so thin, and so tired."

"I am. But we won, Mother. We won." He glanced around. "Is Father here?"

"He is inside, probably collecting money from the other members."

"You mean he made a wager of his own?"

Aouda nodded. "Several of them."

"And he bet that we would win?"

"Of course. You did not suppose he would bet *against* you?" She gave him a slight nudge. "Do not keep him waiting, Hari. He has been very worried about you."

"He told you that?"

She shrugged. "Perhaps not in so many words. But I can tell."

Harry took her arm. "Come with me, Mother."

"No, no," she protested, pulling away. "Women are not permitted in the Club, you know that. I shall go home and have the cook prepare a lovely luncheon for you."

Charles had already entered the Club and, finding the vestibule empty, climbed the stairs to the library. A good half of the members were gathered there, drinks in hand. When he came through the door, they raised their glasses and gave him three hearty choruses of "Hip, hip, hurrah!"

Charles strode over to his father, who shook his hand briskly and handed him a glass of champagne. "Glad to have you back safe and sound," said Julius Hardiman. But he did not look very glad. "Where's young Fogg?"

"He'll be here." Charles took a swig of the champagne and gazed around the room, feeling dazed and disoriented. After three months spent in the backseat of a motorcar and in livery stables, in tents and shabby hotels, the opulent surroundings of the Club seemed unreal. He had supposed that it would be a great relief to return to his old life, but somehow it all seemed rather ordinary and disappointing. He drained the glass and put on a smile. "Well, we did it, Father! We actually drove a motorcar around the world!"

"So you did. I only wish you had taken a bit longer doing it." He leaned closer and said confidentially, "Couldn't you have managed to slow him down some?"

Charles stared at his father. "I understood that I was to be an observer, not a saboteur!"

Julius Hardiman laughed, but it sounded forced and hollow. "Of course, of course. I was merely joking."

"Were you?" Charles set the glass aside. "Father, I must know," he said quietly, grimly. "Did you hire those men to disable the car?"

His father looked genuinely baffled. "What men?"

"A group posing as Luddites. They attacked us just before we reached the Club."

"I give you my word, Charles, I had nothing to do with it."

"Have you any idea who might be responsible?"

Before Hardiman could reply, another chorus of "Hip, hip, hurrah" filled the room. Charles turned to see Harry stride in, grinning triumphantly.

# THE OUTCOME OF THE CONTEST
# IS DISPUTED AND DECIDED

**P**hileas Fogg, who until that moment had remained standing at the window, staring out at
the courtyard, hands clasped behind his back in that
stiff military manner of his, now turned and moved
across the room to greet his son. He looked distinctly
ill at ease, as though he were, for once in his life, at a
loss as to how to act or what to say.

Harry thrust out a hand. His father, clearly relieved
that an embrace was not called for, gratefully grasped
it. "Welcome back," he said. "And congratulations."

"Will you have a drink with us?" asked Flanagan,
one of the parties to the wager.

"No, thank you," replied Harry. "My mother is waiting for me. As you know, she's not permitted to enter

the Club. So if you don't mind, I'll just collect my winnings and go."

"Oh, stay and savor your victory for while," said Flanagan. "Perhaps even gloat a bit."

"Yes, do stay, Harry," put in Dr. Doyle. "We'd all like to hear about your adventures."

"I'm sure Charles will be happy to regale you with stories of the trip."

"He's already revealed that you were attacked by Luddites," said Julius Hardiman. "Was anyone hurt?"

"I don't believe they were Luddites, in fact," replied Harry sharply. "I suspect they were paid to make certain the *Flash* was stopped short of the goal."

"But who would do such a thing?" said Dr. Doyle.

In a quiet but commanding voice, Phileas Fogg said, "I believe I may have the answer to that." He turned toward the window, where a figure had sat unnoticed until now, half concealed in a large armchair. "Mr. Drummond. You were telling me earlier how, once you had my son's vehicle, you would use it as a prototype, to build and sell more motorcars. How disappointed you must be, to have your plans spoiled."

The man who had loaned Harry the money in San Francisco rose slowly from the armchair and turned to the others, looking rather shamefaced. He spread his hands as if in surrender. "All right, I suppose there's no use in my denying it. The Luddite thing was meant only to be a last resort; I stationed men at both ends of the street. But I never imagined that you might actually make it back in time."

Harry could barely restrain himself from punching Drummond right between his ridiculous dundreary whiskers. "And I never imagined," he said, "that you coveted our motorcar so much, you would have us beaten up in order to get it."

"I instructed those men not to harm anyone. They didn't, did they?"

"Not badly—except for the *Flash*, of course."

Julius Hardiman set his drink down so firmly that the glass threatened to shatter. "I'll thank you to leave, now, Drummond," he said coldly. "This is a *gentleman's* club."

"If he may stay just a moment longer," said Harry, "I'd like to pay back the thousand pounds I owe him— minus the cost of repairing the *Flash*, of course. But before I can do that, I must ask you three to make good your wagers."

Hardiman, Flanagan, and Sullivan traded uncomfortable glances. "I'm afraid," said Flanagan, "that I don't have that much on me. Frankly, I didn't anticipate actually having to pay up. I hope you will accept a check?"

Before Harry could reply, Sullivan the banker spoke up. "Just one moment, gentlemen. There's a small matter that must be settled first."

"We followed the rules to the letter," put in Charles, heatedly. "What objection could you possibly have?"

Sullivan turned to him with a smug, superior smile. "The rules state that the motorcar must travel the entire distance under its own power."

"And so she did, except when crossing oceans, lakes, and rivers."

"Are you prepared to swear to that?" asked Sullivan.

"Yes. That is, I—" Charles broke off and gave Harry a desperate glance.

"Isn't it true," Sullivan went on, "that between Rawlins, Wyoming, and San Francisco, California, you were absent from the motorcar—kicked off it, in fact, I believe?"

"How did you—" Charles turned to Drummond. "*You* told him."

Drummond smiled and shrugged.

"Is this true, Charles?" asked Hardiman.

Scowling, Charles grudgingly muttered, "Yes, sir."

"So, you see," said Sullivan, "we have no way of knowing whether or not there were any infractions of the rules during that time."

"You have my *word* on it, sir!" said Harry, his fists clenched in anger.

"I'm afraid that's not enough," replied Sullivan.

Phileas Fogg stepped forward, toe-to-toe and face-to-face with the banker, and said coolly, "If you insult a member of my family, Mr. Sullivan, you insult me. I demand satisfaction."

Sullivan gave a nervous, incredulous laugh. "Are you challenging me to a duel, Mr. Fogg?"

"That is the traditional manner in which gentlemen settle their disputes."

The banker shrank back slightly. "See here, I hardly think that—"

He was interrupted by a disturbance in the hall. A young woman in a long overcoat stormed into the library, shedding drops of water on the expensive Oriental carpet. "I knew it!" she said. "I knew they'd find some objection, some way of making sure they didn't have to pay up!"

"Elizabeth!" cried Charles. "Where did *you* come from?"

"I've been standing in the hall, listening to this—this load of horse manure!"

The doorman, who had entered in her wake, said, "I'm very sorry, sirs. I tried to prevent her from—"

"Are you aware," said Julius Hardiman, "that women are not permitted in this club?"

"Oh, that's another load of horse manure! I am a reporter, and I intend to let my readers know, in great detail, the lengths to which three supposedly respectable businessmen will go to try and weasel out of paying their debts."

"We are simply trying to make certain that the rules were adhered to," protested Sullivan. "And the fact is, for a considerable part of the journey, our impartial observer was not present in the car."

Elizabeth frowned thoughtfully. "That is true," she admitted. Then, slowly, the frown metamorphosed into a sweet, sly smile. "However," she said, "I *was* present during that time, and I give you my word that the *Flash* traveled every inch of the distance under her own power. Now, I *know* that none of you self-professed gentlemen would be so unchivalrous as to question the word of a lady."

Sullivan's mouth moved as though he were about to reply, but there was nothing he could say. He was well and truly defeated, and he knew it. He simply sighed. As though they had been practicing the maneuver, he and his friends reached simultaneously for their checkbooks. Harry held up a hand to stop them. "One moment. To paraphrase Mr. Sullivan, I have no way of knowing whether or not your checks will be valid. I am, however, perfectly willing to wait here while you withdraw the money from your bank accounts."

When the three businessmen had departed, muttering indignant phrases unfit for a lady's ears, Harry turned to Elizabeth. "Thank you," he said.

She shook her head. "No. Don't thank me. It doesn't begin to make up for the trouble I caused you."

"Well, it was hardly your fault," said Harry, "that the *Graphic* sent you off on another assignment. Incidentally, how *were* the whist championships? Riveting, I expect."

Though Elizabeth was momentarily baffled, she did fine job of concealing it. "No, actually," she said, "they were rather tedious. It's a pity the players aren't permitted to place bets. That might have made things a bit more interesting." And though she was grateful to him for keeping her secret, she was careful to conceal that, too. All she did, before she turned to go, was to place a hand briefly and gently on Harry's arm. But he understood.

Phileas Fogg approached his son. "Before you spend all the money on building another motorcar, please remember that a thousand pounds of it is to go back into your trust fund."

Harry grinned. "Yes, sir." The library clock chimed eleven. "I'm afraid I've played havoc with your schedule, Father. You should have left for the dining room ten minutes ago."

"Yes, well, I thought perhaps I'd dine with you and your mother at home, for a change. It will give us an opportunity to hear some of your adventures."

"All right. There're a few adventures, however, that are best left untold, for Mother's sake."

"Yes," said Phileas Fogg. "No doubt you're right."

"And perhaps," said Harry pointedly, "you will tell us some of *your* adventures, in turn."

"But you've heard about my journey a hundred times."

"I was not referring to your journey, sir. I meant your seafaring adventures."

For the first time in Harry's memory, a full-fledged look of surprise came over his father's face.

"You see," said Harry, "I met Captain Keough."

"Ah. Well, perhaps some of those adventures should remain untold, as well. For your mother's sake."

"Fair enough. I'll see you at home, then?"

"Actually," said Phileas Fogg, "I thought I'd help you with the *Flash*—having her towed, or whatever is necessary."

Now it was Harry's turn to look surprised. "Of course. I didn't suppose you'd want to."

"If motorcars are to be the future of transportation," said his father, "it would behoove us all to learn a little something about them, don't you think?"

"Yes, I do. When we've got her running again, perhaps you'd like to take a turn at the wheel?"

Phileas Fogg gave a small, wry smile. "I don't believe I care to know *that* much about them."


Not wanting to lead a flock of newspaper reporters to Johnny, Harry stored the motorcar in a livery stable near Savile Row. A week or so later, when he was sure that the newspapers were done with him, he had the *Flash* towed—embarrassingly enough, by a team of horses— to the blacksmith shop in York Court, where he found Johnny hard at work cleaning up the charred remains of his shed. Harry had intended to share the four thousand pounds that remained, but Johnny refused. "You'll need that money," he said. "For engineering school."

Harry gave him a doubtful look. "You really think I should?"

"Don't you?"

"Well, I could give it a try." Harry scratched his head. "Do you think any decent school will have me?"

"Of course," said Johnny. "You're the famous Harry Fogg."

"But what about our plans to build a new, improved version of the *Flash*?"

"We'll work nights," said Johnny. "And weekends." He sat on the running board and pulled from his trouser pocket a piece of paper covered with mysterious scrawls and sketches. "Want to see my drawings?"

"Does Ganesha have an elephant's head?"

"I don't know," said Johnny.

"Well, he does. Now, let's see what you've got." Though Johnny was not the most communicative person in the world, nor the most skilled draftsman, Harry managed to decipher his drawings and his halting explanation. The new *Flash* would be powered, like the car in Iowa, by electricity. But, unlike Morrison's vehicle, theirs could travel long distances, for the batteries would be recharged by a small, extremely efficient engine like the one patented seventy-five years earlier by another Scotsman named Stirling. Harry wasn't sure precisely how the Stirling engine worked, only that it needed no boiler and burned a fraction of the fuel used by a steam engine.

"This is brilliant, lad!" he said. "When do we start on her?"

"After we clean this up," said Johnny. "And build another workshop."

"Right." Harry doffed his coat and picked up a shovel. "Listen, Johnny, I never apologized to you for selling the *Flash* to Drummond."

"You didn't sell her."

"Well, I nearly did. Anyway, I'm sorry."

Johnny shrugged. "If you hadn't, we'd still be in San Francisco." He set to work shoveling ashes and debris into a cart and Harry followed suit.

They got a welcome respite when Charles Hardiman turned up, carrying the latest edition of the London *Daily Graphic*. "Have you fellows seen this?"

"Seen what?"

"A very extensive and somewhat overwrought account of our journey, written by a certain Miss Annie Laurie."

"Overwrought?"

Charles fished his eyeglasses from his coat pocket. "Listen to this: 'It was at this point that your reporter was compelled to part company with Messrs. Fogg, Hardiman, and Shaugnessey. Even now, she cannot write of her reasons for leaving without suffering acute embarrassment, and yet she feels she owes her loyal readers some explanation of her actions.'"

Harry glanced at Johnny, who had ceased working and was listening intently. "Um, Charles, I think I'd prefer to read it for myself." Perhaps Elizabeth needed to clear her conscience, but there was no need for Johnny to hear it.

With a puzzled look, Charles surrendered the paper. "Yes, all right, but . . ." He trailed off as Harry frowned and gave a slight shake of his head.

Harry found the passage and, sitting on the running board of the *Flash*, scanned it silently:

> . . . owes her loyal readers some explanation of her actions. To put it as delicately and modestly as possible, the situation was similar to that of the familiar syndrome known as *shipboard romance*. That is, the close proximity into which we were necessarily thrown had apparently led to amorous feelings on the part of certain members of the crew, and this unfortunately resulted in another sort of contest, with this reporter's affections as the prize. When the rivalry threatened to erupt into outright hostility, your humble correspondent concluded that it was best for all concerned if she withdrew from the expedition.

Harry grinned and shook his head incredulously. "Well. There's no question that Annie Laurie will become a household name. She clearly knows how to appeal to her readers."

"Someone told me that, since her dispatches began appearing in the *Graphic*, the paper's circulation has nearly doubled."

"What does she say about us?" asked Johnny.

"She says," replied Harry, "that we were the cleverest and most amusing of companions, and that, when we make our next journey, she will insist upon coming with us."

"Our next journey?" said Charles.

"To test the new, improved model," said Johnny.

"What sort of improvements do you mean to make?"

"Actually," said Harry, "we were thinking of building an entirely new and revolutionary sort of vehicle. It will consist of a large covered wagon—"

"A *covered wagon*?"

"Yes, and it will pulled by a giant steam-powered mechanical man."

"Ho, ho. Very amusing."

"Well, I wasn't certain you'd understand if I told you we're going to use a Stirling engine."

"I know what a Stirling engine is," said Charles, a bit indignantly.

"Really? Then perhaps you'll explain it to me."

"It's . . . well, it's an engine that . . . that was designed by Stirling."

"Thank you for that insight."

"You're welcome. See here, Harry, are you looking for investors?"

"Don't tell me your father wants to get into the motorcar business."

"No. Despite everything, he's still convinced that cars are unreliable and impractical. But I have some money of my own, and I'd like to help finance your new, improved model."

"Are you certain? There's no guarantee that you'd make back your investment, you know."

"I'm willing to take that risk."

Harry glanced at him in surprise. "I believe you've learned a new word, Charles."

"*Risk*, you mean?"

"Yes." Harry scratched his head thoughtfully. "Has it ever occurred to you," he said, "how some people—your father, for instance—are like locomotives? Their mind travels on a single set of tracks—tracks that were laid down, often very long ago, by someone else. And then others are like motorcars; they choose their own path."

Now Charles was the one to look surprised. "That's actually a rather profound thought, Harry."

"Yes, it is, isn't it? I've had a number of them lately. It must be all that meditation I've been doing." Harry got to his feet. "Well, that's enough thinking. Time to get back to work. Here." He thrust his shovel into Charles's hands. "If you really want to be a partner in this business, old chum, you'll have to start from the ground up."